Chapter 1

It was Monday morning, and Jack had nipped out to the corner shop to pick up a copy of The Bugle for his ten-pin bowling scores. Meanwhile, I was having a staring competition with next door's cat, Lovely. She was sitting on the fence, glaring at me through the kitchen window. I knew why. She was hoping I'd go outside, so she could bend my ear about Winky; she definitely had the hots for him. Unfortunately for her, Winky didn't want to know.

"You'll never guess what." Jack was back.

"You've realised that ten-pin bowling is boring, and you're never going to play it again?"

"Don't be silly. We've been invited to a party." He held up a small, white envelope.

Just hearing the word *party* had been known to bring me out in hives. "Why is Little Jack throwing a party? Is it to celebrate the launch of his shopping app?"

"The invitation isn't from Little Jack. It's from those new neighbours across the road."

"The Normals?"

"Yeah, they seem like a nice couple. They called me over just now on my way back from the shop."

"Couldn't you have pretended not to hear them?"

"Why would I do that? They seem nice enough."

"Did they mention magnetic fish?"

"What?"

"Never mind. What's the party?"

"It's their housewarming party, obviously. It's on Wednesday night."

"You told them we couldn't make it, right?"

"Why would I do that? We don't have anything

planned, do we?"

"No, but *they* wouldn't have known that."

"It'll be fun. They said that everyone on the street is going."

"That's precisely what worries me. Do you really want to be in the same house as all of our neighbours? They're all misfits."

"Not all of them." He grinned that particular grin of his that usually meant he was about to crack a joke. "The Normals seem normal enough."

See, what did I tell you? My bad joke detector rarely let me down.

"Were they wearing matching clothes?"

"Yes. I thought it was rather sweet. We should do—"

"Don't even go there. If you wanted a bookend for a wife, you picked the wrong woman."

"I still think the jumpers were nice."

"Were they wearing the ones with the Ns on them?"

"Yes. You should ask Mrs V to knit some for us with an 'M' on the front."

"I might ask her to knit one for me that says: I'm not with him." I glanced out of the window. "That cat is doing my head in."

"Lovely? What's wrong with her? She hasn't been doing her business in our garden, has she?"

"No, she's still got the hots for Winky. I think she blames me for keeping the two of them apart."

"Why don't you explain to her that he's not interested?"

"I'm not going to waste my time talking to a cat."

"Don't you do that every day at the office?"

"That's different. Anyway, talking of crazy neighbours, I haven't seen Mr Hosey's tree or bush for a few days."

"Maybe he's invested in a more advanced model that's impossible to spot?"

"Hmm, I hadn't thought of that." I walked through to the lounge, and studied the neighbourhood foliage. "Nah, I don't think so."

That same grin had returned to Jack's face. "Maybe he got tired of it and has decided to *branch* out and do something different." He laughed — no one else was going to. "*Branch* out? Get it?"

"Here's the thing: If you have to explain it, it isn't funny."

Jack was still laughing at his own joke when there was a knock at the door. It was Tony and Clare, and for once, they were sans costumes.

"We're sorry to call so early, Jill, but we wondered if we might have a word with Jack?"

"Hold on, I'll just check if his sides have done splitting." I popped through to the lounge. "It's the next-door neighbours. The cosplayers not the fitness freaks."

"Morning, Tony. Morning, Clare," Jack said.

"Sorry to call so early, Jack, but we have exciting news about TenPinCon," Tony said.

"Come on through to the lounge."

"You can join us if you like, Jill," Clare said.

"That's okay. I'll just pop the kettle on. Tea okay?"

Phew! That had been a close call. I had no intention of getting dragged into the whole TenPinCon debacle. Something was bound to go badly wrong, and I didn't want to be in the same county when it did.

"Tea is served." I took the tray full of cups through to the lounge. And being the hostess with the mostest, I even included a plate of biscuits.

No, of course they weren't my custard creams. I kept a packet of boring digestives in reserve for occasions like this.

"The con is going to be in four weeks' time!" Jack blurted out.

"What? I thought it was next year."

"It was supposed to be," Tony said. "Washbridge Arena has had a cancellation, and they've offered it to us at a massively reduced rate. It was too good to turn down."

"Can you get everything organised by then?"

"We'll have to. Jack has agreed to take on the marketing for the event, haven't you?"

"Yes. It's going to be quite a challenge, but I'm up for it."

"That's great." I edged towards the door. "I'll leave you to it, then. It sounds like you have lots to do."

Oh boy! I'd had grave reservations about this madcap idea when I thought they had a whole year to organise it. But now? It didn't bear thinking about.

***

It was my new office manager's first day in the job. I'd asked him to come in at nine-thirty, so I could be sure I'd be there before he arrived. I was really quite excited at this new stage of the business's evolution. As luck would have it, my accountant, Luther Stone, was due to pay me a visit later today; he would no doubt be impressed with my recent initiatives.

What the—?

I couldn't believe it. I'd deliberately set off from the house earlier than usual, so that I'd be there before Alistair arrived, but now I was sitting in a queue of traffic that hadn't moved for five minutes.

When I could stand it no longer, I turned off the engine, got out of the car, and walked to the front of the queue.

The road was blocked with a temporary barrier, behind which stood two men in high-vis jackets. As far as I could make out, the only thing they were doing was drinking coffee. I wasn't the only one who'd come to see what was happening. There was a crowd of drivers gathered at the barrier; none of them looked happy.

"How long are we going to be stuck here?" someone demanded.

One of the workers shrugged. "It's out of my hands."

"You must have some idea."

"It depends how long it takes the surgeon to get here."

Surgeon? Had there been an accident of some kind? There was no sign of one.

I'd had enough of this, so I pushed my way to the front. "Why is the surgeon needed? Is someone injured?"

Both of the workers laughed.

"Not that kind of surgeon, love." The younger of the two smirked. "We're waiting for a tree surgeon to chop that down." He pointed to a huge tree, twenty yards down the road.

"Why do it in the rush hour? Couldn't you have done it on a Sunday? It's not like it's going anywhere, is it?"

"It was struck by lightning last night, and there's a danger it might fall across the road."

"It looks safe enough to me."

"It's not our call, love. We're only here to make sure no

one goes down this road until it's been felled."

"And you don't know how long that's going to be?"

"Not the faintest."

Great!

That left me with two options. I could sit there like a lemon, waiting for goodness knows how long for someone to come and cut down the tree.

Or I could introduce a little magic into proceedings.

The men in high-vis jackets both dropped their coffees when the lightning bolt struck the tree behind them. They turned around just in time to see the tree fall backwards onto the field behind.

"It looks like the tree's gone," I said.

They were still staring in disbelief at the space where the tree had stood a few seconds earlier.

"Move the barriers!" someone shouted. "I've got work to get to."

Clearly still shell-shocked, one of the men took out his phone and made a call, presumably checking with his superiors. After a brief exchange, he nodded to his pal, and the two of them moved the barrier to the side of the road.

Result! Sometimes, being a witch was really cool.

***

"Morning, Mrs V."

"Good morning, Jill. Mr Song rang a couple of minutes ago to say they'd be installing the replacement sign tomorrow."

"Thank goodness for that. I'll be glad to get that stupid

sign sorted once and for all."

"What time does the new man start?"

"I told Alistair to be here for nine-thirty."

"When he arrives, I'll ask him what colour clown socks he'd like."

"It might be best to let him settle in first."

"You're right. I probably shouldn't trouble him on his first day by asking about the sponsorship either. I wouldn't want to scare him away."

"Sponsorship?"

"I thought I'd told you about it last week?"

"I don't think so."

"The local yarnies are holding their annual charity fundraising event in support of Yarn Aid on Sunday."

"Remind me again what Yarn Aid is."

"It's for those yarnies who are injured in the course of their knitting activities."

"Does that happen a lot?"

"You'd be surprised. I have photos of some of the injuries if you'd like to see them."

"No, thanks."

"Can I interest you in sponsoring me, Jill?"

"What exactly will you be doing? Is it a sponsored knit-in?"

"No, we thought we'd have a complete change this year, so we're holding a sponsored hula hoop."

"Hula hoop? But aren't most of the yarnies rather — err — what I mean is, aren't most of them senior citizens?"

"We can still hula hoop."

"How does the sponsorship work?"

"You pledge so much per minute."

"Fair enough." There was no way Mrs V would be able

to keep a hula hoop going for more than a few minutes. Ten tops. "Okay, you can sign me up for fifty pence a minute."

"Are you sure, dear? That's a lot of money."

"I'm positive." Even if she managed ten minutes, I'd only be out five pounds. "And you can put Jack down for the same amount."

"That's very generous. There is just one other thing that I'm obliged to tell you: The yarnie who keeps their hula hoop going the longest has their sponsorship minutes doubled. Is fifty-pence still okay?"

"Yeah, that's fine. I imagine you'll have to put some practice in?"

"I will if I get the chance, but I used to hula hoop when I was a young girl. I imagine it's much like riding a bike; you never forget how to do it."

As soon as I walked into my office, before I'd even had a chance to speak, Winky shushed me.

He was sitting at my desk, talking to another cat, seated opposite him.

"Okay, Prof, that sounds like a plan. When shall we meet again?" Winky said.

"I should have all the calculations finished later today." The other cat had a scholarly air about him. "How about tomorrow afternoon?"

"Fine by me. Thanks very much for coming by."

"My pleasure, young man. I'll return tomorrow with my detailed proposal."

Once the other cat had disappeared through the window, I hoofed Winky out of my chair. "Who was that?"

"The Prof."

"Professor of what?"

"Physics with a side of engineering."

"Dare I ask what you two are plotting?"

"You can ask, but I'm sworn to secrecy. All I can say is this little project is likely to make me a lot of money."

"How do you keep coming up with all of these schemes of yours?"

"It just comes naturally to me. You had the chance to take advantage of my skillset. All you had to do was allow me to do my job as head of strategic planning, but oh no, you were too busy fairying around."

"I wasn't *fairying* around as you put it. I was helping the floral fairies, and I had a lot of other things on my plate too."

"Whatever. You had your chance and you blew it."

"My new office manager starts today."

"That should be a laugh."

"Before he gets here, I'm warning you: no funny business."

"I can't help being funny. Unlike you, it comes naturally to me."

"I mean no sabotaging the work he's here to do."

"Don't worry. I have much better things to do with my time."

"Like your little project with the professor, you mean? Remind me what that was?"

"It's a—" He caught himself just in time. "Oh no you don't."

"I nearly got you there."

"The day you catch out Winky, will be the day he retires."

"You're doing it again. Referring to yourself in the third person."

"How could you accuse Winky of such a thing?"

***

I thought it would be a nice gesture to greet Alistair at the doors to the office building—that way I could show him around, and introduce him to Mrs V.

Unfortunately, my timing couldn't have been worse. The clown school's first class of the day must have been scheduled to start at around the same time, so when I got outside, there was a crowd of student clowns gathered around the door.

"Excuse me." I tried to thread my way through the assembled masses. "Coming through."

"Did you forget we were supposed to come in our costumes today?" said a clown with really bad makeup.

"I'm not a student."

"Sorry. Are you one of the teachers? I didn't recognise you out of costume. You must be Sneezy."

"No. I have nothing to do with Clown. My offices are at the top of the stairs on the opposite side."

"The private investigator?"

"Yeah, that's me."

"That must be really exciting."

"So people are always telling me."

"If you ever need an undercover clown, I'd be up for it. My name is Seth Ember."

"That's the best clown name I've heard so far."

"That's actually my real name. My clown name is Bungles."

"Right, of course."

"What do you think about me working for you?"

"I'll certainly bear you in mind the next time I need an undercover clown. Now, if I could just squeeze past you?"

When I emerged from the crowd of clowns, I glanced around but there was no sign of Alistair. Then I spotted him—behind me! We must have somehow passed by one another.

Fantastic!

By the time I'd managed to fight my way back through the clowns, and into the building, he was just going into my offices.

Chapter 2

"Jill, there you are," Mrs V said. "I thought you'd gone outside to greet this young man."

"I did, but I got waylaid by a bunch of clowns. I'm sorry that I missed you, Alistair."

"No problem." He walked over and shook my hand. "It's great to be here. I was just telling Annabel how impressed I am by the amount of research into my background you must have done."

"Sorry? I don't—"

"How else could you have known my favourite colour is orange, and my favourite creature is the dolphin." He pointed to his tie, which was orange with a picture of a dolphin on it. "How you managed to find a desk that combined both of those is nothing short of remarkable."

"Nothing is too good for my employees."

"When you interviewed me, you didn't tell me the most exciting aspect of this job."

"I didn't?"

"You didn't mention the clown school next door. I've always loved clowns. They're such fun, don't you think?"

"Well, actually, I—err—"

"According to Annabel, they run evening classes, so I might pop over there in my lunchbreak, to sign up."

"Right."

"And Annabel has even offered to knit me some clown socks."

"That's great." How come the newcomer got to call Mrs V, Annabel?

"I'm keen to get stuck in. Where would you like me to start?"

"Actually, my accountant will be here in a few minutes; I'd arranged the meeting before I knew you'd be starting today. I'm going to be tied up for a while, so why don't you spend some time with Annab, err—Mrs V? She can bring you up to date on our current systems, such as they are. Then you and I can get together later."

"That sounds good to me."

"Where did you find that Gonk?" Winky said. "Why would you trust your business to a man who wears an orange tie with a dolphin on it?"

"Alistair has excellent qualifications and experience."

"Yeah, but does he actually know which is his elbow and which is his—?"

"That's enough of that. I don't want you interfering in the work he's here to do."

"Why would I? It's none of my business if you want to hand over control to some dolphin loving clown."

"Incidentally, your girlfriend is still pining for you."

"If you're talking about that boring Snowdrop who lives next door to you, I'm not interested."

"I feel sorry for her."

"No, you don't. You're just trying to make me feel bad. Well, you're wasting your time. Anyway, I'm seeing someone else now."

"Who is the *lucky* lady?"

"That's for me to know and for you to mind your own business."

"Don't I get to meet her?"

"So you can pass judgement? No chance. And besides, my new lady friend prefers to keep a low profile."

"How intriguing. Now I really want to know who she

is."

"Don't you realise how sad that makes you?"

He wasn't wrong.

***

Luther still had the smoulder factor.

"Good morning, Jill. You're looking very well."

"Thanks. You too. Is that down to Maria?"

"I'm afraid not." He sighed. "We aren't together any longer."

"Really? I'm sorry to hear that. I had no idea."

"It was a mistake for us to ever think we could work together."

"Couldn't you have just stopped working together?"

"It was too late by then. The tension and arguments had already spilled over into our personal life."

"You'll remain friends, though, I assume?"

"I know that's what people are supposed to say under these circumstances, but I'm not convinced that ever really works. Unsurprisingly, she walked straight into another job, and as far as I'm aware, she's happy."

"What about you?"

"I'm fine. I'm giving relationships a break for a while. I'm beginning to think I'm not very good at them."

"Nonsense. You just haven't met the right person yet."

"Unlike you. How's married life?"

"Fantastic, really fantastic. Jack occasionally suggests that we should work together, but I won't hear of it."

"I noticed you have a new member of staff out there?"

"I'll get Mrs V to organise us some drinks, and then I'll bring you up to speed on the new developments in the business."

Once we had our coffee, I updated Luther on my recent entry onto the social media scene, and I explained my thinking in bringing in the new office manager. When I'd finished, I fully expected him to be full of enthusiasm for the new initiatives.

"Oh dear, Jill." He frowned.

Not exactly the reaction I'd been hoping for.

"What's wrong? I thought you'd be pleased. You're always saying that I need to develop the business."

"Yes, and the increased social media presence is definitely a good thing. Particularly as it doesn't seem to have cost very much. It's your new employee that worries me. I'm not sure the increase to the payroll is sustainable."

"But the idea is that he'll pay for himself, and then some. I spend way too much time on admin that I really should be devoting to billable work."

"The theory is sound, but there's one slight flaw in this particular case."

"What's that?"

"I can see no evidence that you've ever spent much time on admin. You've always seemed to fly by the seat of your pants. You've certainly never spent much time on your accounts. If any."

"I think you're being overly pessimistic, Luther. I'm confident that now I have Alistair on board, my billable hours will increase dramatically."

"I sincerely hope you're right, Jill. This could be make or break for the business."

By now, I was feeling totally deflated, but we still had to go through the minutiae of the accounts. Boring!

"There's one thing I need to clarify," Luther pointed to the printout he'd brought with him. "Where exactly are the majority of your clients based? I'd always assumed they were in Washbridge?"

"That's right, but I also get the occasional case from the surrounding areas like West Chipping."

"That's what I thought, so what are all these cases with the letter 'C' next to them? Where are those clients based?"

Oh bum! Those were all the cases I'd worked for clients in Candlefield.

"That's — err — Coventry."

"*Coventry*? That's miles away."

It had been the first place beginning with a 'C' that had come into my mind, but it was a two-hour drive away. What was I thinking?

"That's where my other office is based."

Luther pushed back his chair, and stared at me, incredulously. "What other office? You've never mentioned another office to me."

"Haven't I? Are you sure?"

"I would have remembered. Why have I never seen any bills relating to that office?"

"That's a very good question, and you'll be very surprised by the explanation." Almost as surprised as I would. "It's very simple, actually. The reason there are no bills for the other office is that — err, I share it with an old school friend. I did some work for her years ago, and in return, she's allowed me to share the office at no cost."

"That's incredibly generous of her."

"It is, isn't it?"

"Even so, you really should start recording your

travelling expenses. You must spend a ton of money travelling back and forth between here and Coventry. If these records are accurate, you seem to get almost half of your business from there."

"That sounds about right."

"I still can't believe you've never mentioned it before."

"This is precisely why I need the office manager. He'll make sure there are no omissions like this in the future."

***

"Coventry?" Winky laughed. "How did you come up with Coventry?"

"He caught me off guard."

"There are at least a dozen places closer than Coventry that begin with a 'C'. I can name them if you like?"

"Don't bother. I'm just about to have a meeting with Alistair."

"This should be good. I can't wait to hear what pearls of wisdom dolphin boy has to impart."

"I don't want to hear a peep from you while he's in here. Get on that sofa and keep quiet."

"Your wish is my command."

I called Alistair through to my office, and had Mrs V bring tea in for us.

"Your accountant had a quick word with me on the way out." Alistair took a sip of his tea. "He said I should ask you to update me on Coventry. I didn't realise you had more than one office?"

Neither did I until a few minutes earlier. "I do undertake some cases for clients in Coventry."

"Isn't that rather a long way from here?"

"Yes, but it's a very profitable part of the business, as you'll see."

Just then, out of the corner of my eye, I spotted Winky. He was standing on the sofa, juggling balls.

That wasn't the least bit off-putting.

I waved my hand at him to get him to stop.

"Are you okay?" Alistair said.

"Yes, why?"

"Your hand was shaking."

"That's just a nervous twitch. Take no notice."

The next twenty minutes were spent discussing the way I currently handled case management and billing.

"That's quite an old-fashioned approach," he commented.

"Most of it dates back to the systems originally designed by my father. He started the agency."

"I see. Well, if you don't mind my saying so, it's time for a dramatic update." I was having difficulty focusing on what Alistair was saying because Winky was now playing with a yoyo. "Jill? What do you think? Are you sure you're okay? Your hand is shaking again."

"I'm fine, thanks. I agree with everything you've said. As far as I'm concerned, you have carte blanche to do whatever you feel is necessary to get this place working like a well-oiled machine."

"Excellent. I'll complete a thorough review, and get back to you with a series of suggestions by the end of next week, if that works for you?"

"That's fine. I look forward to seeing it."

He was on his way to the door, but hesitated. "I don't want to speak out of school, but I wondered if you were aware that Annabel seems to spend most of her time knitting?"

"Yes, that's perfectly okay. Mrs V isn't actually on the payroll. She comes here because she enjoys the company. I'm quite happy for her to knit when she has no other work to do."

"Fine. I just thought I should check."

"What a snitch that guy is," Winky said, once Alistair was out of the room.

"I thought I told you to stay quiet while we were having our meeting?"

"I was quiet. You never said anything about juggling or yoyoing, though."

***

My first new client of the week was a Mrs Bernadette Sparks. I hadn't taken the initial phone call, but according to Mrs V, her visit was related to her late husband's death.

"Please have a seat, Mrs Sparks."

"I prefer Bernie."

"Okay, and I'm Jill. My PA said you wanted to speak to me about your late husband?"

"That's right. Kirk died five months ago. You may have seen the article in The Bugle. The headline they used was an absolute disgrace, but then I'd expect nothing else from that sordid rag."

"I didn't see it, but I do my best to avoid that horrible publication."

"Kirk was a reporter with The Chips."

"That's the West Chipping newspaper, isn't it?"

"That's right. An altogether different proposition from The Bugle. The Chips is well respected throughout the industry. That's what attracted Kirk to the job." She hesitated. "I still find it very difficult to discuss his death."

"Take as long as you need."

She took a deep breath, and then continued, "He was crushed to death by two dice."

I had been in this business for some time, but that was a new one on me.

"Did I hear correctly? Did you say dice?"

"Do you know the Lucky Thirteen Casino?"

"I can't say I do."

"It's located halfway between Washbridge and West Chipping, on a small retail park. Kirk had been working on some kind of big exposé about the casino. That's why the so-called *accident* happened, I'm convinced of it."

"The dice, you mean?"

"Yes. The signage for the casino comprised of a huge roulette wheel and two large dice. The official story is that lightning struck the building, causing the dice to fall to the ground. My only consolation is that Kirk can't have known anything about it."

"Wrong place, wrong time?"

"That's what they say, but I don't buy it. Someone was worried about the story Kirk was about to run, and they wanted him out of the way. There wasn't even a thunderstorm that day; the sky was clear."

"What did the police have to say?"

"Not much. After the inquest delivered a verdict of death by misadventure, they said there was nothing for them to investigate."

"What about the fact that there was no thunderstorm?"

"A freak lightning strike, they reckon. It happens, apparently."

"Do you know exactly what would have been in your husband's article?"

"No, he never discussed his investigations with me."

"What about the other staff at the newspaper? Would anyone there know more about the story?"

"No. They all keep their stories close to their chest until they're published. It's a very competitive environment."

"Did he have a computer at home? Might there be something on there that I could use as a starting point?"

"Kirk didn't trust computers; he was scared of getting hacked. He kept all of his notes in small notebooks."

"Do you have those?"

"Yes. They're locked away in a cupboard back at the house."

"Okay. I'm going to need to see the notebook he was using just before he died."

"Of course. Sorry, I should have thought to bring it with me."

"That's okay. Perhaps I could pop around tomorrow and collect it?"

"Of course. Do you think you'll be able to find out what really happened to Kirk?"

"I'll do my best."

Chapter 3

Not long after Bernie Sparks had left, Mrs V came through to my office. "Could I have a quick word, Jill?"

"Of course. Is it about the hula hoop?"

"No, it's about Alistair."

"Oh? Nothing wrong I hope?"

"No, not really. He seems a perfectly nice young man. It's just that—err—never mind, it doesn't matter."

"It obviously does, or you wouldn't have brought it up. He hasn't upset you with something he's said, has he?"

"No. In fact, he's barely looked up from his work since his meeting with you. He seems very industrious."

"What is it, then?"

"It's the whistling."

"*Whistling*?"

"Yes. I'm not even sure he's aware that he's doing it, but he's been whistling practically all morning."

"Is he whistling anything in particular?"

"Nothing I recognise. It isn't very tuneful at all."

"I'm not really sure what I can do about it. I can hardly tell him to stop whistling, can I? It would seem a little heavy-handed on his first day in the job."

"You're right, dear. He's probably just nervous. If he doesn't stop, though, I'll have to bring in my earmuffs tomorrow."

"Fair enough."

"I told you dolphin boy was trouble." Winky had to have his say as usual.

"It's nothing."

"Thin end of the wedge if you ask me."

"Which I most certainly did not."

"It sounded to me like your accountant was of a similar mind. He said you couldn't afford dolphin boy."

"Will you please stop calling him that; his name is Alistair. And Luther didn't say anything of the kind."

"Yes, he did. I heard him."

"I'm not going to debate the complexities of accounts with a cat."

"Why not? I like nothing better than to talk trial balances, balance sheets and P&Ls. Not that you'd have a clue what any of those are."

"Of course I do."

"Okay. Explain to me what a balance sheet is."

"It's obvious from the name, isn't it?"

"I'd still like to hear your definition."

"It's the sheet that balances the—err—" Much to my relief, my phone rang.

"Jill, it's Amber. When you're not busy do you think you could pop over to Cuppy C?"

I glanced at Winky who was still waiting to hear my definition of a balance sheet. "Okay, if it's that urgent, I'll be straight over."

"No, it isn't urgent."

"Right. In that case, I'd better come over now."

"But, Jill, I just said—"

I ended the call. "Sorry, Winky, I'd love to talk trial profit sheets with you all day, but there's an emergency that requires my immediate attention."

***

When I arrived at Cuppy C, Amber and Pearl were

seated at a corner table.

"You didn't need to come straight over if you were busy," Amber said.

"That's okay. I was only discussing the business's finances. It's nothing that can't wait."

"Can I get you a drink, Jill?" Pearl offered.

"A caramel latte would be nice."

"And a muffin?"

Why did I get the sense that they were up to something?

"Yes, please. How come you two are in the shop today? I thought Monday was your day off?"

"It is. We just popped in for a quick drink, and then we're going shopping."

"Where are the little ones?"

"Alan and William have got them. We're going to meet up with them this afternoon in the park."

Pearl was back with my drink and muffin.

"How much do I owe you?"

"Nothing. It's our treat."

That clinched it; there was definitely something going on. "What are you after, girls?"

"What do you mean?" Pearl tried but failed to look innocent.

"You obviously want something. You might as well spit it out."

"Well, actually." Amber twiddled with one of the buttons on her cardigan. "There was *something* we wanted to ask you."

"I'm listening."

"Hello, you three." Aunt Lucy appeared at the table. "What are you plotting?"

"Nothing," Pearl said. "We're just chatting."

"Come and join us." I tapped the chair next to me.

"Thank you, Jill."

"Why don't you go and get your mum a drink?" I said.

"Fine!" Amber stood up. "Tea, I assume?"

"That would be lovely."

"Have you asked Jill about the circus?" Aunt Lucy said.

"She won't want to come with us." Pearl rolled her eyes. "Have you forgotten? She's afraid of clowns."

"I'm not afraid of them," I protested.

"Not afraid of what?" Amber was back.

Aunt Lucy took the cup of tea from her. "I was asking Pearl if you two had asked Jill if she wanted to come to the circus with us."

"You should definitely come," Amber said. "Pearl and I are going."

"What about the little ones?"

"They're a bit too young."

"I'm going too." Aunt Lucy took a sip of tea. "And you don't need to worry about the clowns because I read an article in The Candle that said the clown troupe had quit Candlefield Circus."

"I'm not scared of them anyway."

"Will you come, then?"

"Sure, why not? When is it?"

"A week on Wednesday."

"Okay. Count me in." I turned to the twins. "You were going to ask me something before Aunt Lucy arrived."

"Yeah." Pearl nodded. "Amber and I have been talking, haven't we?"

"And the guys too," Amber said.

"We all agree it would be for the best, don't we, Amber?"

"Yeah."

"I have absolutely no idea what you're talking about. I was having a much more intelligent conversation with my cat just before I came over here."

"You discuss your business's finances with your cat?" Pearl raised an eyebrow.

"Never mind that. What is it that you've all been discussing?"

The twins each seemed to be waiting for the other one to speak up; it was Amber who finally cracked. "We're all agreed that it would be a good thing if Lil and Lily were to grow up knowing both the sup and human worlds. That's why we intend to take them on regular visits there. Starting right now."

"I'm not sure that's such a good idea," Aunt Lucy said. "They're still very young."

"We knew that's what you'd say, Mum," Pearl said. "That's why we weren't going to tell you until it was all arranged."

"Actually, I think the twins are right," I chipped in. "It'll be much easier for their two girls to adapt to life in the human world when they're adults if they've been used to visiting there regularly."

"Thank you, Jill." Pearl beamed. "See, Mum, Jill thinks it's a good idea too."

"You all seem to be assuming the girls will want to go to the human world when they grow up. Not all sups do. Some prefer to stay here in Candlefield."

"Like you, you mean?" Amber snapped. "That's why you never took us there, isn't it? And it's why we're stuck here now."

"I'm sorry I was such a terrible mother." Aunt Lucy was

clearly upset.

"I never said that, Mum." Amber tried to backtrack.

"It's alright." Aunt Lucy stood up. "My opinion is clearly not wanted here."

"Aunt Lucy, wait." I tried to grab her hand, but she pulled away.

"It's alright. I have a lot to do today. I'll see you all later."

Oh bum!

"That's why we didn't want to say anything in front of her." Amber sighed. "We knew how she'd react."

"I'm sure she'll come around," I said. "She just needs time to get used to the idea. To be honest, I think she finds the human world a little scary."

"Precisely," Amber said. "And that's why we don't want our kids to grow up afraid of it."

"For what it's worth, I think you're doing the right thing."

"We were hoping you'd say that, weren't we, Pearl?"

"Yeah, that makes it easier for us to ask you."

"Ask me what?"

"We were thinking we might start by taking the girls over to the human world next weekend, and we were kind of hoping—" Her words trailed away.

"Hoping what?" That's when I realised I'd sealed my own fate. "That you could stay at my place?"

"Thanks, Jill," Pearl said. "It would only be for the one night. You won't even know we're there. We thought we'd take the kids around Washbridge on Saturday, and then go back to yours in the evening. We'd just need you to pick us up from Washbridge. And we'll leave on Sunday morning. We won't be any trouble, I promise."

"Please say yes, Jill," Amber pleaded.

"You did say you thought that it was a good idea." Pearl reminded me.

"Okay, but I can't promise to do this every time you come over if this is going to be a regular thing."

"That's okay. We'll look out for a cheap hotel that we can use, if you aren't able to put us up in future."

"It's going to be so great!" Pearl gushed.

Oh boy.

A few minutes later, the twins said their goodbyes, and set off on their shopping expedition. What had I just done? How had I allowed myself to agree to letting them stay the night? If I'd had my wits about me, I would have realised where the conversation was headed, and I could have sided with Aunt Lucy.

While I was in Cuppy C, I decided to take another look at the creche. I was still feeling a little uneasy about what I'd witnessed on my earlier visit. Maybe a second visit would put my mind at ease.

Just like last time, there were no sounds coming from the creche as I made my way upstairs. I was probably worrying about nothing. Maybe it was just that Belladonna had managed to create an incredibly relaxed atmosphere that fostered a calmness in both the children and their parents.

As I approached the creche, I could see that they were all fast asleep: the children and their parents. In fact, the only person not sleeping was Belladonna who was in a chair, reading a book. She gave me a little wave, and came over to join me.

"Nice to see you again, Jill. Did you want something?"

"Err, no. I've just had a drink with the twins, and I thought I'd pop up to see how things were going."

"It's all going splendidly so far."

"Everyone's asleep?"

"That's right."

"Isn't that a little strange?"

"Not really. If you'd been here half an hour ago, you'd have seen all the little ones running around. They've tired themselves out, so now they're having a rest."

"What about their parents?"

"Bringing up a youngster can be pretty tiring; you have to grab your sleep when you can. Would you like to stay a while until they wake up?"

"Err, no thanks, I'd better get going."

"Okay. Pop in anytime."

This couldn't be right, could it? On my first visit, the children had all been behaving like little angels; not a single tantrum to be seen. And this time, all of the kids and their parents were fast asleep. Did the twins know what was going on in their creche?

***

It was late afternoon when Mrs V came through to my office.

"A woman dropped this off just now." She held out a small, white envelope.

"Who was she?"

"I don't know, dear. She rushed in and out so quickly that I didn't have the chance to ask her."

"Okay, thanks. How's the whistling going?"

"He hasn't done it once all afternoon."

"That is good news. Perhaps it was just his nerves."

"Hmm." She sighed. "It's not just the whistling, I'm afraid."

"What else is he doing?"

"It'll sound like I'm deliberately picking fault with him, and I'm not, honestly."

"What's he done?"

"Every time I've looked at him this afternoon, he's had a finger up his nostril."

"Picking his nose?"

"Yes, but I really shouldn't complain about him because he's just sponsored me for the hula hoop event. One penny a minute."

"That was very nice of him." One penny? What a tightwad.

I tore open the envelope to find an invitation to a gathering of W.O.W. ladies at the house of Charlotte Greenmuch. According to the note, there was to be a small get together at her house on Friday. Tea and cake would be provided.

Normally, I would have avoided that kind of thing like the plague, but as a new member of W.O.W, I felt I should show my face at at least one or two of these functions. And besides, the invitation had included the magic word: cake.

There was no request for me to RSVP, so presumably I should just show up on the day. Maybe Grandma would be there too. I could always hope not.

***

By the time I'd wrapped up for the day, Mrs V had already left. Alistair, though, was still busy at his desk.

"You should have gone home by now, Alistair."

"I'd like to get this section finished before I leave." Thankfully, he removed his finger from his nostril before he spoke to me.

"Did you change your tie?" I pointed to the blue tie with a picture of an elephant on it.

"Err, yeah. I spilt coffee on the other one."

"Don't stay too late, and remember to lock up when you leave."

"Will do."

I couldn't fault the guy's enthusiasm. I'd just have to hope that his annoying little habits were a temporary blip brought on by first day nerves.

***

As soon as I pulled onto the drive, I spotted it in the Livelys' front garden. Mr Hosey might be able to fool most people with his new high-tech surveillance tree, but he couldn't fool me.

"This is a vast improvement, Mr Hosey. It's much more realistic than the previous one." He didn't reply; he was obviously afraid of giving himself away to other passers-by. "It must have cost you an arm and a leg."

"Are you okay, err —?"

I turned around to find Britt and Kit standing behind me.

"Her name's Jill." Kit prompted his wife.

"Sorry, of course it is. Are you okay, Jill?"

"Yes, thanks."

"It's just that it looked like you were talking to our new tree?"

"*Your* tree?"

"We thought the front garden looked a little bare, so we had it planted this afternoon," Kit said. "Do you like it?"

"Yes, I was just admiring it." I patted the trunk. "You're a real beauty."

Just then, Lovely began to weave in-between my legs. If the Livelys hadn't been standing there, I would have shooed her away, but to be polite, I bent down and gave her a stroke.

"Where's Winky?" Lovely asked me.

"He's back at the office."

"Who's back at the office?" Kit said.

Oh bum! What was I thinking? "Err, Jack is back at the office. In case you were wondering where he was."

"Right?"

"I'd better get going. It's my turn to make dinner. Catch you later."

When I got inside the house, I glanced through the window. The Livelys were still in the front garden, no doubt discussing their crazy neighbour who not only liked to get naked in the back garden, but also talked to trees and cats.

Chapter 4

"Do you think we should buy some toys before they come?" Jack was eating a banana for breakfast.

Ever since I'd told him that the twins and their little ones would be staying over on Saturday night, he'd been buzzing with excitement.

"I don't think that's necessary. They'll only be here overnight, and I'm sure the twins will bring the babies' favourite teddy bears or cuddly giraffes with them."

"No one has a cuddly giraffe."

"I did. His name was Neckie."

"You've just made that up."

"It's true. Ask Kathy the next time you see her."

"Do you still have him?"

"Neckie? Of course I don't. I threw him away when I was a teenager."

"How could you do that? I still have Kidney."

"*Kidney*?" I laughed. "What on earth was Kidney?"

"A teddy bear. My parents gave him to me when I was two or three years old."

"Why did you call him Kidney?"

"His name was supposed to be Sidney, but for some reason I always pronounced it as Kidney and the name just stuck."

"How come I've never seen him?"

"He's in one of the drawers in my bedside cabinet. The one in the spare room."

"Aww, that's so sweet. Do you go and give him a cuddle every now and then?"

"See, this is precisely why I've never mentioned Kidney to you before. Have you given any thought to where the twins and the babies are going to sleep on Saturday night?"

"I hadn't really thought about it. In the lounge I suppose."

"They're our guests. You can't expect them to sleep in the lounge."

"Guests are people that you've invited to stay. They invited themselves."

"Even so, we can't let them sleep downstairs. They can have our bedroom and we'll sleep down here."

"Are you insane? I'm not sleeping on a sofa. We'll have to clear out the spare bedroom before weekend. The twins can have that."

"What will we do with my furniture?"

"We can throw it all away. Or burn it."

"No way. I love that furniture. We'll have to put it in storage."

"That'll cost a small fortune. There is another option, but it would require a waiver of the no-magic pact."

"What do you have in mind?"

"I could shrink it. That way we could store it in something like a shoebox until the twins have left, then I'll magic it back to its normal size."

"That sounds like a plan."

"Yes, but we did say we wouldn't break the no-magic pact unless it was an emergency. I'm not sure this qualifies."

"So you'd rather pay the storage fees, would you?"

"I'll shrink the furniture."

"What time are the twins actually coming to the house?"

"They're going shopping in Washbridge during the day,

and they'll give us a call when they want us to pick them up. Talking of magic, don't forget that the twins don't know that you know about me."

"I know they don't know that I know. But you already know that."

"Could you repeat that?"

"Probably not."

After Jack had finished his banana and I'd eaten my cornflakes, we took our coffee through to the lounge.

"I never got around to asking you last night. How's the new office manager settling in?"

"Okay, so far. He seems very industrious."

"Is he getting on alright with Mrs V?"

"More or less, I suppose."

"You don't sound too sure."

"Everyone has annoying habits, don't they?"

"What does he do?"

"Whistles. A lot."

"That's not so bad."

"And picks his nose."

"Yuk."

"It's probably just the initial nerves. He does seem to share Mrs V's love of clowns, though."

"I bet you're thrilled about that."

"He's sponsored her too."

"Sponsored her to do what? Another knitathon?"

"No. She and the other yarnies are going to be hula hooping."

"Isn't that dangerous at their age?"

"You'd better not let Mrs V hear you say that. She bit my head off when I suggested that it was a strange choice of event for seniors."

"I hope you've sponsored her."

"We both have."

"*Both,* as in you and me?"

"Yeah. I knew you'd want to get involved."

"I do, but I remember what happened the last time you talked me into sponsoring something. It ended up costing me a small fortune."

"There's nothing to worry about this time. After all, how long can Mrs V possibly keep a hula hoop going? The most it will cost us will be a fiver each."

"Fair enough." He walked over to the window. "Did you see that the Livelys have planted a tree in their front garden?"

"Have they? I hadn't noticed."

What? I wasn't about to let Jack know what a fool I'd made of myself.

When I was ready to leave, Jack was still in the lounge, scribbling notes in his TenPinCon file.

I popped my head around the door. "Aren't you going to be late for work?"

"There's so much to do for this con. It was bad enough being the creative director; I should never have agreed to look after the marketing too."

"What have you come up with so far?"

"Zilch. I don't have a clue where to start."

"You'll just have to tell Tony and Clare that you can't do it."

"I can't let them down now." Suddenly, his face lit up. "I've had an idea."

"There, I knew you'd come up with something."

"Your grandmother could help."

"Grandma?"

"You're always saying she's a marketing genius."

"And she is, but what makes you think she'd agree to help you?"

"She'd help *you* if you asked."

"No, she wouldn't, and besides, I'm not getting involved."

He stood up, pulled me into his arms, and gave me a kiss. "There must be something I can do to change your mind."

"That's not going to work, buddy." I pushed him gently away.

"Please, Jill. I'm desperate. Won't you at least speak to her?"

"She'll say no."

"Will you at least try? Please."

"Okay, I'll ask her, but don't get your hopes up."

He pulled me back in for another hug and kiss. "You're the best."

***

Jack and I eventually left the house together. As we did, Kit Lively was just coming out of his door.

"Morning, Kit!" Jack called.

"Hi there, you two."

"We were just admiring your new tree."

"Thanks. Jill was actually talking to it yesterday. Is that a naturist thing? Talking to trees, I mean?"

Jack shot me a puzzled look.

"I thought I'd explained that I'm not a naturist," I said.

"Of course not." Kit winked as he got into his car. "It's okay. Your secret is safe with us."

After he'd driven away, Jack turned to me. "Were you talking to the tree?"

"Of course I wasn't." I scoffed. "All that exercise has clearly scrambled his brain."

Mr Ivers was on duty at the toll bridge.

"Good morning, Jill. Isn't it a beautiful day?"

"Lovely." I held out the cash, but he ignored it.

"I saw two frogs earlier."

"That's nice."

"I suppose they could have been toads. I'm never quite sure what the difference is."

If he didn't take my cash soon, he'd find out at first hand.

"The toll fee, Mr Ivers." I thrust my hand closer to his face.

"Of course, but first, you'll want to hear my exciting news."

"I'm actually running a little late."

"The first all-new edition of the movie newsletter will be available on Friday."

Whoop-de-doo. "That's great."

"You haven't heard the best part yet."

"I really do need to get going."

"I've decided to produce an audio version of the newsletter too."

"I think I'll just stick with the printed version."

"I know what you're thinking: More expense. But you'd be wrong. An audio copy will be made available free of charge to all subscribers."

"That's very generous of you."

"No prizes for guessing who'll be providing the narration."

"Could it be you by any chance?"

"Correct. And although I do say so myself, I have the perfect voice for it. I've often thought I could have been a voice-over artist. What do you think, Jill?"

I think that if you don't take this cash within the next thirty seconds, I won't be responsible for my actions. "You have a great voice, Mr Ivers. Now, the cash?"

"Thank you." He took the money, and raised the barrier.

As I drove away, he was still rattling on about his prospects as a voice actor.

***

"Morning, Mrs V. Morning, Alistair."

"Good morning, Jill." Alistair glanced up only briefly from his work.

Mrs V was wearing earmuffs, and she obviously hadn't heard me come in, so I waved my hand in front of her face.

"Sorry, Jill." She lifted the earmuffs from one ear. "I didn't hear you." She puckered her lips, and gestured towards Alistair.

From that, I gathered that my new office manager had been whistling again. At least he didn't have his finger up his nose.

"I see you managed to get your tie cleaned, Alistair," I said.

"Sorry?"

"You said you'd spilled coffee on it?"

"Oh yes, that's right. It's as good as new now."

"Do you need anything else from me?"

"Not yet, thanks. I've got plenty to be getting on with."

"Excellent."

"I signed up for the clown school last night," he said.

"Great."

"Now all I have to do is come up with a good clown name. I don't suppose you have any suggestions, do you, Jill?"

"No, sorry. I'm not really the person to ask about matters clown related."

"Jill is scared of clowns," Mrs V chipped in.

"No, I'm not." I rolled my eyes. "I've just never seen the point of them, that's all. Anyway, I'd better get going. Lots to do."

"Have you considered therapy?" Winky said.

"For what?"

"Your fear of clowns."

"Why does everyone think I'm afraid of clowns? It's a ridiculous notion."

"It just so happens that I'm a qualified therapist. And as luck would have it, I specialise in coulrophobia."

"In what?"

"The irrational fear of clowns. The first step in the process is for you to own your fear, so why don't you start by admitting it?"

"Because it isn't true. And even if it were true, which it isn't, the last person I'd turn to for help would be you. Now if you don't mind, I have work to do."

"There's no helping some people."

The situation at CASS was still weighing on my mind. Left to his own devices, Maligarth would destroy everything that was good about the school.

But not if I had anything to do with it.

Grandma had come up with a good suggestion: I needed to start by contacting the school governors, to find out as much as possible about the man, and to ask them why they'd appointed him.

The one person I knew I could trust at CASS was the caretaker, Reggie, so I gave him a call.

"Reggie, it's Jill."

"I take it you've heard."

"Heard what?"

"Maligarth has sacked me."

"When?"

"The day after you were over there. He made me pack my bags and leave the same day."

"Are you back in Candlefield?"

"Yeah. I'm still unpacking."

"I'm so sorry, Reggie. How are you?"

"Not great, to be honest. CASS was my life. I don't know what I'm going to do now."

"Keep your chin up. All may not yet be lost."

"What do you mean?"

"I'm not prepared to stand by while this man singlehandedly destroys the school."

"What can you do to stop him?"

"I don't know yet, but would you be willing to help?"

"Of course. Just tell me what you need, Jill."

"Why don't we meet up and we can discuss it?"

"Okay. Where?"

"What about Cuppy C?"

"Fine by me. When?"

"There's no time like the present. If that's okay with you?"

"I'll be there in a few minutes."

When I arrived at Cuppy C, Amber and Mindy were behind the counter.

"Hey, you two. I'm meeting Reggie here in a few minutes. Give him whatever he wants, and I'll settle up with you later. And I'll have my usual, please."

"Are you feeling okay?" Amber smirked.

"Fine. Why?"

"You just offered to pay for someone else's drinks. You never do that."

"Of course I do. You make me sound like a real cheapskate."

"That's because you are."

"Rubbish." I checked to make sure Belladonna wasn't anywhere around. "How's the creche going?"

"Fantastic. It's one of the best decisions we've ever made."

"And Belladonna?"

"She's great. We couldn't have recruited anyone more suited to the job."

"Did she mention I'd popped up there a couple of times?"

"Yeah." Amber grinned. "She reckons you were checking up on her."

"No, I wasn't. I was just curious to see how things were going. Mind you, I did find one thing a little weird."

"What's that?"

"The first time I went up there, the kids were playing in silence. There was no screaming, no tears or tantrums."

"That just proves how good she is. The children all react really well to her."

"It felt a little weird, that's all. Then, yesterday when I took another look, everyone was asleep. The kids *and* their parents."

"That's down to the relaxed atmosphere Belladonna has created."

"Something just didn't feel right."

"You're doing what you always do, Jill. You're seeing problems where there aren't any."

"Maybe, but that first time, there was one particular little girl with her mother. As soon as her mum told her to put down a toy because it was time to go home, the girl did as she was told without a word of complaint. No tears, no backchat or tantrums."

"What's wrong with that?"

"Nothing. Except that when I saw the same little girl and her mother out on the street just a few minutes later, the child was being a total monster. She was having a real strop about something. It was as if she was a different person."

"Which just underlines how good Belladonna is. There's no wonder we're getting more and more parents and kids here every day. If the numbers continue to grow, we may have to start a waiting list."

Chapter 5

"I'm sorry I'm late, Jill." Reggie was struggling to catch his breath; he'd obviously been running. "I couldn't find my other shoe."

"That's okay. You didn't need to rush over here. Go and get yourself something from the counter; I've told them to put it on my account."

"That's very kind of you." When he eventually joined me at the table, he had a milkshake and a plateful of buns. "I hope this is okay. I was only going to have one of these, but the young woman who served me insisted that you'd want me to have them all."

Behind the counter, Amber was grinning from ear to ear.

"That's fine."

"I'm starving." He took a huge bite out of one of the buns. "I haven't got around to getting any food in yet; I wasn't expecting to be home until half-term."

"What Maligarth has done to you is disgraceful."

"I don't think it would have mattered what I did or how hard I tried to please him, he'd already decided he wanted me out."

"What will you do now?"

"I have no idea. CASS is all I've ever known. Who'd want a big lummox like me?"

"Don't be silly. With all the experience you have under your belt, you shouldn't have any problems finding another job. Have you ever thought of looking for work in the human world?"

"I'm not sure if I could work alongside humans."

"They don't bite. They're not that much different to

sups really."

"I may have to consider it, if I can't find anything here in Candlefield. It isn't going to be easy because I don't have any references, and Maligarth isn't likely to give me one."

"I'm sure Ms Nightowl would."

"If I can find her. No one knows where she's gone. It's like she's just disappeared. Anyway, enough about me. I'll be okay. You said you needed my help."

"There must be a way to stop Maligarth, and if there is, I intend to find it. First, though, I need to find out as much about the man as I can."

"No one seems to know anything about him." Reggie was on his second bun. "Even Ms Nightowl said she knew nothing about the man."

"That's pretty much what she told me too, but his appointment must have been approved by the school governors. They must know something about him."

"I guess so."

"I have no idea who the governors are," I said. "And I don't really want to make enquiries at CASS because I might alert Maligarth to what I'm doing. I was hoping you might be able to find out who they are."

"I'll definitely try. I still have a lot of contacts there. I'll see what I can find out."

"Great. You'll need to do it on the quiet. Like I said, I don't want Maligarth to get wind of what I'm doing."

"Don't worry, Jill. I'll be the soul of discretion."

***

I'd promised that I'd drop in at Kathy's shop because

she wanted me to meet Pippa, the witch who would be managing the new shop in West Chipping. It was Pippa's first time working in the human world, so I had no doubt she would be doubly nervous.

When I arrived at the shop, Kathy was busy with a customer.

"Good morning, madam, how can I help you today?" The eager young woman had dimples and a dazzling smile.

"Pippa?"

"That's right. How did you know?"

"I'm Kathy's sister."

"Jill? Thank you so much for getting me this job."

"I'm pretty sure you did that yourself. All I did was put your name forward."

"Thanks anyway. I thought it might take a while for me to find something."

I lowered my voice to a whisper. "Have you moved here yet or are you magicking yourself back and forth every day?"

"I'm living here in Washbridge now with my boyfriend, Howie."

"He's a human, right?"

"That's right. Butter told me that you live with a human too."

"Jack, yeah."

"Has it been difficult? Keeping your secret, I mean?"

"It was tricky at first, but it gets easier. What does your boyfriend do?"

"He's a policeman."

"Really? So is Jack. Where's Howie stationed?"

"Here in Washbridge."

"Jack used to be, but he got a transfer to West Chipping."

"I see you've met my new manager." Kathy had finished with her customer.

"Pippa's boyfriend is a policeman."

"I know. She told me when I interviewed her."

"When does the new shop open?"

"A week tomorrow. You'll have to come to the big launch."

"I will if I can, but I—"

"There'll be cake."

"I'll be there. What time does it start?"

***

As I made my way back up the high street, Betty came out of She Sells.

"Hi, Betty." Whatever I did, I mustn't look at her eyebrows. Too late, I was already transfixed.

"What do you think, Jill?"

"What do you mean?"

"You were staring at my eyebrows. Deli has been pencilling the left one in for me."

"It's amazing. I wouldn't even have known one was missing if you hadn't reminded me."

"She certainly makes a better job of it than I ever could."

"Deli told me that you'd come to an amicable agreement."

"I'm not sure I'd call it amicable, but it is acceptable."

"I'm sorry, I was the one who recommended you go to that salon."

"It isn't your fault. It's that lunatic husband of hers.

Whenever I go in there now, he always disappears into the back. I think he's scared of what I might do to him."

I wasn't particularly hungry, so I just grabbed a sandwich for lunch on my way back to the office.

There was no sign of Mrs V, but Alistair was at his desk, eating a Pot Noodle.

"I hope you don't mind me eating lunch at my desk, Jill?"

"Of course not. I see you swapped your tie again?"

"Err, yeah. I dropped some noodles on it."

"Just as well you keep a change of tie with you."

"I like to be prepared."

"I'm surprised you didn't want to take a walk outside in your lunch break, to get a little fresh air."

"I would have done, but I thought I might bump into one of those clowns." He gave a little shiver. "They give me the creeps."

"Right? I'll leave you to it, then."

Winky and the professor were at my desk; they seemed oblivious to my arrival.

"Excuse me." I cleared my throat. "That's my desk."

"We're almost done." Winky was studying the paperwork in front of him. "Okay, Prof, I'm happy with that." He scribbled his signature at the bottom of the last page, and then slid the papers over for the professor to sign. "A pleasure to do business with you, Prof."

"Likewise."

Once the professor had disappeared out of the window, I shooed Winky out of my chair. "What was that all about?"

"We've just signed a contract for our joint venture: Cat Zip.

"Don't you mean cat nip? You're a bit late to the game there, aren't you?"

"Not cat nip. That's just a big con, anyway."

"What do you mean?"

"You two-leggeds are so gullible. Do you really think that cat nip has any effect on cats?"

"Of course it does. I've seen it."

"You mean something like this?" He started to walk around the office as though he was inebriated. "Look at me. I've just sniffed some cat nip."

"Are you telling me that it doesn't really have any effect?"

"Of course it doesn't, but every cat that gets their owner to buy some receives a small commission on the sale. You have to hand it to Conor. It's a work of genius. I only wish I'd thought of it."

"Who's Conor?"

"Conor the Con. He's a brilliant con artist. He was the one who came up with the idea of cat nip."

"And this Conor, he's a cat, I assume?"

"Of course. No way a two-legged could have come up with something as brilliant as this."

"So what's Cat Zip, then?"

"First, I'll need you to sign this." He produced a sheet of paper from somewhere. "It's a standard NDA."

"Okay." I signed the agreement and handed it back to him.

"What would you say is the biggest cause of feline injury and death in a city like Washbridge?"

"Err, I don't know."

"Come on, Jill. It really isn't that difficult."

"The roads? Being hit by a car?"

"Bingo, and that's where Cat Zip comes in. Answer me this, why did the chicken cross the road?"

"What does that have to do with anything?"

"Humour me."

"To get to the other side."

"Precisely, and that's exactly why so many felines are injured on the roads. Because they're trying to get to the other side."

"Duh! I would have thought that was obvious. I still don't understand how your project is going to reduce the number of cats who are injured or killed on the roads."

"It's really very simple. Cat Zip will give them a safer way to get across the road."

"How?"

"It's in the name."

"Zip? I don't get—wait a minute, you don't mean—you can't possibly mean—"

"Zip wires, yes. Ingenious or what?"

"You are certifiable. Are you seriously proposing to have cats traversing the roads on zip wires?"

"Not just any old zip wire. Cat Zips."

Oh boy.

I sometimes think that I should write a book about my life, but who would buy it? I mean, who in their right mind would want to read about cats traversing the roads on zip wires? They'd have to be completely crazy.

Yes, I'm looking at you.

***

I needed to collect the notepad from Bernie Sparks, so I gave her a call just to make sure she was in, and told her I'd be over there in thirty minutes.

Mrs V was back at her desk, but she was no longer wearing the earmuffs. Alistair had finished his pot noodle, and now had one finger up his left nostril.

"I'm nipping out to see Mrs Sparks. I'm not sure how long I'll be or even if I'll be back today."

"Okay, dear." Mrs V looked up from her knitting. "Isn't Mr Song supposed to be installing the replacement sign today?"

"I'd forgotten all about that. When he comes, would you please check and double-check the new sign before he puts it up? If there's anything wrong with it, don't let him install it — just give me a call."

"Will do, dear."

***

Bernie Sparks lived only five minutes from Kathy's house.

"This is Kirk." She handed me a framed photograph of herself and a man, standing on a beach. "That was taken in Hawaii three years ago. We went there for our crystal wedding anniversary."

"He was a very handsome man."

"Kind too. I was blessed to share my life with him."

After Bernie had made the tea, she handed me a small notepad.

"I'm not sure how much help this is going to be, Jill.

Kirk always said that he was the only one who would understand his cryptic notes. I think that was deliberate, so that if anyone got hold of this, they wouldn't be able to make head nor tail of it."

"I'll take it anyway. It can't do any harm. You said that your husband didn't discuss the articles he was working on, but do you happen to know what prompted him to investigate the casino in the first place?"

"Actually, I do. It was purely by chance that it came about. Kirk didn't go out without me very often, but this particular day, it was the birthday of one of his friends. There were four of them—four guys. After they'd been drinking in Washbridge, someone suggested they end the evening at the casino. Kirk had never been there before, and to be honest, I don't think he was very keen on the idea, but he allowed his friends to talk him into it. When they arrived at the casino, the doorman refused to allow Kirk in."

"Just Kirk?"

"Yes, the others had already walked by the doorman before Kirk was stopped."

"Why wouldn't they let him in?"

"The doorman insisted Kirk was drunk, but that was nonsense. None of them were drunk, and if anything, the other three had had more to drink than Kirk."

"I assume the others didn't stay there after Kirk was refused entry."

"They were going to leave, but Kirk insisted that they stayed. He said he was tired, which was true, and that he wanted to get back home anyway. They took a little persuading, but in the end, they went inside, and Kirk got a taxi home."

"And that's what got him interested in the casino?"

"Yes. He told me he thought there was something dodgy about the place, and it seems his instincts were right."

"But he never actually told you what he'd discovered?"

"No."

"What about the three friends who were with him that night? Do you have their contact details?"

"Yes, I'll write them down for you before you leave."

"Thanks. Is there anything else you can think of that might help my investigation?"

"No." She hesitated. "Well, there was one thing."

"What is it?"

"It's just that I found something strange in Kirk's jacket. It's probably nothing."

"Tell me, please."

"It was a receipt for a meal in a restaurant called Wonders."

"What's unusual about that?"

"Maybe nothing. But I can't find any trace of a restaurant called Wonders anywhere."

Chapter 6

"Yes!" I shouted, drawing a few curious looks from passers-by.

I didn't care what anyone thought; I was so excited at having got my new sign. It was now perfect in every way.

Jill Maxwell

Private Investigator

It had taken much longer than it should have, but all's well that ends well.

Alistair was beavering away at his desk, with the obligatory finger up one nostril.

"Could I have a word please, Jill?" Mrs V said.

"Sure, what is it?"

"In your office, please."

"Okay."

After she'd made a point of closing the door behind her, she said, "It's about Alistair."

"If it's the nose-picking thing, I—"

"It isn't that, although that is quite disgusting."

"What is it, then?"

"I'm not sure how to put this."

"Has he said something to upset you?"

"Yes. No, at least not in the way you mean. It's all very strange."

"Just tell me what's happened."

"Do you remember he mentioned that I was going to knit him some clown socks?"

"Yes?"

"Well, just now, I showed him what I'd done so far, and he said he hated clowns. That they gave him the creeps."

"It's funny you should say that because he said something similar to me, but I didn't really think much of it at the time."

"I know that some people are afraid of clowns. You for example."

"I'm not actually."

"But he said he'd signed up for the clown school. Why would he do that if he doesn't like them?"

"Beats me. It's all very strange. How's the whistling going? I noticed you didn't have the earmuffs on when I came in just now."

"That's another weird thing. The mornings are terrible. It's whistle, whistle, whistle — non-stop. But then, after lunch, there's not a whistle to be heard."

"That's good at least."

"But that's when the nose-picking begins."

"Oh dear."

"Another thing, Jill. Have you noticed he changes his tie at lunchtime?"

"That's because he spilled coffee on it yesterday."

"And today?"

"Noodles, he said."

"I just don't know what to make of him, Jill."

"I realise it must be difficult having to share the office with someone after having it to yourself for so long."

"It's not that. I shared with Jules and that was okay."

"If I remember correctly, you two had your moments."

"Only when she first started."

"Exactly, and it's only Alistair's second day. You have to give him a chance to settle in."

"You're right. I'm being very unfair to the young man."

"Not at all. You were right to come and talk to me about

it, but let's give it a couple of weeks to see how things develop. I'm sure it will all work out fine. Can you do that?"

"Of course. What do you think I should do about his clown socks?"

"I'd hold off on those for the time being if I were you."

"What did I tell you?" Winky jumped onto my desk. "The new guy is a cheese short of a mousetrap."

"That isn't even a saying. And coming from someone who is considering selling zip wires to cats, I'm not sure you're in any position to talk."

"You only have to look at the guy to see he's a nutjob. I mean, those ties? Where did he get those from? Ugly Ties Inc?"

"I'm not going to discuss members of my staff with a cat."

"Please yourself. I'm only trying to help. Don't blame me when the men in white coats come knocking at the door, and take doliphant boy away."

"What's a doliphant?"

"Haven't you noticed? He wears a tie with a dolphin on it in the morning, and one with an elephant on it in the afternoon. Dolphin plus elephant equals doliphant."

"Don't you have zip wires to sell?"

I'd be lying if I said I wasn't beginning to have a few doubts about my new office manager, but like I'd said to Mrs V, it was only day two. Things were bound to get better.

Weren't they?

I'd been hoping that Kirk Sparks' notepad might give me some clues into what he'd discovered about the Lucky Thirteen Casino, but I was to be sorely disappointed. His notes weren't so much cryptic as non-existent. In fact, under the heading **Lucky Thirteen** there were only three scribbled lines of text:

No 5 allowed.
Got it wrong. Some 5 allowed.
Only 5 win.

And when I say scribbled, I really do mean that. His handwriting was even worse than mine, and that was saying something. I had no idea what those three lines of text were supposed to mean, but it seemed clear that the number *five* was the key. All I had to do now was find out what the *five* represented.

I searched the online archives for articles on the casino. The most recent, unsurprisingly, covered the death of Kirk Sparks. After seeing The Bugle's headline, I could understand why Bernie had been upset. Apparently oblivious to the effect their words might have on the deceased's relatives, they'd chosen to go with the headline: **Unlucky Strike**.

The other newspapers had resisted the temptation to use the sensationalist, insensitive approach employed by The Bugle, but they all agreed that a freak lightning strike had dislodged the stone dice that had crushed Kirk Sparks.

By digging further back into the archives, I hoped that I

might uncover more information about the casino. Maybe even some hint of a scandal that might give me a pointer towards what Kirk had been investigating.

Unfortunately, I was to be disappointed. The oldest article dated back to five years earlier when the casino had first opened. Neither Washbridge nor West Chipping councils had wanted the casino, but permission had eventually been granted for it to be located on the retail park halfway between the two. The owner was a Mr Orville Ringstone, about whom I could find no other information. It was almost as though he hadn't existed prior to opening the casino.

Since then, there had been precious few articles relating to the casino until the recent tragic incident. The few pieces I did find were all innocuous; mainly related to special events that had taken place there.

I finished my research feeling that I was no further forward. Hopefully, the three men who had been with Kirk on the night that he'd been turned away from the casino would be able to help.

Mrs V came through to my office. "A woman has just dropped this off for you."

"Who was she?"

"I don't know. I did try to ask her, but she was in and out like a flash."

I opened the envelope to discover an invitation to another W.O.W. gathering to be held at the home of Camilla Soapling on Monday next week.

"What's a beetle drive, Mrs V?"

"Goodness, it's a long time since I've been to one of those."

"But what are they?"

"It's a game. You throw a dice and draw a beetle. It's really fun."

"It sounds like it." Yawn.

"Who's invited you to a beetle drive?"

"It's—err—one of our new neighbours."

"I wonder why she didn't introduce herself."

"She's a busy woman."

"Will you go? To the beetle drive?"

"I'll think about it. Probably not. I'm going to shoot off in a few minutes because I need to call and see Grandma before I head home."

"Alright, dear. I'll see you tomorrow."

"Beetle drive?" Winky laughed. "Don't you have to be over ninety to play that?"

"I hadn't heard of it until just now."

"Still, thinking about it, you'd probably enjoy it. It's about your pace."

***

When I arrived at Ever, I half expected to find the Everettes continuing with their protest outside the shop, but there was no sign of them.

Julie, the head Everette, was still dressed in canary yellow, but she looked much happier than the last time I'd seen her.

"Hi, Jill."

"Hi. I take it the protest is over?"

"Yes. I'm pleased to report that your grandmother decided to see sense and allow us to go back to the red uniforms."

"That's great." To say I was surprised would have been an understatement. Grandma rarely backed down over anything. "When will you get them back?"

"Get what back?"

"The red uniforms?"

"We're wearing them." She gave me a puzzled look.

"Right, yes, of course. Sorry, I'm not on my 'A' game today."

"I have days like that too." She smiled.

"Is she in her office?"

"Yes. She was drinking a strange, green concoction when I popped my head around the door a few minutes ago. Some kind of herbal tea I imagine."

"Do you have a minute, Grandma?"

"As long as it's quick. I'm working on an upgrade to ForEver Young."

"Your anti-ageing cream?"

"Yes. Have you tried it yet?"

"I don't need anti-ageing cream."

"Hmm."

"I see the Everettes are back at work."

"And not before time. How am I supposed to run a business with those girls walking around on the pavement outside?"

"Julie seems to think you backed down."

"She does, doesn't she?" She cackled.

"She also seems to think that the yellow uniform she's wearing is red."

"Does she?" She cackled even louder. "Isn't that strange? Perhaps she's colour blind?"

"You can't go around casting spells on people willy-nilly."

"Did you come down here to ask me something or just to shoot the breeze? Because if it's the latter, I don't have the time to waste."

"I need your help."

"Again? What is it this time?"

"Actually, it's for Jack."

"That's your human, isn't it? Why would I want to help him?"

"Because he's my husband."

"Don't remind me. I've tried to block that out."

"Will you help him or not?"

"With what?"

"He's agreed to help with the marketing for a convention, but there's one slight problem."

"Which is?"

"He doesn't have a clue what he's doing. He's never done any marketing before."

"So you told him that I'd be able to help him?"

"Actually, it was Jack's idea. He's been very impressed by some of the recent marketing you've done. Like the Surfing Extravaganza for example. He said if anyone could do it, you could."

"He did, did he? Maybe that human has more sense than I credited him with. What exactly is this convention?"

"TenPinCon."

"What's that?"

"It's for people who like ten-pin bowling, and for cosplayers."

"What's a cosplayer?"

"It's—err—kind of difficult to explain. Basically, they're people who like to dress up as their favourite comic book characters."

"Just when I was beginning to think there was some hope for humans. Who would want to attend such an event?"

"Ten-pin bowling enthusiasts and cosplayers. It's actually our next-door neighbours who are organising it. They're hardcore cosplayers; they go to a different one almost every week."

"They're humans too, I assume?"

"Yeah."

"When is this convention?"

"In four weeks' time."

"That doesn't give us very long. What has Jack done so far?"

"Well, err—actually, nothing."

"What's the budget?"

"There isn't one."

"If there isn't any cash, what am I supposed to do?"

"I thought you could—err, you know."

"I have no idea what you're talking about."

"Yes, you do. You could use magic."

"Let me get this straight. You're the one who's always preaching to me that I shouldn't use magic in the human world, but now because it suits you, you're encouraging me to do it. Do you know what I call that?"

"Hypocritical?"

"No." She grinned. "Inspired. You're getting more like me every day."

"Right. Thanks." That was possibly the worst thing anyone had ever said to me. "Does that mean you'll do it?"

"Why not? How difficult can it be to persuade a few thousand dumb humans to go to some kind of stupid convention?"

"Thanks, Grandma."

"You will of course owe me a favour."

"*A favour*?" A shiver ran down my spine as I recalled the last time I'd agreed to owe her a favour. Those bunions still gave me nightmares.

"It's only fair, isn't it?"

"I suppose so."

"Off you pop, then. I have cream to develop."

"Okay, thanks." I started for the door, but then hesitated. "Do the ladies of W.O.W. go in for a lot of informal gatherings?"

"A few, but it's a while since I went to one."

"Right. Okay, thanks again."

Julie gave me a wave on my way out. She was still looking resplendent in yellow.

Based on what Grandma had just told me, I could only conclude that she hadn't been invited to either of the two W.O.W. gatherings. I'd considered mentioning them to her, but I didn't want to cause friction unnecessarily.

***

When I arrived home, Britt was out front, watering her flowers. Lovely, meanwhile, was using the new tree as a scratching post.

"Stop that!" Britt tried to shoo the cat away from the tree, but Lovely ignored her, and continued her assault.

"Hi, Britt," I said.

"Hi there, err—"

"Jill."

"I don't know what's wrong with Lovely. She's usually so well behaved."

"Cats can be testing at times. I can certainly vouch for that."

"She seems to have gone off her food too. I wonder if it's because she's missing that cat of yours. Wonky."

"It's Winky, and I wouldn't think it's that. It's more likely to be the upset of moving to a new house. It can be quite traumatic for a cat."

"I suppose you're right."

Just then, a phone rang inside Britt's house. "Sorry, err—" She hurried to the door. "I'd better go and get that."

"Okay. See you."

Before I could go inside, Lovely came hurrying over to me. "Hey, Jill!"

How come the cat could remember my name, but her owner couldn't?

"If you're going to ask about Winky, I—"

"It's not that. He had his chance and blew it. I was going to ask you a small favour."

I glanced around quickly to make sure none of the other neighbours were around. "What kind of favour?"

"My two-leggeds have taken it upon themselves to change my food. That slop they've bought for me is horrible."

"That's why you're not eating?"

"Yeah. Memory woman thinks I'm pining for Winky, but I just want some decent nosh."

"I'm not sure what I can do about it."

"Have a word, will you?"

"What would I say?"

"You'll think of something. Please. If things carry on like this, I'll have to find myself a new home. I don't suppose you'd consider taking me in, would you?"

"I'll have a word with Britt and Kit about the food."

"Thanks. Winky said you were a star."

I very much doubted that.

Chapter 7

"Kathy called while you were in the shower," Jack said when I came downstairs for breakfast.

"Is everything okay?"

"I think so, yeah. She's going to pop over in about ten minutes."

"Didn't you tell her I'd be on my way to work?"

"No, I said you'd have a cup of tea waiting for her."

"Thanks. Did she say what it was about?"

"I got the impression it wasn't something she wanted to discuss with me. I did tell her the twins were coming over this weekend, though."

"Please tell me you're joking?"

"I didn't realise it was supposed to be a secret. She seems really keen to see them."

"Great."

"Are you sure your grandmother didn't give you an idea of what she had in mind for the promo when you spoke to her yesterday?"

"No, I told you last night. She just said she was prepared to do it. She did say that I'd owe her a favour in return, though."

"That's not so bad, is it?"

"It was the last time."

"Why? What did you have to do?"

"Trust me, you're better off not knowing."

"Maybe I should contact her, suggest that she and I get together to brainstorm a few ideas."

"That's definitely not a good idea. She isn't exactly a team player, and besides, she doesn't have a very high opinion of — err — "

"Of what? Of me?"

"Of humans in general. It's nothing personal."

"It sounds kind of personal."

"This is no time to be offended. She's said she'll help, and I'm sure she will."

"I hope you're right because I promised Tony and Clare that I'd take care of it."

"You were the one who wanted her help. You've seen what she's capable of, so now you need to let her do her thing."

"Okay, you're right. I just don't like handing over control, that's all."

"I thought I was supposed to be the control freak in this family."

"Talking of which, have you and the office manager come to blows yet?"

"Of course not. He's going to spend the first two weeks reviewing the business, and then he'll present me with his findings and suggestions."

"That's when the sparks will fly."

"Not at all. I'm open minded enough to embrace new ideas."

"O-kay." Jack laughed.

"You'll see."

"We need a few things from the shop. Will you have time to call on your way home tonight?"

"There's no need. We can use Little Jack's new shopping app."

"He's got an app?"

"I thought I'd told you about it." I grabbed my phone. "Look."

"Cool. Have you tried it yet?"

"No, this will be the first time. What do we need?"

Jack reeled off a list of everything we were short of, and I added them to the app's shopping basket.

"That's it," he said.

"I don't think so. You've forgotten the most important item."

"What's that?"

"Seriously? You have to ask?"

"Custard creams?"

"What else?"

"I have to get going or I'll be late." He gave me a kiss. "I'll leave you to finish off the order. Have a good day. Love you."

"Love you, too."

Now, how many packets of custard creams should I order? Two? Maybe three. Four would just be greedy.

This was the first item where I'd needed to order more than one unit. I clicked on the quantity button and scrolled until it reached four.

Hold on! What was going on? The quantity field wouldn't stop scrolling no matter how many times I clicked on it. It eventually came to a halt when it reached the maximum of twenty-five. Even I didn't need that many custard creams, so I tried to adjust the quantity, but the stupid thing wouldn't let me do it. It was stuck.

What should I do? I didn't want to abandon the order altogether. If I did that, I'd have to start over again, and I didn't trust myself to remember everything that Jack had listed. Fortunately, there was a comments box on the checkout page, so I entered a note to say the quantity of custard creams was incorrect, and that I actually only wanted four packets.

I confirmed the time slot I wanted, and then placed the order.

Job done!

I was expecting Kathy at any minute, so I put the kettle on. With almost perfect timing, she arrived just as it boiled.

"Why didn't you tell me that the twins were coming over this weekend, Jill?"

"I thought you'd be busy with the new shop."

"Not too busy to see the twins and their darling babies. What time are they coming?"

"They're going to spend most of Saturday shopping in Washbridge, then either Jack or I will pick them up and bring them here. They're staying with us on Saturday night and going back on Sunday morning."

"We'll come over Saturday evening, then. It'll just be me and Lizzie because Mikey is going fishing with Pete. Lizzie is going to be so excited to see the babies. Where are they all going to sleep? You're surely not going to make them sleep in the lounge, are you?"

"Of course not. What kind of host do you think I am? They'll have the spare room."

"Isn't that full of Jack's furniture?"

"It is at the moment, but we'll have it cleared out by the time they arrive. Anyway, what did you want to see me about?"

"It's nothing, really. I'm probably worrying needlessly."

"Is it Lizzie again?"

"Yeah.

"The ghost thing?"

"No. I've stopped worrying about that because she

rarely mentions it these days."

"What's up, then?"

"It's stupid. You'll think I'm crazy."

"You're here now, so you might as well tell me."

"Over the last week or so, Lizzie has been really upset every morning when she wakes up. Because of her dreams."

"Is she having nightmares?"

"No, that's just it. She's upset because she says she can't dream anymore."

"We all have periods like that."

"I know. I've tried to explain to her that it's not that she isn't dreaming—it's just that she can't remember them. It doesn't do any good, though. She's convinced that she'll never dream again."

"Poor little mite. Is there anything I can do?"

"Not really, no. I imagine it's just another phase that will pass, like the ghosts. I don't really know why I came over here. I guess I just needed someone other than Pete to talk to."

"What does he say about it?"

"That I worry too much." She forced a smile. "I know he's right, but I can't help it. You'll understand when you have kids of your own."

That was my cue to get out of there. "I really do have to get going."

"Me too. Sorry to burden you with my problems."

"That's okay."

"There was one other thing while I'm here. I need a favour, actually."

"What is it this time?"

"Pete and I have been invited to a do in London next

Monday. It's a dinner sponsored by one of the top landscape gardening magazines. It's all very prestigious, but it will mean an overnight stay. Pete's parents are going to see to the kids during the daytime, but they have something arranged themselves that night. I wondered if you and Jack might be able to come over to our place to babysit for the night?"

"Wouldn't it be easier for the kids to stay here?"

"It's just that they have school the next day. I think they'll settle better in their own beds. Would you be able to do it?"

"I suppose so. Monday, you say?"

"Yeah. You wouldn't need to be there until seven o'clock. Pete's parents will be there until then."

"Okay."

"You're the best, sis."

So everyone kept telling me.

***

I was halfway up the stairs to my office when I heard it: the tuneless whistling.

The source of that awful noise was wearing his dolphin tie. "Morning, Jill."

"Morning, Alistair."

Mrs V pulled the earmuffs away from one ear. "Morning, Jill."

"Hi. Any messages?"

"Mr Macabre phoned a few minutes ago. He said he's going to pop in to see you tomorrow."

"What does he want?"

"He wouldn't say. Only that it was important."

"It can't be about the sign. I've only got the one now. It's a pity he hasn't got anything better to do with his time."

"By the way, Jill," Alistair said. "I've decided on RibTickle."

"Sorry?"

"For my clown name. What do you think?"

Now I was thoroughly confused. It was only yesterday afternoon that he'd said clowns gave him the creeps.

"I—err—it's a very good name."

"I thought so. I wanted to go for something different. All I need now are my clown socks."

"Right. Anyway, I'd better crack on."

Winky was standing on the window sill; he appeared to be signalling to someone across the way.

"Excuse me," I said.

He almost toppled out of the window. "Are you trying to kill me? Why would you creep up on a person like that?"

"Sorry. I didn't realise you hadn't heard me come in. What are you up to anyway?"

"Isn't it obvious?" He shuffled to one side to give me a better view.

"You've got the zip wire installed."

"It's a Cat Zip."

"Sorry. That was quick."

"This is only the prototype. We're going to run tests before starting full-scale production."

"Is that the professor over there?" I pointed to the figure in an open window on the fourth floor of the building across the road.

"Yeah." He spoke into a small walkie-talkie, "Winky to the prof, come in."

"Prof receiving, loud and clear. Over."

"How's it looking, Prof? Over."

"So far, so good. I need to do a few more checks before we test it. Over."

"I hear you loud and clear, Prof. When will it be ready to test? Over."

"Hopefully, tomorrow. Over."

"Great stuff, Prof. Over and out."

"When you say, test it?" I said. "What does that entail exactly?"

"What do you think? There's only one way to test a Cat Zip."

"That's what I thought. So the professor is going to zip from that window to this one?"

"Not the professor. He's an academic. I couldn't expect him to do that."

"I suppose not. So who will be testing it?"

"Me, of course."

"But it's dangerous. You could be killed."

"Rubbish. The professor knows what he's doing. Once he's declared it safe, the test will just be a formality. I'm actually looking forward to it."

***

I was doing my best to focus on the Sparks case, but it wasn't easy because I kept seeing flashes of Winky zip wiring high above the road. He seemed very confident in the professor, but what if his calculations were wrong?

My phone rang, and to be honest, I was quite pleased

for the distraction.

"Aunt Lucy?"

"Do you think you could pop over, Jill?"

"Sure. Is everyone okay?"

"Everyone's fine. There's just something I need you to see."

As soon as I walked through the door, I knew exactly why she'd asked me to go over. Every wall in the hallway was covered in pictures, which appeared to have been created using crayons. They looked like the sort of thing a toddler would produce.

Aunt Lucy was in the lounge; the walls in there too were covered in similar pictures.

"I take it Barry did these?"

"Who else?"

"They're terrible."

"I know. It wouldn't be so bad but he's churning them out at an alarming rate. When he asked if I'd mind if he put them up on the walls, I assumed he meant they'd just be in the spare bedroom, but now they're all over the house."

"We're going to have to be cruel to be kind. I'll tell him that these are awful, and that he should focus on quality rather than quantity."

"You'll be wasting your time. When Dolly came around yesterday, she heaped praise on him for the work he's been producing."

"Dolly? She can't draw for toffee herself."

"Try telling Barry that."

"I'll go and have a word with him."

Barry came charging over to me. "I'm sorry, Jill, but I

don't have time to go for a walk today. I'm too busy with my drawings."

"Hi, Jill!" Rhymes popped his head out from under the cupboard. "Do you know when I'll get my books?"

"I'm not sure. I'll ask Jack."

"I've changed my mind about publishing a book," Barry said.

"Oh? I thought that's what all these pictures were for?"

"They were, but then Dolly persuaded me it would be better to hold my own exhibition. Isn't that a great idea?"

"Err, I'm not sure. Aren't those expensive and difficult to organise?"

"Dolly says she's going to do it for me. I'm going to be a famous artist, Jill."

"That's great."

"Did you come upstairs to tell me something?"

"Err, no. I just popped up to say hi."

"Well?" Aunt Lucy was waiting at the bottom of the stairs. "Did you break the bad news to him that he's never going to be an artist?"

"Not exactly."

Poor Aunt Lucy. She soon wouldn't be able to move in that house for Barry's pictures.

I asked her if she wanted to come with me to Cuppy C, but she was expecting Lily to wake up at any moment, and she'd need feeding.

Pearl and Mindy were behind the counter, and for a change, it was Mindy who couldn't wait to tell me her news.

"Miles is moving to the human world."

Miles Best was Mindy's ex-boyfriend who had been a

long-time thorn in the twins' side.

"How come?"

"He's got himself a new girlfriend. A human, apparently."

"What's happening to Best Cakes?"

"He's sold it."

"I didn't see a For Sale sign."

"There wasn't one. It seems he found a buyer privately. I don't know who it is."

"How did you find out that he was moving?"

"He came to see me. He was actually quite sweet about it. He apologised for being a horrible boyfriend and wished me luck."

"I still wouldn't trust him as far as I could throw him," Pearl said.

"Me neither." I'd had more than my fair share of run-ins with Miles. "I've just come from your mum's."

"Have you seen all those awful pictures?" Pearl laughed. "I don't know why she doesn't just burn them."

"She can't do that. Barry is hoping to have his own exhibition."

"Poor thing. He'll be a laughing stock."

"Anyway, the reason I popped in was—"

"We know. A caramel latte and a muffin."

"Yes, but apart from that, I wanted to warn you and Amber that Kathy and Lizzie will be coming to my house on Saturday, to see you and the little ones."

"That's great. It'll be nice to see them again."

"You'll both have to be on your best behaviour."

"What do you mean?"

"I mean magic-wise. You mustn't use any magic in front of them."

"We're not stupid, Jill. And, anyway, we wouldn't have been able to use it in front of Jack even if your sister wasn't coming over."

"Yeah, right, of course. I knew that. How's business upstairs?"

"The creche? It's been busy all morning." She checked the clock on the wall behind the counter. "In fact, it's probably time you were going up there, Mindy."

"Do you work up there too?" I said.

"I just cover Belladonna's lunch hour." She smiled. "That's plenty long enough for me, to be honest."

"It can't be that bad, can it? When I was up there, the kids were really quiet or fast asleep."

"I don't seem to have Belladonna's magic touch. As soon as I get up there, they all go crazy. I'm exhausted by the time Belladonna gets back."

Chapter 8

Cuppy C was busy, so Pearl wasn't able to join me at my table. Normally, I liked to take my time with a muffin, and savour every mouthful, but today, I finished it in record time. Likewise with the coffee.

No, it wasn't gluttony. I wanted to be ready for when Belladonna came downstairs, which sure enough, a few minutes later she did. I waited until she was out of the door, and then shouted my goodbyes to Pearl.

The twins seemed delighted with their new employee, and there was no doubt that the creche was a resounding success, but I still had my reservations about Belladonna. Mindy's comments had just served to increase my doubts. Why were the kids so subdued and well behaved for Belladonna, but then loud and disruptive as soon as Mindy took over? It reminded me of the little girl, Tiffany, who I'd first seen in the creche and then, only minutes later, out on the street. She'd acted like two different children.

It was quite possible that I was being overly suspicious; it wouldn't be the first time. Still, it wouldn't do any harm to find out a little more about the strange young woman who had such a penchant for purple and black.

Fortunately, the street outside Cuppy C was busy, so I was able to follow Belladonna without fear of her spotting me. It soon became obvious that she was headed for the market square. To pick up lunch? Why wouldn't she eat in Cuppy C? The twins gave all of their staff a discount. Maybe she just preferred to get out into the fresh air.

When she reached the market, she walked down one of the aisles of stalls. I took the one that ran parallel to it, from where I still had a good view of her. Halfway down the aisle, she stopped at a flower stall, and it was obvious she was making a purchase. From my vantage point, I couldn't see what she'd bought, but when she continued on her journey, and I got close to her again, I saw the black and purple flowers.

Once we were out of the market square, the streets were much less crowded, so I made myself invisible, just in case she looked behind her. I needn't have worried because she never once looked back. After a few minutes, I realised where she was headed. The last time I'd been to this graveyard was when I'd attended my mother's funeral, shortly after the revelation that I was a witch. The weather that day had been grey and wet, but today the sun was beating down from a cloudless sky.

Once inside the graveyard, she slowed her pace a little. The area just inside the gates was well maintained, but she seemed to be headed for the far side, which was overgrown and neglected. The grass was waist high; weeds had covered most of the fallen and crumbling headstones. Eventually, she came to a halt in front of one of the few headstones that were still upright. With her head bowed, she mouthed a few words before placing the flowers on the grave. Moments later, she turned away and hurried past me towards the exit. As she did, I could see the tears in her eyes.

I felt a little guilty at having spied on such a private moment, but the guilt wasn't enough to suppress my curiosity entirely. Once I was sure Belladonna had left the graveyard, I reversed the 'invisible' spell, and then walked over to take a look at the headstone where she'd laid the flowers.

It was blank.

***

Lawrence Lawson was one of the men who had been with Kirk Sparks on the night that he'd been refused entry to the Lucky Thirteen casino. He'd agreed to meet me in Java's coffee shop.

"Thank you for seeing me."

"No problem." Lawrence was in his early forties and looked as though he might once have been an athlete. "Kirk and I had been friends for ages. I still can't believe he's gone."

If we hadn't been in such a public place, I'm not sure he would have been able to suppress the tears I could hear in his voice.

"You know his wife, Bernie, I assume?" I said.

"Of course. How's she doing?"

"Not great, but mainly she's angry. She doesn't believe Kirk's death was an accident."

"If I thought for one moment that it was anything but a tragic accident, I'd move heaven and earth to find out who was behind it, but it's obvious the lightning strike dislodged those dice. I hate to see her wasting her money trying to find someone to blame."

"You may be right about it being an accident, and I can promise you if that's the case, then I'll tell Bernie just that. But if there's even the smallest possibility that foul play was involved, wouldn't you want those responsible to be brought to justice?"

"Of course."

"That's why I wanted to talk to you. I need to know more about the night of the birthday celebrations when you visited the casino and Kirk was turned away."

"It was Fred's birthday."

"That's Fred Marlow, right?"

"Yes. Have you spoken to him yet?"

"No, I haven't been able to contact him, but I plan to."

"The thing that haunts me is that it was my idea."

"To go to the casino?"

He nodded. "I was the only one who'd been there before."

"You'd all been drinking?"

"Yes. In Washbridge from about eight o'clock."

"Were you drunk?"

"Merry, maybe, but definitely not drunk. And Kirk wasn't even merry; he'd moved onto cola while the rest of us were still on beer."

"And yet, he was the only one the doorman barred from entering the casino."

"That's right. The rest of us were already inside."

"What did you do when you realised he wasn't with you?"

"We went back to the door and tried to reason with the doorman, but he wasn't having it, so we were going to leave too."

"But you didn't?"

"Only because Kirk insisted that we stay. He said he was tired, and that he was going to get a taxi home. I wish we'd left with him now."

"I'm not sure that would have changed anything."

"Maybe, maybe not. He definitely had a bee in his bonnet about the casino after that night."

"What did he say about it?"

"Not much. He didn't go into detail — he never really talked about any of the stories he was working on, but I got the impression that he'd dug up something about the casino. Something bad."

***

When I arrived home, Britt was in the front garden again.

"Hi, err — ?" she called to me.

"Jill."

"Sorry, Jill. I will get it eventually, I promise. I have a photographic memory for most things, but I struggle with names for some reason."

"At this rate, you'll be putting our garden to shame."

"Gardening is a passion of mine."

Just then, Lovely appeared at Britt's feet. When I glanced down at her, she winked at me and gestured towards Britt.

"Is your cat eating okay now?"

"No, she still won't touch her food. I think it must be what you said: the stress of moving to a new house."

"Actually, I was thinking about that. Maybe she doesn't like the new food that you've swapped to."

Britt looked puzzled. "How did you know that we'd changed her food?"

That was a very good question.

"I — err, I guess Kit must have mentioned it to me."

"Oh? Right." She looked down at Lovely. "Is that it, girl? Don't you like the new food?"

In response, Britt heard the cat meow loudly, but I

heard her say, "It's revolting. Bring back the old stuff."

"I'd better get going." I started for the door.

"Will you and Jack be going to the Normals' housewarming tonight?"

Oh bum! I'd blocked that out of my mind. "I'm not sure. I think we might have something else planned."

"Do try, even if it's just for half an hour."

"We'll do our best."

***

"There must be some way we can get out of this," I said.

"I don't want to get out of it." Jack was busy trying on different ties. "It'll be fun."

"It's a housewarming party. How is that going to be fun?"

"There'll probably be lots of cake."

"You don't know that for sure. The Normals probably don't even eat cake. They look like the kind of people that would maintain a no-cake diet."

"Now you're just being ridiculous. It'll be nice to have a chance to see all of our neighbours in one place."

"But they're all weirdos."

"Mr Hosey's a bit weird, I grant you."

"A bit? The man dresses up as a tree."

"The other neighbours are okay, though."

Before I could disagree, there was a knock at the door. "I'll get it," Jack volunteered.

I knew why he'd offered to get the door; it was because I was winning the argument about the neighbours. They were all weird—there was no getting away from that. Jack and I were an oasis of normality in a sea of crazy.

What do you mean I only got that half right?

"Jill!" Jack shouted from downstairs. "I think you'd better come and see this."

That sounded like bad news.

Outside the door, there were two young people on bikes. One of them was Lucy Locket; the young man, though, I didn't recognise.

"I think you'd better sort this out, Jill." Jack stood to one side.

"Hi, Lucy." I stepped forward.

"Hello, Jill. This is Peter."

"Peter Piper." He smiled.

"Nice to meet you, Peter. What seems to be the problem?"

"These." Lucy pulled back the cover from Peter's basket.

"Do you see the issue now?" Jack chipped in.

"Why do you have so many packets of custard creams in there?" I tried to count them, but gave up at twenty-two.

"It's your order. There are forty packets."

"I didn't order all those."

"Your order was actually for twenty-five packets."

"That was just a mistake. The quantity button on the app wasn't working properly. Didn't Little Jack see the note I made in the comments section? It said the quantity should have been four."

"I tried to tell him that," Lucy said. "But he insisted that at the rate you went through custard creams, four couldn't possibly be right. He thought that once you'd realised the quantity maxed out at twenty-five, you'd tried to enter a comment saying you wanted forty packets."

Little Jack and I eventually reached a compromise. I agreed to keep ten packets of biscuits, and he put the rest back into stock. I also got him to agree to investigate the problem with the quantity button on the app. He said he'd also increase the maximum quantity to fifty, just in case I needed that many in future.

**

My last-minute plea that I wasn't feeling well had fallen on deaf ears, so I was now resigned to an evening with the Normals. All the time we were getting changed for the housewarming party, Jack had a stupid smirk on his face.

"You'd better not mention the custard creams when we get to the party," I threatened him.

"Why not? It'll make a great ice-breaker."

"I'm warning you. I don't want everyone thinking I'm some kind of custard cream junkie."

"That would never do."

"What's that?"

"It's a welcome to your new home card." Jack locked the door behind us.

"You bought them a card?"

"And a gift voucher for Washbridge Department Store."

"We barely know them."

"Of course we barely know them; they've only just moved in. That's why it's called a housewarming party."

"I hope you didn't spend too much."

"Definitely not as much as you spent on custard creams."

"Are you ever going to let me forget about that?"

"Probably not."

Norm and Naomi Normal were waiting by the door to greet their guests.

"Hi, you two." Norm beamed. "I'm so glad you could make it."

"Everyone else is already inside," Naomi said.

"I'm sorry we're a little late." Jack handed over the card. "Jill had a custard cream emergency. Ouch!" He began to hop around.

My kick to his shin may or may not have had something to do with that.

Inside, were all the usual suspects: Tony and Clare (minus any costumes), Jimmy and Kimmy (also minus their costumes, thankfully), Britt and Kit, and a few others who I didn't know, other than to say hello to.

We'd only been there a few minutes when Jack became engrossed in conversation with Tony and Clare about TenPinCon. Fascinating as that was, I managed to drag myself away.

"Hey, Jill," Britt called to me.

"You remembered my name."

"It always takes me a while with new people, but I get there in the end. I just wanted to thank you for suggesting that Lovely might not be eating because we'd changed her food. You were right. As soon as we gave her some of her old stuff, she wolfed it down."

"That's great."

"The strange thing is that Kit doesn't remember telling you that we'd swapped her food."

"He must have done. How else could I have known? It's

not like Lovely could have told me, is it?"

"Who's the guy with the leaves in his hair?" Jimmy said.

"That's Mr Hosey. He's in charge of the local neighbourhood watch."

"Do you think I should tell him he has leaves in his hair?"

"Are you interested in trains?"

"Not particularly."

"In that case, I definitely wouldn't bother."

"Is it true what I heard?" Kimmy said.

"What's that?"

"A little bird told me you like to−err−" She blushed. "Become one with nature, so to speak."

"No, no! That was all just a big misunderstanding."

"That's a pity. I've always thought naturism could be something I might enjoy."

"Err, I think Jack's calling me. Excuse me, would you?"

I grabbed Jack by the arm. "Sorry, Tony, Clare. I just need to borrow my husband for a minute."

"What's up?" Jack said.

"You deserted me."

"I was just talking to−"

"I know what you were doing. While you've been talking TenPinCon, I've been cornered by every nutter in the place. Let's go home."

Just then, Norm Normal called for silence. "Neighbours, thank you all for making us feel so welcome. And thank you too for your very generous gifts."

"Generous?" I mouthed to Jack who ignored me.

Naomi spoke next, "Norm and I have a favourite parlour game that we'd like to share with you tonight. Bring it through, Norm."

It took him a few minutes to set it up, and only when he'd finished did I realise what it was.

"Come on." I tugged at Jack's arm. "Let's go."

"Hold on. I want to see what this is."

"We had this giant edition of the magnetic fishing game specially commissioned for tonight," Norm said. "We're sure that you'll enjoy it."

"Come on, Jack, that's our cue to leave."

"We can't leave now. That game sounds like fun."

Oh bum!

Chapter 9

"I thought you said you weren't a bad loser." Jack smirked, as he poured out a bowl of muesli.

"I'm not a bad loser."

"Why are you still sulking then?"

"I'm not sulking. I'm still half asleep. If we'd left the Normals' house when I wanted to, I would have got a good night's kip."

"But then we'd have missed all the fun."

"By *fun*, I assume you're referring to magnetic fishing?"

"It was brilliant, wasn't it? Remind me again who won?"

"Catching four magnetic fish isn't anything to brag about."

"How many did you manage to catch?"

"I wasn't even trying. It's a stupid game."

"I seem to recall that you didn't catch any."

"Okay, if we're going to talk fishing, why don't you tell me again how you did in your sea-fishing contest with Peter?"

"That's a low blow."

The bin was only half full, but I decided to take the rubbish out anyway. Anything to get away from Jack's magnetic fishing braggadocio.

"Thanks for putting my two-leggeds right about the food, Jill." Lovely was on the fence. "That's the first decent meal I've had since we moved here."

"No problem. I'm glad to have been of assistance."

"Assistance with what?" Kit came around the corner of his house.

Oh bum!

"Err, Jack was just shouting to me." I pointed to the upstairs bedroom window. "I've been helping him to—err—choose which tie to wear for work."

"Oh? Does he always do that?"

"Most days. Jack values my input when it comes to matters sartorial."

"Right. By the way, Britt tells me that we have you to thank for getting Lovely to eat again."

"It was just a hunch."

"She seems to think that it was me who told you about the change of food, but I'm pretty sure I didn't say anything about it."

"Britt must be mistaken. I think she actually told me herself."

"Right, well thanks anyway. We were beginning to worry about this little one." He stroked the cat.

Lovely purred, and said to me, "Winky told me you could lie for England."

"Did I hear you talking to someone out there?" Jack said.

"Yeah. Lovely and Kit."

"Not both at the same time, I hope?"

"No, but I'll have to be careful when Lovely's around. She seems to have taken a shine to me."

"She can tell you're a cat person. Oh, by the way, we might have to get some new cupboards in here."

"Why?" I glanced around the kitchen. "What's wrong with these?"

"They're beginning to warp under the weight of all the custard creams."

"There you go again. Not being funny."

"You just don't understand my sophisticated sense of humour."

"That's true."

"I have an interesting day lined up today. We've got one of the country's leading experts coming in to talk to us about cybercrime. What about you? Have you got anything exciting planned?"

"Not really. Except that Winky will probably be testing his zip wire. That's all."

"Did you just say zip wire?"

"I thought I'd told you about it. He and this professor type cat have gone into business together. They're going to be selling zip wires for cats, or as he insists on calling them: Cat Zip."

"Why would a cat need a zip wire?"

"To get across the road safely of course."

Jack rolled his eyes. "It's so obvious now that you say it."

***

When I arrived at work, Mrs V was by herself in the office.

"Morning, Mrs V. No Alistair?"

"He called a few minutes ago. He's got a flat tyre, so he'll be a little late."

"Are the two of you starting to gel yet?"

"Sometimes I think we're beginning to, but he's so unpredictable."

"How do you mean?"

"You've seen how he is about the clowns. One minute,

he can't stop talking about them, and the next, it's like he hates them."

"That is a bit weird."

"It isn't just that. I made him a cup of tea yesterday morning, and he said the one teaspoon of sugar wasn't enough, so I added another. In the afternoon, I put two spoonsful in, and he said he couldn't drink it because he didn't take sugar in his tea. I'm going to let him put his own in from now on."

"You do right. You have enough on without having to pander to people's weird sugar needs."

"Hmm."

"It's not long now until your hula hoop thingy."

"It's a *marathon*."

"Sorry." A marathon that would last all of five minutes. Snigger.

"I managed to get in a little practice last night. I wasn't as rusty as I thought I'd be."

"Don't go overdoing it. You don't want to burn yourself out before the big day."

Just then, the door opened, and in walked Alistair. "Sorry I'm late, Jill. Did Annabel tell you what happened?"

"Yes, no problem. Did you manage to get the tyre sorted?"

"Yes. That's the second new tyre I've had to buy this month. That car is costing me a small fortune." He took something from his coat pocket. "Look what I bought yesterday, Annabel." He put on a large red nose. "It's the snozzle25, what do you think of it?"

"It's very nice." Mrs V seemed genuinely impressed, if not a little jealous.

"Admit it," Winky said. "You're starting to have doubts about doliphant boy."

"Rubbish. I'm very pleased with him so far."

"Really? Even though the guy is sitting out there, wearing a clown's nose?"

"We all have our own interests and hobbies."

"Except that he doesn't know if he likes clowns or not. One minute he does, and the next he doesn't. He's clearly a whack job."

"You're just picking fault with him."

"It's better than picking my nose. Or whistling."

"I'm not discussing this anymore. Alistair is here to stay, so you may as well get used to it. Anyway, shouldn't you be thinking about your zip wire test?"

"How many times do I have to tell you? It's Cat Zip. The professor and his crew will be setting it up this morning. If all goes to schedule, I should be able to test it first thing this afternoon."

"Are you sure you know what you're doing?"

"Never more so."

***

I wasn't going to admit it to Winky, but I was a little concerned about some of Alistair's *quirks*. Still, it was way too soon to start panicking.

I'd just finished my bi-weekly paperclip sort when Mrs V came through to my office. Not more Alistair problems, hopefully.

"Mr Macabre is here."

"I'd forgotten he was coming today. Give me a minute

and then send him through, would you?"

"Will do."

"Winky, get behind the screen. And keep quiet."

"I'm expecting a call from the professor any minute now."

"I don't care. Turn off your phone, and get behind that screen."

"This is most inconvenient."

"Good morning, Mr Macabre. What brings you here today? I know it can't be about the sign because that's all sorted now, as you no doubt saw on your way in."

"Unfortunately, Mrs Maxwell, it is indeed about the sign. It's in contravention of the lease."

"No, it isn't. I replaced the two signs with a single one, as per your request."

"You did indeed."

"So what's the problem?"

"Clause 32A, sub-section vi, is quite unambiguous."

"About what?"

"The maximum dimensions of the sign that can be displayed. Your sign is two centimetres too wide."

"Two centimetres? That's nothing." I illustrated the point using my thumb and first finger. "What possible difference can a measly two centimetres make?"

"It's the difference between compliance and non-compliance with the terms of your lease, and if you continue to be in non-compliance, I'll be forced —"

"Let me guess. To kick me out?"

"Much as it would distress me to do so."

"Okay, I'll get it sorted."

"Excellent. I'll expect you to be in compliance by the

end of next week."

"Right. Is there anything else?"

He sniffed the air. "I thought I caught a whiff of cat?"

"You're mistaken. There are no animals in here because that would be against the terms of my lease."

"Clause 15D, sub-section ii, to be precise."

"Is there anything else?"

"No, that's everything. It's been a pleasure as always, Mrs Maxwell."

"Why don't you just turn that guy into a cockroach?" Winky emerged from behind the screen.

It wasn't a bad suggestion.

***

It was time for me to take a look at the Lucky Thirteen casino for myself. Like a lot of casinos, it never closed, but I figured mid-morning would be as quiet a time as any. Although the building was situated on a retail park, it was on the opposite side of the car park from all the shops.

There was no sign of the huge roulette wheel which had once been mounted on the front of the building alongside the dice. I assumed that it must have been removed after the tragic incident, which had resulted in Kirk Sparks' untimely death.

"Morning," I said to the doorman—a giant of a werewolf.

"I'm sorry, but you can't come in."

"Are you closed? I thought you were open twenty-four seven?"

"The casino is open, but you're not allowed inside."

"Why not?"

"No sups allowed."

"That's outrageous."

"I don't make the rules, love. Sorry, you can't come in."

It would have been a trivial matter to use magic to gain entry, but I elected not to—not yet, at least.

Even though I hadn't managed to get inside the casino, I had learned something very interesting. Kirk's friends were under the impression that he'd been turned away because he'd had too much to drink. Maybe that wasn't the case. Perhaps it was because he was the only one in the group who was a sup. He obviously wouldn't have been able to tell his human companions the real reason he'd been refused entry, which is why he fed them the line about the drink. If my hunch was correct, then Bernie too would have had no idea that she was married to a sup, which is why Kirk had been forced to tell her the same lie.

I checked the restaurants in Candlefield, and sure enough, there was one there called Wonders. That explained why she'd been unable to find any trace of it in the human world.

*　*　*

Back at the office, it was business as usual: Mrs V was wearing her earmuffs while knitting clown socks. Alistair was still sporting his clown nose, and whistling some nondescript tune.

But there was no sign of Winky.

"Where are you?" I checked behind the screen, but he wasn't there. "Stop messing around!" There was still no sign of him.

But then I spotted the machinery that had been attached to the window frame; it was clearly the Cat Zip. On closer investigation, I found that a wire had been installed between my office building and the one opposite. That's when I saw Winky, standing in the open window of a room on the fourth floor of the building across the road. He was wearing a crash helmet, and a harness.

He must have seen me too because he waved.

"This doesn't look safe!" I yelled.

He put a paw to his ear and shook his head.

"Don't do it!"

He obviously couldn't hear a word I said.

I was still trying to figure out how I could stop him from going through with this insanity when he pushed off from the window sill. I didn't want to watch, but I seemed to be frozen to the spot.

To my amazement and relief, all seemed to be going well. Maybe this wasn't such a crazy idea after all. He was already halfway across. Another few seconds and he'd be safe.

Snap! The wire broke, and his expression changed from one of exhilaration to one of blind fear, as he plunged towards the ground.

From that moment, everything seemed to happen in slow motion. A soft-topped lorry was headed this way, but it wouldn't be level with my building soon enough.

If I didn't act quickly, Winky would be splattered across the road.

The spell wasn't the most elegant I'd ever cast, but it slowed Winky's descent long enough for the lorry to reach a spot underneath him. Moments later, he landed on top of the vehicle with a thud.

Had I done enough? Had the impact still injured him? Or worse?

As the lorry continued down the road, I hardly dared to look. For the longest moment, he didn't move, but then, he slowly got to his feet. As the lorry disappeared into the distance, he gave me a little wave.

Phew!

I was still standing next to the window when Mrs V came through to my office.

"Are you alright, Jill? You're as white as a ghost."

"Yeah, I'm fine."

"I didn't get the chance to ask you earlier. What did Mr Macabre want?"

"Nothing, it was just a routine catch-up." There was no way I was going to tell her about the latest issue with the sign. I would handle that without Mr Song this time.

"Where's the cat?"

"Winky? Err, I'm not sure. He must have nipped out."

She walked over to the window. "What's this contraption?"

Oh bum! "Err, that's a — err — "

"There's a wire hanging from it."

"Yes, it's a fire wire."

"A what?"

"If there's a fire, I can just slide down the wire."

"But we already have a fire escape."

"Belt and braces, Mrs V. Belt and braces."

Still unconvinced, she left me to it.

Thank goodness I'd been in the office when Winky made his test run. If I hadn't, I would have been scraping him off the road. Just think of the mess that would have made of my clothes.

What? I was only joking. Sheesh!

I would have worn overalls, obviously.

Chapter 10

My phone rang.

"Hello, Grandma."

"It's an outrage." Oh no. Had she got wind of the attempted coup at W.O.W? "They've raised the price of cockroach crunch. That's the second time this year."

"That's terrible. Is that the reason you called?"

"Of course it isn't. I've finalised the marketing plans for your human's silly convention."

"Would it kill you to call him by his name?"

"What is it again?"

"You know very well that it's Jack."

"You'd best pop down here, and I'll run through what I have in mind."

"Shouldn't we wait until Jack can be there too?"

"That won't be necessary. I'll explain it to you, and you can translate it into human-speak."

"Okay. When shall I come down?"

"My bunion lady is due any minute, so give it an hour."

"You have a chiropodist?"

"No, why would I need a chiropodist?"

"You just said—"

"That my bunion lady was coming, yes. Rita Greendeer is Candlefield's leading authority on bunions, and do you know why?"

"I couldn't even begin to guess."

"I'll tell you why. Because she's a specialist. You won't get corn or verruca treatment from Rita. It's strictly bunions only."

"Yuk, what a job."

"Pardon?"

"Nothing. I'll come down in about an hour then, shall I?"

"Yes, but I should warn you that the ointment Rita uses has a rather pungent aroma."

"Great. Can't wait."

Alistair popped his head around the door. "Do you have a minute, Jill?"

"Sure, take a seat."

"I just wanted to—" His nose crinkled, and he began to blink.

"Are you okay?"

"Err, yeah. It feels like my allergy is coming on, but it can't be."

"Hay fever?"

"No. I'm allergic to cat fur, but there's obviously no cat in here."

"Actually there is. There's Winky."

"Who?" He sneezed.

"He's my cat. He lives in this office."

Alistair looked around the room through streaming eyes. "I don't see him anywhere."

"He had to zip out. Don't you remember? I mentioned him during the interview when you asked who else I employed."

"Oh yes, I remember now." He sneezed again. "I'm sorry, Jill. Maybe we could do this at my desk later?"

"Yes, of course."

***

The Everettes were still blissfully unaware of their

yellowness.

"Hi, Jill." Julie was all smiles.

"Hi. Is Grandma alone?"

"Yes. There was someone with her for a while, but she just left."

"That must have been Rita Greendeer."

"That's her. Do you know her?"

"Only by reputation."

"She's a little strange if you ask me. I said hello to her, and she asked if there was a history of bunions in my family."

"That's kind of her speciality. Bunions, I mean."

"How horrible. I sometimes think that this job can be trying, but dealing with people's bunions all day?"

"It doesn't bear thinking about, does it?"

Grandma had not been exaggerating when she said the bunion treatment had a pungent aroma.

"Can't we go outside to discuss this, Grandma? That smell is making me feel ill."

"I can't walk anywhere for another hour. I have to give the treatment time to work. Pull up a chair, and stop your moaning."

It was my turn to endure watery eyes.

She continued, "For maximum impact, we'll stage the promotion a couple of weeks before the event. That seemed to work well for the surfing extravaganza."

"Okay. That makes sense."

"I suggest we commandeer the high street on the Saturday after next."

"We'll have to get permission to close off the road, I assume?"

"Don't be ridiculous."

"What do you have planned?"

"The marching band was quite popular last time, so we'll include them again."

"Right."

"And then I thought a team of jugglers but with a twist."

"What kind of twist?"

"They'll all be juggling skittles."

"They're actually called pins." She fixed me with an icy gaze. "Not that it matters. Obviously."

"And then for the pièce de résistance."

"Was that supposed to be a French accent?" I laughed, but not for long. "Sorry, you were saying?"

"I was saying that the centrepiece will be a giant game of skittles on the high street."

"It's ten-pin bowling."

"Same difference. There'll be ten giant skittles at one end of the street, and members of the public will be able to take turns bowling a giant ball at them."

"When you say *giant*, how big do you mean exactly?"

"About half the size of the surrounding buildings."

"That's huge. How is that going to work? Will you be using holograms?"

"Of course not. I'll get regular skittles and a ball, and use magic to make them giant size."

"I think I see a slight flaw in your plan."

"What's that?"

"The giant ball and skittles will destroy the high street."

"That's okay. We'll make sure they aren't anywhere near Ever or Ever A Wool Moment."

"What about the rest of the shops?"

"Collateral damage."

"No, it's much too dangerous. People could get crushed."

"So what? They're only humans."

"No, I'm sorry. I like the idea of the giant ten-pin bowling game, but you're going to have to come up with something less dangerous."

"How many human casualties would be acceptable?"

"None."

"You like to make life difficult, don't you? I suppose I'll have to have a rethink."

"Okay, thanks. While I'm here, Grandma, could I ask you about Candlefield cemetery?"

"I hope you're not thinking of buying me a plot for my birthday."

"No, it's nothing like that. It's just that I was in there yesterday."

"Do you often hang out in graveyards?"

"Of course not. I was following someone."

"Who?"

"Belladonna, the woman who's working in the creche at Cuppy C. Have you met her?"

"Not yet. Why were you following her?"

"I don't really know. There's just something about her that bothers me. Anyway, she went to the overgrown section of the graveyard. The graves there have mostly been neglected and are overrun with weeds. Are you familiar with it?"

"You're talking about The Shadows."

"Am I?"

"Yes, it's the area of the graveyard where the evillest sups are buried. Are you familiar with Brynn Bonetaker?"

"No."

"Delia Deathdrop?"

"No."

"You really do need to brush up on your Candlefield history. Those are two of the most notorious sups who ever lived. They're both buried in The Shadows. There are many others too. What was the name on the headstone that Belladonna visited? I assume you had enough gumption to check?"

"I did, but that's the strange thing. The grave she visited was well maintained but the headstone was blank. I was wondering if you had any idea how I can find out whose grave it is?"

"You could start by talking to the churchwarden, I suppose."

"Right, thanks. I'll do that."

I left Grandma to ponder how to stage a non-lethal TenPinCon promotion.

On my way back up the high street, I had a case of déjà vu. Betty Longbottom was walking towards me, and she was covering one of her eyes with her hand. It was obvious even before she spoke that she was furious about something.

"This time I'm definitely suing them!"

"What's wrong, Betty? I thought you and Deli had reached an agreement."

"I'll see that woman in court!" And with that, she stormed off.

What could have made her so angry?

When I arrived back at the office, there was still no sign

of Winky. I was just wondering how I could check on him when the cat himself came through the window.

"Are you okay?"

"Just a couple of bruises. That lorry broke my fall."

"You have me to thank for that. I used magic to make sure you had a soft landing."

"Couldn't you have picked a local vehicle? I had to wait until he stopped at the motorway services before I could get off."

"Pardon me for saving your life. How did you get back from there?"

"I hitchhiked of course."

"Who would stop to give a cat a lift?"

"A couple of pretty witches pulled up. I think they took quite a shine to me."

"That's nice."

"They run a recruitment agency over the other side of Washbridge. They said I was welcome to move into their offices anytime I want."

"Don't let me stop you."

"You pretend you wouldn't care, but I know you'd be devastated if I left. Don't worry, I couldn't do that to you. Now, where's that salmon?"

"What are you going to do about Cat Zip?" I asked while he tucked into his food.

"I'm done with that. I thought the professor knew his onions, but the man almost killed me. There are easier ways to make money."

"What about all the chickens?"

"What chickens?"

"The ones that are still waiting to cross the road."

"That isn't even in the same postcode as funny."

***

It had been Fred Marlow's birthday the day that Kirk Sparks had been refused entry to the Lucky Thirteen casino. I'd eventually managed to get hold of him and he'd agreed to drop by the office.

"Thanks for coming in to see me, Mr Marlow."

"It's Fred. Lawrence told me you'd spoken to him already."

"That's right. Can I get you a drink?"

"No, thanks. I grabbed a coffee on my way here." He shuffled around on the seat as though he was trying to get comfortable. "Although I'm beginning to wish I hadn't."

"Oh?"

"Are you familiar with that coffee shop on the high street?"

"Coffee Games?"

"That's the one. I've never been in there before, and I won't be going back."

"What happened?"

"I was standing at the counter, waiting for my Americano, when some idiot wearing a blindfold stuck a pin in my—err—" He shuffled around again.

"Oh dear. Why would someone do that?"

"I was going to thump the guy, but he apologised and said something about it being pin the tail on the donkey day."

"Right. Would you like a cushion to sit on?"

"No, it's okay."

I ran through the story that Lawrence Lawson had told me about the night they'd all visited the casino.

"Yeah, that's pretty much what happened," Fred said. "There's no way Kirk was drunk that night."

I was in no doubt that he was right about that. It was now obvious to me that the real reason Kirk had been turned away was because he was the only sup in the group.

"Is there anything else you can tell me, Fred? Any idea at all what Kirk was working on?"

"Not really, although he did ask if I'd mind paying another visit to the casino."

"To do what exactly?"

"Just to observe really. He wanted me to take note of who the winners were. He said I should focus on the craps table. So that's what I did. I stayed there for a couple of hours and made a note of those players who were on a winning streak."

"Then what?"

"Kirk was waiting for me in the car park. When I left the casino, I assumed we'd go straight back to his place, and I'd tell him what I'd observed. But he insisted that we stay there until the early hours of the morning, so that I could point out the winners as they came out."

"And did you?"

"Yeah. There were about five of them altogether."

"Then what?"

"Then nothing. Kirk seemed quite excited by it all, but I have no idea why."

"Didn't you ask him?"

"Of course I did, but he said he didn't want to say anything until he was sure his hunch was right."

"And he didn't tell you what that hunch was?"

"No, and by then, I was past caring. I just wanted to get

home to my bed. I'm not sure how any of this helps. Lawrence told me that Bernie still doesn't believe it was a tragic accident."

"That's right."

"My heart goes out to her, but I don't really see what other explanation there can be, do you?"

"That's what I intend to find out. Thanks very much for coming in today."

"No problem." He winced again as he got out of the chair.

Things were slowly starting to make sense. When I'd first seen the cryptic notes in Kirk's notepad, I'd been flummoxed by the references to the number five, but I now realised that the '5' wasn't a five at all. It was the letter 'S'. And the 'S' stood for sups.

No 5 allowed. Was actually *No sups allowed.*

After he'd been refused entry into the casino, Kirk must have jumped to the conclusion that no sups were allowed inside.

Got it wrong. Some 5 allowed. Was actually *Got it wrong. Some sups allowed.*

His subsequent visits to monitor the casino must have made him realise that some sups were being allowed inside.

Only 5 win. Was actually *Only sups win.*

This final entry was the most significant. Kirk had asked his friend, Fred Marlow, to point out the big winners. And those big winners had all been sups.

At last, I felt I was making some progress on this case, but to get any further, I would need to get inside the casino.

When I called it a day, Winky was still busy dismantling the remains of the Cat Zip. Mrs V had already left, and Alistair was just about to leave.

"I'm sorry we didn't get the chance to get together this afternoon, Alistair. I got caught up with a few other things. Maybe we can do it tomorrow."

"No problem." He pulled something out of his coat pocket, and then bent over and began to fiddle with his trouser bottoms. It took me a few seconds to realise what he was doing.

"Bike clips?"

"They're a nuisance really. They ruin my trousers, but better safe than sorry."

"You're on your bike?"

"Yes. I cycle everywhere."

As I walked out of the door, I almost ran into a man in overalls, carrying a large tool bag.

"Sorry, lady. Are you okay?"

"I'm fine. Are you here for the clown school?"

"Me? No." He laughed. "Not really my thing. I've been carrying out some minor repairs for your landlord."

"Macabre."

"What is?"

"The landlord: Martin Macabre."

"Oh yeah, that's the guy."

Chapter 11

It was the next morning, and Jack and I had just finished breakfast.

"When are you going to shrink the furniture and move it out of the spare bedroom?" he said.

"There's plenty of time."

"The twins are coming tomorrow."

"I know, but there's no need to panic. Once I've shrunk everything, it'll only take a few minutes to put it in a shoe box. We can do it tonight."

"Okay, if you're sure."

"Have I ever let you down?"

"Hmm. I still don't understand why you won't tell me about the ideas your grandmother came up with for marketing TenPinCon."

"It's like I said last night, the plans need some tweaking."

"You could at least give me some idea of what she has in mind, couldn't you?"

"If I told you, it would scare you to death."

"No, it wouldn't. I'm a big boy."

"Okay. Don't say I didn't warn you. Her idea was to have a giant bowling ball and pins in the high street."

"That sounds cool. What's wrong with that?"

"Nothing much, provided you aren't worried about the damage that would be done to the surrounding buildings. Oh, and then there are all the people who would be crushed. Other than that, it sounds like a fabulous idea."

"I see what you mean about scaring me to death."

"I told her she had to go back to the drawing board, and come up with something that didn't involve devastation on the scale of a small earthquake."

"Okay, thanks."

"By the way, how did the talk from the cybercrime expert go yesterday?"

"It didn't. Someone hacked his satnav, and he ended up at the wrong police station."

***

When I left the house, I heard a sound I hadn't heard for some time. It was Bessie's whistle. Mr Hosey brought the train to a halt in front of our house.

"Morning, Jill."

"Good morning, Mr Hosey. What happened to your face?"

It was covered in red blotches.

"It seems I'm allergic to tree bark."

"Oh dear. I'm sorry to hear that."

"The doctor has told me I have to give up the tree camouflage."

"What about the bushes?"

"He recommended I stay away from those too, just to be on the safe side."

"What will you do now?"

"I'll have to scale back the surveillance until I can come up with another camouflage idea. Unless—"

"Yes?"

"Are you allergic to bark, Jill? Maybe you could stand in for me until I find an alternative."

"I'd love to, but I suffer from leafitus. It's a rare allergy which affects only one person in every hundred thousand. If I go anywhere near a leaf, I get a rash similar to yours."

"That's a shame."

"You should ask Jack. He's quite partial to camouflage."

"Thanks, I'll do that."

Snigger.

***

"Your wait is over, Jill." Mr Ivers had a smile twice as wide as his face.

"Sorry?"

"You're such a kidder. Pretending that you don't know what I mean."

I didn't have the first clue what he was talking about.

Until he held out the newsletter.

"Of course." I tried, but failed to sound enthusiastic. "How could I have forgotten?" I threw it on the passenger seat, and was about to drive off.

"Wait! You've forgotten the audio version." He passed it to me.

"Cassette?"

"You'll be able to listen to it while you drive."

"Right, thanks." That went onto the seat too.

"Let me know what you think of it. I've included a recap of all the big movies released while I've been away."

"Will do."

Two miles down the road, I pulled into a layby, and hurled the newsletter (printed version and cassette) into the rubbish bin.

***

There was a clown sitting on the bottom step of the

stairs to my office. Normally, I'd have given him a wide berth, but he was in tears.

"Are you okay?"

"Someone has stolen my shoe." He pointed to his feet. "They cost me a fortune."

I could see why. The one remaining shoe was at least three feet long.

"Maybe you've just misplaced it?"

"How could I misplace something this size?"

He had a point. "What makes you think someone deliberately stole it? Surely, one shoe wouldn't be any good to anyone."

"I'm not the first person this has happened to. Coco had one of his stolen yesterday, and the day before it was Bonkers."

"What was bonkers?"

"That's his clown name. Bonkers had one of his shoes taken too."

"That is strange. Is it always the same shoe?"

"No. We all have our own shoes."

"I meant is it always the same foot: left or right?"

"They took my right shoe. I don't know about the others. Why?"

That was a very good question. Why did it matter? "No reason. I'd better get going. I hope you find your shoe, err —?"

"Bingo."

"Right. Good luck, Bingo."

It was obvious that Alistair had made it to work on time today because I could hear his whistling even before I reached the top of the stairs.

"Morning, you two."

"Morning, Jill." Mrs V was speaking much louder than usual. No doubt because of the earmuffs she was wearing.

"Morning." Whistling boy looked up from his work.

"Did you drive or come on the bike, Alistair?"

"In the car of course. I never did get the hang of riding a bike."

"But I thought—never mind. We can have that get together later today if you like?"

"I'm not ready yet, Jill. I'd rather wait until I have something meaningful for you to see."

"Oh? I thought you said—err, my mistake. Carry on. Give me a shout when you're ready."

"Will you and Jack be coming to the hula hoop marathon on Sunday, Jill?" Mrs V had now removed her earmuffs.

"I'm not sure if we'll be able to make it. We have my cousins and their babies staying with us this weekend."

"You must take photos of the little ones for me to see."

"I will, and if we can get to the hula hoop thingy, we will."

"Morning, Winky." I laughed. "What on earth are you doing?"

"What does it look like?"

"It looks like you're trying to hula hoop. Emphasis on *trying*."

He spun the hoop around his middle and made a few clumsy gyrations, presumably in an attempt to keep it spinning.

"I think I'm getting the hang of it."

"No, you're not. You don't have a clue."

"Okay, smarty pants." He stepped out of the hoop. "If you're so clever, why don't you show me how it's done?"

"It's years since I did any hula hooping."

"That's what I thought. You're all talk, as usual."

"Give it here." I couldn't possibly be any worse than he was.

I stepped into the hoop, lifted it to waist height, and spun it. "See, that's how it's done." I managed to keep it up for half a dozen spins before it dropped to the floor.

He took it from me and tried again, with no more success. "This is stupid." He kicked the hoop across the floor in frustration.

"You should ask Mrs V to give you lessons."

"The day I need the old bag lady's help with anything is the day I throw myself out of the window."

"Didn't you do that yesterday? How is the Cat Zip business, by the way?"

"Kick a man when he's down, why don't you?"

***

Charlotte Greenmuch had a delightful cottage in Washbridge Heights. The invitation to the W.O.W. gathering had said there would be tea, cakes and lots of sparkling conversation. I was looking forward to the tea and cakes, but not so much the conversation—sparkling or otherwise.

"Jill." Charlotte hugged me like a long-lost friend. "I'm so pleased you made it. I wasn't sure if you'd come after what happened at the HQ."

"Thank you for inviting me. This is my first time at one of these gatherings."

"Come through and meet everyone."

Waiting for us in the lounge were several other witches, some of whom I recognised from my HQ talk. I was quite relieved to find that Belinda Cartwheel wasn't amongst those present.

Almost everyone went out of their way to make me feel welcome. There was just one lady who seemed to be doing her best to avoid talking to me. Twice I approached her, and both times she made an excuse to move away.

After about an hour, Charlotte tapped a spoon against her cup to get everyone's attention. I assumed she was going to make a speech, but she turned to me.

"Jill, we're so pleased that you came here today."

"Thank you for inviting me. It's very nice to meet you all."

"The pleasure was all ours, but I have to come clean and tell you that there was another reason why we wanted you to come."

"You're not going to propose I stage a coup against Grandma, are you? I've already made my position clear on that."

"No, it isn't that," Charlotte said. "Quite the opposite in fact. We were all appalled by what Belinda did the other day at our HQ. Your grandmother is an amazing person. We can't imagine what W.O.W. would be without her as the chairman."

"I don't understand. The impression I got at the HQ was that she had the support of everyone there."

"That's not true." A witch who had earlier introduced herself as Yasmine Younglove spoke up. "Belinda is a very intimidating individual. The truth is that most of the members are afraid to go against her."

"Surely she can't be more intimidating than my grandmother?"

"It's a close-run thing."

Charlotte chipped in, "That's why we wanted this opportunity to let you know our true feelings."

"I definitely appreciate you doing that, but there are far fewer people here than there were at HQ. How do the others feel?"

"I'd say the vast majority still back your grandmother."

"That's reassuring. It makes me feel much better about turning Belinda down."

"She wasn't expecting you to do that. She was sure you'd jump at the chance to oust your grandmother."

"She obviously doesn't know me very well."

"Doesn't she?" It was the woman who had done her best to avoid me all morning. "Are you sure about that?"

"Sorry, I don't know your name. We didn't get a chance to talk."

"Not today, maybe. But you had plenty to say when I saw you yesterday."

"Sorry?"

"Don't pretend you don't know what I'm talking about."

"I don't. I have no idea."

She turned to the others, who were obviously as surprised by her outburst as I was. "Don't fall for this act. Jill came to see me yesterday, and spent twenty minutes trying to persuade me that I should back her in her attempt to oust her grandmother."

"That's nonsense," I said. "I've never seen you in my life before this morning."

"I'm not staying here to listen to these lies." She started

for the door. "And if the rest of you have any sense, you'll leave too."

No one else did, but the atmosphere changed dramatically. Although on the surface everyone continued to be friendly towards me, it was obvious that at least a few of those still present now had their doubts.

It came as a great relief when Charlotte finally called an end to proceedings.

"Jill, stay for a moment, would you?"

I did as she asked, and when everyone had left, I said, "I honestly have no idea what that woman was talking about."

"I believe you. Everyone does."

"I'm not sure they all did. Who was she, anyway?"

"Gina Justice. She's usually one of our more reserved members. I've never seen her like that before."

"Do you think it would do any good for me to speak to her in private?"

"I'm not sure it would."

I left Charlotte's house feeling totally confused. Why had Gina Justice been so adamant that I'd spoken to her, and that I'd tried to persuade her to move against Grandma? The only explanation I could come up with was that she'd aligned herself with Belinda Cartwheel, who must have been stung by my rebuttal. Either that or Gina was delusional.

***

I'd just parked my car when I got a call from Bernie Sparks.

"Hi, Jill. I just wondered if you were making any progress?"

That wasn't an easy question for me to answer. The truth was I had a strong lead, but I could hardly tell Bernie because that would have meant trying to convince her that her late husband had been a sup.

"It's slow progress so far, I'm afraid. I've spoken to Lawrence Lawson and Fred Marlow, but they weren't able to tell me anything I didn't already know. I really need to get inside the casino. I'm going to give it a try tonight."

"Will you keep me posted, please?"

"Of course. The moment I have anything to report, I'll update you."

"Hey, Jill!" Deli called from across the road.

I thought I might get away with a quick wave, but she waited for a gap in the traffic, and hurried over to join me.

"I saw Betty yesterday," I said. "She was beside herself with rage. She's threatening to sue you again. I thought you two had reached an agreement?"

"It's all that idiot husband of mine's fault."

"Nails? What did he do this time?"

"While I was pencilling in Betty's eyebrow, Nails was putting together a new poster to advertise the spray tanning. The idiot put a permanent marker on my tray of brushes and pencils. I was so busy chatting to Betty that I picked it up by mistake."

"But surely you must have realised it wasn't the eyebrow pencil once you had it in your hand?"

"Of course I did, but Nails had seen me pick it up and he panicked. He tried to grab my arm and I lost my balance. The next thing I knew, I'd drawn a line across Betty's forehead."

"Oh no."

"She went crazy, and I don't blame her. That marker will take ages to wear off."

"What are you going to do?"

"I don't know. I tried offering free spray tans for a year, but she told me where to shove them. Will you have a word with her, Jill? She might listen to you."

"I can try, but she wouldn't even talk to me yesterday."

"Men, they're useless. The lot of them."

Chapter 12

Back at the office, Mrs V was on the phone. "Are you absolutely sure you didn't leave it in the car? Have you checked the boot? Alright, we'll have to sort it out tonight. Okay, bye." With the call ended, she sighed. "Men! They'd lose their heads if they were loose."

"Was that Armi?"

"Yes. He's only gone and lost one of his clown shoes. I ask you, Jill, how do you lose something that big?"

"Maybe he didn't *lose* it."

"He just told me that he has."

"I don't doubt that he has one missing, but he may not have lost it."

"I don't understand."

"On my way into the office this morning, I bumped into a clown on the stairs. He was upset because someone has stolen one of his shoes. He said it had happened to two other clowns too."

"That's terrible. Why would someone go around stealing clown shoes?"

"And why only one of them?"

"You should investigate, Jill."

"I'm not sure that would be a good use of my time." I turned to Alistair who was making himself a cup of tea. "What do you think, Alistair?"

"Sorry, Jill, I was miles away."

"Do you think it would be a good use of my time to pursue the case of the missing clown shoes?"

"With my office manager's head on, I'd be forced to say no. But with my red nose on, I hate to think of my fellow clowns being deprived of their footwear."

"Okay, I'll see what I can do, but I'm not promising anything."

"Jill, just a second." Mrs V caught me just as I was about to go through to my office. "I had a phone call from Reginald Crowe while you were out. He's going to pop in later. I told him I wasn't sure if you'd be able to see him, but he said he'd take his chances."

"Okay."

Winky was still practising the hula hoop, but he wasn't getting any better.

"It's time to give that up, I think," I said.

"Rubbish. I'm improving with every attempt."

"At this rate, you'll soon be able to keep it going for ten seconds."

"It's precisely that defeatist attitude that has held you back all of these years."

"What are you talking about? I've always had a *can-do* attitude."

"*I can* eat custard creams, and *I can* eat muffins, doesn't really count."

"I'll ignore that remark. You wouldn't happen to know anything about some missing clown shoes, would you? It seems someone is stealing them."

"Have you checked the online auction websites? I imagine they'd fetch a pretty penny."

"Whoever is behind this can't be trying to sell them because they're only taking one shoe from each pair."

"That's kind of weird."

"I promised Mrs V and Alistair that I'd investigate."

"That sounds like a good use of your time. I thought doliphant boy had come here to improve your productivity?"

"He has."

"And yet, he's just suggested you devote time and energy to finding a few clown shoes. Will anyone be paying you to do that?"

"Well, no, I don't suppose—"

"I rest my case."

***

Reggie's hair was even more unruly than usual, and I couldn't help but notice that it was now more grey than black. Had that happened recently or had I simply not noticed until today?

"Hi, Jill. I hoped I'd catch you. I have the contact details for the school governors that you asked me to find."

"You needn't have made a special trip just to bring me those. You could have phoned. Or are you here for Jenga day again?"

"Not this time." His grin revealed a missing tooth, which I hadn't noticed before. He must have realised that I'd seen it because he touched a finger to the gap. "I have to get that fixed."

"What happened?"

"Someone must have heard I'd been enquiring about the school governors, and sent some thugs around to warn me off."

"Who were they?"

"There were two of them—werewolves—big guys. They didn't take kindly to my telling them to sling their hook."

"Are you okay? Apart from the tooth, I mean?"

"A few bruises. Nothing serious."

"I'm sorry I put you in that position, Reggie."

"Don't give it a second thought. I'm a little worried about you, though. If they're that upset at my asking questions, they're going to be livid when you talk to the governors. Why don't you let me come with you?"

"That won't be necessary. I can handle myself."

"So I hear. Actually, the reason I came over in person is because I'm job hunting."

"Here in the human world?"

"Yeah. I figured if I was going to make a new start, I might as well go the whole hog."

"Do you know anyone over here?"

"I know you." He smiled, a little more self-conscious now. "A few other people too, but I haven't seen any of them for years."

"What sort of work are you looking for?"

"Anything really. I can turn my hand to most things."

"My brother-in-law has a landscape gardening business. He's set on a few people recently. I could put a word in with him if you like."

"That would be great. Thanks, Jill."

I really liked Reggie. Hopefully, Peter would have a job for him. As for the governors, something told me I was onto something there. Why else would someone have felt the need to try to put the frighteners on Reggie?

***

I wanted to speak with the churchwarden at Candlefield cemetery. Grandma had suggested that they might be able to throw some light on who was buried there.

The church's noticeboard confirmed the warden's name was Albert Cruikshank. His address was church cottage, which turned out to be only a hundred yards from the church itself.

Ivy had almost totally swallowed the tiny building. The only gaps in the foliage were where it had been cut away from the door and windows.

I hadn't called ahead, so I had no idea if I'd even find him at home, but I was in luck.

"Yes, young lady?" The man was wearing a nightshirt, and judging by his tired eyes, he must have been asleep when I knocked at the door.

"I'm sorry. Did I wake you?"

"That's okay. I'm not normally in bed at this time of day. I seem to have picked up an awful cold." As if on cue, he sneezed. "And I can't seem to shake it. Are you here on church business?"

"Kind of, I suppose."

"Could it possibly wait a couple of days?" He sneezed again.

"It's just a quick question, really. There's a grave in The Shadows section of the graveyard that has a blank headstone. I wondered if you might have any idea who it belongs to?"

"I'm very sorry." He blew his nose. "I've only recently taken over as churchwarden. The previous incumbent passed away six months ago. You could always try Rufus. He might know."

"Who's he?"

"Rufus Alldig. He's the gravedigger and has been for some time. If anyone would know, it would be him."

"Do you know where I might find him?"

"He lives near Candlefield Park. I'm afraid I don't have his address handy."

"That's okay; I'll find it. Thanks very much for your help. I hope you feel better soon."

He sneezed a goodbye.

I had no idea how long it would take me to find Rufus Alldig's house, but I needn't have worried because, when I reached the park, the first person I asked was able to give me directions.

The narrow terraced house looked out over the park.

"I'm sorry, we never buy at the door." The witch was a similar age to Aunt Lucy.

"I'm not selling anything."

"They all say that, dear." She began to close the door in my face.

"Honestly, I'm not selling anything. My name is Jill Maxwell."

"Don't I know you from somewhere?"

"It's possible."

"Didn't you win the Candlefield darts competition?"

"Err, no, that wasn't me."

"Are you sure? You look just like her."

"It definitely wasn't me. Actually, I was hoping to speak to Mr Alldig. Are you Mrs Alldig?"

"I am. I'm Alice. What did you say your name was again?"

"Jill Maxwell."

"You'd better come in. Rufus is just re-lacing his boots." She led the way to the small kitchen at the back of the house. "Rufus, this young lady would like a word with you. Don't you think she looks like the witch who won the

Candlefield darts competition last year?"

"She looks nothing like her." He was surrounded by a pile of boots, all minus their laces. "The witch who won the darts had a crooked nose."

Alice gave me another quick glance. "I still say she's the spitting image of her. Can I get you a drink, Jill?"

"No, thanks. I can't stay long."

"I'll leave you two to it, then."

"Sorry about Alice." Rufus put one boot down and picked up another one. "She never was very good with faces."

"You have a lot of boots."

"One pair for each day of the week. These are Monday's."

They all looked identical to me, and I was tempted to ask how he could tell them apart, but I thought better of it.

"New laces?"

"No. I like to wash the laces once a week. My old mum always used to say that you could tell a lot about a man by his laces."

"Right."

"I'm sure you didn't come here to discuss my boots."

"Err, no. Albert Cruikshank gave me your name."

"How is he?"

"Still made up with cold."

"He doesn't eat enough greens. I've told him."

"Right. Anyway, he said you might be able to identify one of the graves in The Shadows."

"I try not to spend any more time in The Shadows than I have to. It gives me the creeps."

That seemed a strange comment coming from a gravedigger, but I pressed on regardless. "There's one headstone which is unmarked. I wondered if you knew whose grave it was?"

"I know the one you mean. It's the only grave in that section that is well maintained. Someone leaves fresh flowers there all the time, and they're always black and purple."

"Do you know whose grave it is?"

"I don't, I'm afraid. It was already there when I started work at the graveyard."

"How long have you worked there?"

"It's just coming up to my centenary."

"Right. Well, thanks for your time, anyway."

"Hold on a minute. My father had this job before me. I still have all of his journals. You might find something in there."

"Did he use the journals to record details of the people he'd buried?"

"They're not official records if that's what you mean. They're personal journals in which he recorded anything of interest to him. He was always fascinated by the people who were buried in The Shadows. I can't imagine why. Still, it might be worth a look."

"Could I borrow them?"

"You haven't told me why you're so interested in that particular grave."

"Just curiosity, really. I've always been interested in Candlefield history. When I saw the blank headstone, my curiosity was piqued."

"Okay. You can borrow the journals, provided you take care of them."

"Of course. You have my word."

When Rufus had mentioned the journals, I certainly hadn't anticipated there would be twenty-five of them. They came in three large cardboard boxes, which weighed a ton and were covered in dust.

After magicking myself and the boxes back to Washbridge, I put them in the boot of the car and drove home. Normally, I would have taken the boxes up to the spare bedroom, but with the twins expected the next day, I figured it would be best if I left them in the car.

I intended to visit the casino that night, so I was hoping to grab a few hours' sleep in the afternoon. At least now that Mr Ivers had moved out, I didn't have to worry about being disturbed by one of his hot tub parties.

I curled up in bed and was soon fast asleep.

What the—?

I checked my phone to find that I'd been asleep for less than an hour. Something had woken me, but what? Maybe I'd just had a bad dream?

I'd no sooner put my head back on the pillow than I heard the most awful noise.

Great! Just great!

I jumped out of bed, walked across the landing, and looked out of the front window. Mr and Mrs Normal were standing on their front garden, holding the most enormous horns. The instruments were at least ten feet long with the bell section resting on the lawn in front of them. They were taking it in turns to blow them.

You have got to be kidding me.

I threw on some clothes, and went outside. As soon as Norm spotted me, he tooted his horn and waved.

"Hi, Jill," Naomi shouted.

I walked across the road to get a closer look at these instruments of aural torture.

"Those are very big," I said, stating the obvious.

"They're alphorns," Norm said, proudly. "We're not very good on them yet."

You think? "Did you have to import them from Switzerland?"

"Goodness no." He laughed. "We picked them up at a car boot sale in Wolverhampton."

"Really?"

"We know they're rather loud. That's why we're only going to play them in the daytime. We wouldn't want to disturb anyone's sleep."

"That's very considerate. Actually, I was just—"

"Of course you can have a go," Norm said. "Be our guest."

"Err, no. Thanks, anyway, but I have a sore throat; I think I may be coming down with a cold. I wouldn't want to pass it on to you."

"Maybe another time?"

"Yeah, maybe."

As I walked back across the road, I was serenaded by a cacophony of tuneless horns.

Chapter 13

Thankfully, the alphorn duo ran out of breath twenty minutes later, so I was able to grab a little more sleep. I had hoped that Jack would be back in time to make dinner, but whilst I'd been in bed, he'd sent me a text saying that he had to work late. Undeterred, I resorted to one of my emergency microwave meals, which when cooked looked nothing like the picture on the packet. Having managed to eat only half of it, I was pretty sure the cardboard packaging would have tasted better.

When I left the house at nine o'clock, Jack still wasn't home.

Rather than resorting to invisibility to get into the casino, I used the 'block' spell, which would prevent any other sup realising I was a witch. I was in luck because the doorman on duty wasn't the same one who had turned me away on my previous visit. This time, I breezed past him, no questions asked.

Inside, it was nothing like I'd imagined it would be. I'd expected to find rows and rows of slot machines, and for the place to be filled with noise and flashing lights. In fact, there were very few slot machines; I counted no more than a dozen. The lighting was subdued, the furnishings tasteful, and the noise levels generally low except for the crowd around the craps tables. The casino was split-level, with a bar and craps tables occupying the lower level. On the upper level were the card tables and roulette.

The drinks were remarkably cheap, but I figured that was a deliberate policy. Happy customers were more likely to stay longer, and in most cases, the longer they stayed, the more money they would lose.

"Lime and soda, please. No ice."

"Coming right up." The young barman was a human. "I don't think I've seen you here before, have I?"

"It's my first time. I thought I might try the craps table."

"Here's hoping the dice roll for you." He passed me the drink.

"Didn't you used to have two large dice on the front of the building?"

"We did, but there was a tragic accident a few months ago. A lightning strike brought them down, and a man was killed."

"How terrible. I didn't hear about that."

The mix of customers reflected the casino's policy of turning most sups away. I estimated it was ninety-five percent humans to five percent sups. And those five percent were all witches and wizards. The only other sups present, a few vampires and werewolves, were all on the staff.

If I'd understood Kirk Sparks' cryptic notes correctly, he'd concluded that sups were the big winners in the casino. With that in mind, I joined the small crowd gathered around the craps table. Although the precise rules of that particular game were beyond me, it was easy enough to tell if someone was a winner or a loser. For the first twenty minutes, a procession of humans took their turn as the 'shooter'. Their fortunes were mixed, but generally they came away as losers or small winners.

The first sup to pick up the dice was a witch, who looked remarkably bored. Even her celebrations when she won, which she did big time, seemed rather subdued.

Everyone around the table was cheering her on, much more excited at her 'good fortune' than she appeared to be. Although it was quite obvious to me that she was using magic to affect the outcome of the dice, the humans present had no idea that anything untoward was taking place.

I wasn't too familiar with the rules of the card games, so I headed next to one of the roulette tables. Unsurprisingly, the vast majority of punters gathered around the table were humans, but I did spot one wizard. Over the next hour, the chips flowed back and forth. There were several small winners, but far more losers. The biggest winner was the wizard, who used magic to influence the roulette wheel. Just like the witch, he showed little or no emotion.

Over the course of my visit, I drifted between the various tables, and witnessed a similar pattern each time. The characters changed: witches and wizards came and went, but they were always the big winners.

By three o'clock in the morning, I could barely keep my eyes open, so I called it a day. My visit had served to confirm Kirk's own conclusions: Most sups were turned away from the casino, but a few witches and wizards were allowed inside, and they always turned out to be big winners. But what did that mean? Who were the 'chosen' few? And why did the owners turn a blind eye while they used magic to win?

***

Jack, AKA sleeping beauty, was dead to the world when I arrived home, so I slid into bed beside him, and was fast asleep as soon as my head hit the pillow.

"Jill! Quick! Wake up!" Jack was hopping around the bedroom, trying to put his trousers on.

"What's up? Where's the fire?"

"Kathy and Lizzie are outside. Peter has just dropped them off."

"What time is it?" I grabbed my phone from the bedside cabinet. "Eleven? Why didn't you wake me earlier?"

"I was asleep too. I didn't get in until after midnight."

"You'll have to go downstairs and let them in. I need time to come around."

"You don't have time. You've got to clear the spare bedroom."

"What?" My brain was still in neutral.

"You were supposed to shrink the furniture last night, remember?"

"Oh yeah. I forgot all about that."

"You'll have to do it now while I stall Kathy and Lizzie."

"Great." I crawled out of bed, and tried to find my clothes. "Don't let them come upstairs, whatever you do."

"Okay, but you'll have to be quick." Still minus one sock, Jack disappeared out of the bedroom.

I should have sorted out the spare room before I went to the casino, but all was not lost. It would only take me a few minutes to shrink the furniture, gather it all together and put it into the shoe box.

As I walked across the landing, I heard Jack welcoming Kathy and Lizzie. Once inside the spare bedroom, I closed the door behind me before casting the 'shrink' spell. I had to be careful as I walked around the room, collecting the tiny furniture, because if I trod on anything, I'd never hear the end of it from Jack.

Five minutes later, I'd got all the furniture in the shoe box. I intended to hide it at the bottom of my wardrobe, and cover it with a few jumpers.

Once again, Jack had been panicking over nothing.

"Kathy? Lizzie?"

I'd stepped out of the spare bedroom just as the two of them reached the top of the stairs.

"Morning, Jill," Kathy said. "Lizzie is bursting for a pee, aren't you, pumpkin? Off you go."

Lizzie didn't answer; she just rushed towards the bathroom.

"What's that?" Kathy was staring at the shoe box.

Oh bum!

"It's err—"

"Did you buy those for Lizzie?"

"I—err—"

"That's a really lovely thing to do." Before I could stop her, she'd taken the box from me. "These are great. Where did you get them from?"

"I—err—"

"Lizzie is going to love them. I didn't realise you knew she had a dolls' house."

Just then, the toilet flushed, and Lizzie came to join us.

"Hi, Auntie Jill. I'm sorry I didn't say hello before, but I needed the loo."

"Look what your Auntie Jill has got for you." Kathy held out the box.

Lizzie's face lit up. "Thank you, Auntie Jill. "Can I take them home with me?"

"Well, I—err—"

"Of course you can," Kathy said. "Auntie Jill bought them for your dolls' house, didn't you, Auntie Jill?"

Before I could speak, Jack came upstairs to join us.

"Look what I've got, Uncle Jack." Lizzie held up the box.

Jack's face was a picture. "Err, where did you get those from?"

"We bought them for Lizzie," I said. "Don't you remember?"

"Oh yes." If looks could kill, I'd have been stone dead. "I'd forgotten about that."

"Kathy, would you mind helping yourself to a cup of tea or coffee? Jack and I were still in bed when you arrived. We need to take a shower."

"No problem." She winked at me. "You newlyweds."

Jack closed the bedroom door behind him. "Are you insane? You've just given Lizzie my furniture."

"It's your fault."

"How is it my fault?"

"You were supposed to keep them occupied downstairs while I shrank the furniture and hid it."

"Lizzie was bursting to go to the loo. What was I supposed to do?"

"You should have told her to hold it."

"What are we going to do about my furniture?"

"What can we do? Do you want to tell Lizzie she can't have it?"

"This would never have happened if you'd cleared the spare bedroom last night like you said you would."

"I was working until three this morning."

Jack and I showered and dressed, and then went downstairs.

"Look, Auntie Jill." Lizzie had arranged the furniture across the lounge floor. "Mummy says it's the best she's ever seen."

I could feel Jack's eyes burning into the back of my head. "It's very nice, but to be honest, I was in two minds when I bought it. The shop had some more modern stuff. Maybe I should take this lot back and get it swapped?"

"No." Lizzie looked horrified. "I like these."

"The attention to detail is amazing." Kathy picked up the small bedside cabinet. "Some of the drawers even have things inside them. Look, there's a tiny teddy bear in this one."

"That's Kidney," Jack said.

I shot him a look.

"Sorry?" Kathy seemed puzzled by Jack's contribution.

"Err, I think Jack meant the bear was a funny shape, didn't you?" He just glared at me. "It's kind of kidney-shaped."

As we would be having dinner with the twins that evening, Jack volunteered to make sandwiches for lunch. While Kathy and Lizzie were preoccupied, I went through to the kitchen to see if I could make the peace.

He was buttering the bread, so I came up behind him, and put my arms around his waist. "I'm really sorry. Do you forgive me?"

"You admit that it was your fault, then?"

"Well, I—err."

He turned to face me. "Jill?"

"Yes, it was my fault. I should have done it earlier in the

week. I'll try to figure out a way to persuade Lizzie not to take the furniture home with her."

"You can't do that now. You've seen how much she loves it. And besides, it was only rotting away in the spare bedroom."

"But we were going to swap it with my furniture at some point."

"You were never going to let me have my stuff out. You hate it."

"Only because it's ugly."

"No, it isn't, but that doesn't matter now. If it makes Lizzie happy, I'm cool with it."

I gave him a kiss. "Have I ever told you that you're the bestest husband in the whole wide world?"

"Only when you want something." He kissed me this time. "There is just one thing I need you to do, though?"

"Anything. Just name it."

"I don't want to lose Kidney."

"Leave it with me. I'll see what I can do."

After lunch, Kathy and I were in the kitchen. Jack was in the lounge, playing dolls' house with Lizzie—something he seemed to enjoy way too much.

"Thanks, Jill." Kathy gave me a hug.

"Put me down."

"I'm lucky to have such a lovely sister."

"Have you been at the wine?"

"That was an awesome thing you did, buying the dolls' furniture for Lizzie. She's been down in the dumps most of the week because of that stupid dream business."

"Is she still on with that?"

"Yeah. It's got to the point where I dread the mornings.

She still insists she can't dream. Hopefully, the dolls' furniture will take her mind off it. By the way, I hope you've got plenty of cake in because from what I remember, the twins have a sweet tooth."

"I haven't had the chance. I've been so busy at work; I was working undercover until three this morning."

"Why don't I nip out and get some? Where's the nearest shop?"

"The corner shop is just down the road. Why don't you ask Jack to show you?"

While Jack and Kathy went in search of cake, I got down on the lounge floor with Lizzie who was still enthralled by her new toys.

"Having fun?"

"Yes, thanks, Auntie Jill. I like the bed best."

"It's a bit too creaky for my liking."

"How do you know?"

"Oh? I—err—it just looks like it would be. Your mummy told me you've been a little upset about your dreams."

"A bit."

"Everyone has periods when they can't remember them."

"That's what Mummy said, but it's happened to other kids at school too."

"Oh?"

"Yeah, lots of them. Donna was crying about it in class yesterday."

When Jack and Kathy got back, they were weighed down with bags.

"Just how many cakes did you two buy?"

"We've got biscuits too." Kathy put the bags onto the kitchen table. "There are some very weird people in your neighbourhood."

"Oh?"

"The guy in the shop was walking around on stilts."

"The stilts are new. He used to stand on a box."

"And then there was the guy in the train."

"Mr Hosey? Don't you remember? He was the one who took me to the hotel when we got married."

"He was having the weirdest conversation with Jack. How's Lizzie?"

"She's fine."

Kathy went through to the lounge, leaving Jack and me to unpack the bags.

"What was Hosey talking about?" I said.

"You might well ask," he snapped.

"What's wrong?"

"He seems to be under the impression that I have a thing for camouflage."

Oh bum!

Chapter 14

The twins had phoned to say they were ready for us to collect them. Jack was playing with Lizzie, who seemed to be impressed by his in-depth knowledge of the dolls' furniture, so I said I'd go and collect Amber and Pearl.

"I'll come with you," Kathy said.

"Don't you want to stay here with Lizzie?"

"No, she won't miss me. She and Jack are having a whale of a time. He's really good with kids, isn't he?"

"Yeah. I'll just let him know we're going."

Neither Jack nor Lizzie noticed me walk into the lounge.

"Do you like this, Uncle Jack?" Lizzie held up the miniature wardrobe.

"I do, it's nice. I used to have a wardrobe just like that."

"What happened to it?"

"Your Auntie Jill threw it away."

I cleared my throat to let them know I was there. "Auntie Jill didn't throw it away, Lizzie. She gave it to someone who would appreciate it much more. Didn't I, Uncle Jack?"

"That's what I meant." He glared at me.

"Kathy and I are going to pick up the twins. Will you two be okay here playing with the dolls' furniture?"

"Yes, thank you, Auntie Jill." Lizzie beamed. "Uncle Jack is telling me what everything is."

"Okay, have fun, you two. We won't be too long."

Kathy was waiting by the car. "Are those two okay in there?"

"Yeah, they're having a ball. If I'd realised how much Jack was into that kind of thing, I'd have bought him a dolls' house for Christmas."

"Where did you say you'd pick up the twins?"

"On the side street, just around the corner from your shop."

"I'm really looking forward to seeing Crystal and Emerald again."

"It's Amber and Pearl."

"Is there any wonder I don't remember their names. I get to see them so rarely."

"I just hope they haven't overdone it with the shopping."

But, of course, they had. And then some.

The two of them were standing on the corner of the street, prams by their side. And at their feet, were a thousand carrier bags.

"We should have brought both cars," I said, as I pulled in next to them.

Kathy was out of the car almost before it had stopped. "It's so lovely to see you both again. And look at these two little darlings. Which one is which?"

"The pretty one is Lily," Pearl said.

"She wishes," Amber shot back.

"Okay, you two." I had to nip that in the bud. "Let's try and get this lot into the car. Why don't you two get in the back with the little ones while Kathy and I try to get all this shopping into the boot."

"There won't be room in the back for us both," Pearl said. "Not once we've put the baby seats in."

"Right, so how are we going to do this, then?"

"Jill, why don't you take one of the twins and her baby?" Kathy said. "And the rest of us can take a taxi."

"Okay. I guess that would work."

"I'll go with you, Jill." Amber was already in the car, fixing the baby seat in place.

"I'll put as much of this shopping in your boot as I can." Kathy picked up several carrier bags. "Pearl and I will bring the rest in the taxi."

"That sounds like a plan."

"Jill! Why do you have these dusty boxes in here? They seem to be full of old books."

Oh bum! I'd forgotten I had Rufus Alldig's father's journals in there. "They're for a case I'm working on."

"You should have taken them out. There's hardly any room left in here."

"Just put in what you can."

Eventually, Amber, Lil and I were all set to go.

"We'll see you back at the house," I said.

"We shouldn't be long." Kathy checked her watch. "They said the cab would be with us in ten minutes."

"Okay, bye."

"Thanks for letting us stay tonight, Jill," Amber said.

"No problem. It looks like you two have had a good day's shopping."

"Most of that stuff is Pearl's. You know what she's like. Spend, spend, spend — she's always been the same."

"Hmm."

***

Amber and I were still unpacking my car when the taxi turned up with Kathy, Pearl and Lily. Between us, it took a good ten minutes to get the prams and all the shopping into the house.

"I'm sorry about all this lot," Pearl said to me while Amber and Kathy were in the house. "Most of this stuff is Amber's. You know what she's like."

"Spend, spend, spend?"

"Exactly."

Jack had had the good sense to get Lizzie to put all the dolls' furniture into the shoe box before we got back. Had it been left on the floor, it would no doubt have been trampled underfoot.

"Hi, you two." Jack gave both of the twins a hug. "Lovely to see you both again."

"Where shall we put all of our stuff?" Amber said.

Before I could guide them to the spare bedroom, Jack jumped in, "We've put you in our bedroom. Jill and I are going to take the spare room."

"That wasn't necessary," Pearl said. "We could have slept in there."

"We wouldn't hear of it," Jack said. "Our bedroom is much bigger. You'll need the additional space with those two little ones. Come on, I'll show you to your room."

The twins, with their babies, followed Jack upstairs.

"That was a nice gesture," Kathy said to me.

"It was, wasn't it?"

"Shall I put the kettle on?"

"Yes, please."

"I'll help you, Mummy." Lizzie followed her into the kitchen.

Moments later, Jack came back downstairs, so I grabbed him by the arm and took him through to the lounge.

"What were you thinking? I thought we'd agreed that

the twins would have the spare room?"

"We did, but that was before you made one tiny little mistake."

"What are you talking about?"

"Look in there." He pointed to the shoe box full of dolls' furniture. "What do you see there on top?"

"It's a bed."

"Precisely. It's a bed."

"Oh bum!"

"Oh bum, indeed. You weren't supposed to shrink the bed. That room is empty now. How could I let the twins have the room without a bed in it?"

"I could have reversed the spell on the bed."

"And how would you do that with Kathy and Lizzie in the house?"

"Where will we sleep, then?"

"That's a good question."

"It's okay. I have a plan."

"Tea or coffee, you two?" Kathy appeared at the door.

***

While Kathy and Lizzie spent time with the twins and the little ones, Jack and I made dinner. Lizzie was thrilled because the twins had allowed her to hold each of the babies in turn.

"What's this plan of yours?" Jack said while peeling the potatoes.

"I'm not telling you because you'll only give the game away."

"Should I be worried about it?"

"Of course not. I have everything in hand."

"I hope so. I don't fancy sleeping on the floor."

"By the way, you'll never guess what the Normals were up to yesterday."

"Was it the magnetic fish again?"

"Much noisier than that. I was trying to catch a few hours' sleep before I went undercover at the casino, but they woke me up with their stupid horns."

"Why were they hooting their car horns?"

"I don't mean they were hooting their car horns. They were playing alphorns."

"Aren't they those whopping great things?"

"They are. They were out on the front garden with them."

"Are they any good?"

"They were terrible. It was an awful noise."

"Where did they get them from? Switzerland?"

"No."

"Austria?"

"No. A car boot sale in Wolverhampton, apparently."

"Poor you." He grinned. "Didn't you get much sleep, then?"

"Luckily, they ran out of breath after a few minutes. So, when do you make your debut as a bush? Or do you have your heart set on being a tree?"

"I suppose you think that's funny."

"Come on. In my position, you *wood* too." I dissolved into laughter. "*Wood*? Do you get it?"

"I get it; it's just not funny."

"I know you're not really angry. Your *bark* is worse than your bite."

"Any more?"

"No, I'm done. I'll *leaf* it at that."

"Pathetic."

***

The twins had fed the two little ones before we sat down to eat, so we were able to get through dinner without being disturbed. The meal seemed to go down a treat with everyone.

"That was delicious, Jack," Kathy said.

"Yeah, thanks, Jack." Amber nodded her approval.

"You're a great cook, Jack," Pearl added.

"Excuse me," I objected. "This meal was a joint effort."

For some reason, that seemed to amuse everyone around the table.

"It's a lovely evening," Pearl said. "Why don't we go out into the back garden?"

"Actually, Lizzie and I had better be making tracks." Kathy stood up. "Pete and Mikey will be back by now, and we promised to go to his mother's tonight. Go and get your shoe box, Lizzie."

"I'll run you home while Jack tidies up here," I volunteered, selflessly.

"I've really enjoyed today, Jill." Kathy was in the front with me, as we drove back to her house.

"I did, too," Lizzie said from the back seat. "Can we go to the twins' houses sometime? I've never been there."

"That would be nice," Kathy agreed.

"It's not easy. They live such a long way away."

"Where exactly is it they live again?" Kathy said. "I've never been sure."

"It's err—did you remember to bring the shoe box with you, Lizzie?"

"Yes, I've got it here."

"So?" Kathy said. "What do you think about us going to visit the twins?"

"It's a great idea. I'll mention it to them."

"Don't forget you and Jack are babysitting for us on Monday, will you?"

"Of course not. It's in my diary."

"Do you actually keep a diary?"

"No, but if I did, it would be in it."

When I got back, I went to join the twins.

"Hi, girls. I'm back."

"Lizzie is such a darling," Amber said. "And she's so good with Lil and Lily."

"Yeah. Not awkward like you, Jill."

"What do you mean? I'm not awkward with them."

"You look terrified when you're holding them."

"Rubbish. Kathy asked when she and Lizzie can visit you."

"What did you tell her?"

"I stalled her. Hopefully, she'll forget all about it."

It had been a hectic couple of days, and I was glad for the chance to sit back and enjoy what was left of the evening sun.

What the—?

The two prams began to move back and forth across the patio. It took me a moment to realise what was happening; the twins were controlling them with magic.

"What do you two think you're doing?"

"The little ones love it."

"You can't use magic here." I pointed to the house. "Jack might see."

"Sorry."

"We forgot."

They both cancelled the spells.

"How do you manage to keep it a secret, Jill?" Pearl said. "That you're a witch, I mean?"

"It isn't easy."

"You must be tempted to use magic sometimes." Amber began to rock her pram in the more conventional way.

"No," I lied. "I never am."

"I don't think I could ever get used to it," Pearl said. "I mean, just imagine not being able to use magic to do things like housework."

"It doesn't bear thinking about," Amber agreed.

"You get used to it," I said.

Jack joined us a few minutes later, and the four of us enjoyed a drink and the delicious chocolates, which the twins had bought as a thank you for letting them stay.

When one of the babies started to cry, the other soon joined in.

"They're ready for their feed," Amber picked up Lil.

"We'll take them inside." Pearl grabbed Lily.

"I'll show you where everything is." Jack followed them into the house.

I was about to do the same when Britt appeared next door. "Hi, Jill. I see you have guests."

"That's Amber and Pearl, my cousins. And their little ones."

"I saw them from the bedroom window. I didn't realise

they made prams that could move back and forth by themselves?"

Oh bum! "Err, yeah. They're good, aren't they? It's remarkable what they can do these days."

"My sister is expecting a baby soon. I'm sure she'd love one of those. Could you find out where your cousins bought them?"

"Err, yeah. I'll ask them. Anyway, I'd better get inside. Catch you later."

***

At just after ten, the twins decided to call it a day. Jack and I bid them and the babies goodnight, and waited until we had heard them close the bedroom door.

"Phew! Thank goodness that's over." I breathed a sigh of relief.

"I've enjoyed today."

"Me too, but it was exhausting. While you were in the house, the twins were using magic to move the prams back and forth."

"It's a good job I didn't see them." He grinned. "I might have thought they were witches."

"It's not funny. Britt saw the prams moving by themselves."

"What did you say?"

"I made up some rubbish about the prams being the latest hi-tech models."

"It's a good job you're such a great liar."

"The only problem is she wants to know where to buy one. Her sister is expecting a baby, apparently."

"Oh dear. What did you tell her?"

"That I'd try to find out where the twins bought them. Hopefully, she'll forget about it."

"I'm shattered. Where are we going to sleep?"

"I told you I had a plan, didn't I?" I picked up my handbag, and took out the miniature bed.

"How did you get that?"

"I sneaked it out of the shoebox while Lizzie wasn't watching."

"She's bound to realise."

"I know. I'll just say we found it after she left. We can drop it off tomorrow after the twins have gone home."

"You're a genius."

"That's not all." I took out the little bear.

"Kidney!" He hugged the tiny thing. "Do we have to give him back tomorrow too?"

"I don't think Lizzie will miss the bear. Come on, let's find out if this bed still creaks."

Chapter 15

"Good morning, sweetie." Jack woke me with a kiss.

"Is it really morning already?"

"It's almost eight. The twins are already up; I heard them go downstairs ages ago."

"One of us ought to get up and make breakfast for them." I yawned. "They're bound to want a fry-up."

"Are you volunteering?"

"You're so much better at fry-ups than I am."

"And you're so much better at fawning." He grinned. "Do you think they would have heard the bed creaking last night?"

"Nah. They were way across the landing, and besides, they probably slept like logs after the busy day they'd had."

"You're probably right. I'll grab a shower and go and get breakfast started."

"Have I ever told you that you're the best husband ever?"

"Yeah, every time you get your own way."

Harsh but true.

I didn't rush my shower because I figured if I took my time, breakfast should more or less be waiting for me when I got downstairs.

And it was.

"Cornflakes?" I stared at the bowl.

"You're welcome to have the same as us if you like?" Jack held up the box of muesli.

It was only then that I realised the twins were eating that mush too.

"Muesli?" I glanced back and forth between Amber and Pearl. "I thought you two would want a good old-fashioned fry-up."

"We get those all the time at Mum's." Amber shoved a spoonful of sawdust into her mouth.

"Yeah." Pearl managed through a mouthful of the stuff. "This makes a nice change."

Freaks, all of them.

Rather deflated, I poured myself a bowl of cornflakes.

"Did you manage to get any sleep last night with the little ones?" I said.

"The babies didn't keep us awake, but the creaking did." Amber smirked. "Didn't it, Pearl?"

"Yeah, and it seemed to go on for ages."

"I didn't hear any creaking." I shrugged. "Did you, Jack?"

"I—err—" His face was the colour of beetroot. "Does anyone want toast?"

After we'd finished breakfast, Jack volunteered to tidy the kitchen.

No, I *didn't* volunteer him. I had the distinct impression that he was glad to get away from us. If I wasn't mistaken, he was feeling a little intimidated by being outnumbered three to one. Five to one if you counted the little ones who were now being bottle fed by the twins in the lounge.

"What shall we do about magicking ourselves home, Jill?" Pearl said.

"Don't worry, I'll keep him occupied while you do it."

"Won't he think it's strange if we just disappear?"

"Not if you've already said your goodbyes. I'll distract him and then say you've taken a taxi to the station."

Not long after the babies had been fed, the air was filled with a pungent aroma that could mean only one thing.

"We'll take the little ones upstairs to change them." Amber picked up Lil.

"Do you want to do it, Jill?" Pearl said. "The practice might come in handy."

"That's a very generous offer, but I got all the practice I needed when you two were laid up with the sup flu. When you come back downstairs, you'd better say your goodbyes to Jack."

"I was just telling the twins they should come over again next Saturday," Jack said, as he hugged them both goodbye.

Had the man lost his mind? Once a year was more than enough.

"You didn't tell us about the big event that Grandma has organised, Jill," Amber said.

"What big event?"

"The promo for TenPinCon," Jack said.

"I didn't think it was worth mentioning."

"Jack says there's going to be a parade and a band, and then giant skittles."

"They're pins."

"It sounds like fun," Pearl said. "Maybe we'll pop over."

"Isn't it a long way to come just for a few hours, though?"

"It'll be worth it. We might ask Mum to come with us."

"Aunt Lucy? You'll be lucky. You know how she feels about the human—"

Terrified that I was about to let the cat out of the bag,

Amber spoke over me. "Mum would enjoy a trip to Washbridge."

"You should all come," Jack said. "It's going to be great."

I took Jack through to the kitchen, so that the twins could magic themselves home.

"Have you recovered?" I asked him.

"What do you mean?"

"I've never seen anyone blush as much as you did when the twins mentioned the creaking bed."

"I wasn't blushing. I—err, just—err, anyway, why did the twins take a taxi? We could have run them to the station in both cars."

"They haven't taken a taxi. And they aren't going to the station."

"But they said they were."

"Come on, Jack. Just think about it for a minute."

I could almost see the penny drop. "Oh yeah. Of course. You'd think I'd be used to all of this magic stuff by now."

"Talking of which, why did you ask them to come over again next Saturday?"

"I thought they'd enjoy it."

"You're supposed to think they live several hours away. You have to be careful that you don't let on that you know where they really live."

"Sorry, I wasn't thinking. Do you reckon they cottoned on?"

"No. Luckily, the twins are away with the fairies most of the time. You'll need to be much more careful if Aunt Lucy does come over. And you'll definitely have to watch what you say around Grandma. She doesn't miss a thing."

"Okay. I will. I promise."

"If I shrink the bed, can you take it around to Kathy's while I tidy up here?"

"Sure."

"It might be an idea to tell her it needs oiling."

***

While Jack went to Kathy's, I tidied the kitchen and took the rubbish out to the bin.

"Jill!" Britt called to me over the fence. "Are your cousins still here? I was hoping I might see their little ones."

"They've already gone home, I'm afraid."

"Oh? I didn't see them leave."

"Yeah, just now."

"Did you ask them where they bought their prams from?"

"I did, yes, but it seems they're not on general sale yet."

"Oh?"

"They're a prototype. The twins signed up to test them."

"That's disappointing. My sister would have loved to have one of those."

"Maybe they'll be on general release soon. I'll ask the twins to keep me posted."

"Thanks. Are you and Jack doing anything interesting for the rest of the day?"

"Nothing much."

"Kit and I are taking part in the West Chipping half-marathon later."

Of course you are. "Nice."

"Did you see those big trumpets that the Normals were playing yesterday?"

"Alphorn."

"Alf who?"

"No. That's what they're called: Alphorns. They made an awful noise, didn't they?"

"Kit and I quite enjoyed it. We were thinking of asking where they got them from. It would be nice to play a musical instrument."

"Might it be better to start with something a little smaller?" And quieter?

"You could be right. I used to enjoy playing the triangle when I was at school."

"No! Not the triangle!"

"Sorry?" She looked understandably surprised by my extreme reaction.

"Err, you can do better than the triangle. How about a tambourine?"

"Perhaps. I'll need to discuss it with Kit. Maybe you and Jack could join in too? Do either of you play an instrument?"

"Not me. I'm tone deaf. Jack is a bit of a whizz on the glockenspiel, though."

"Really? That's fantastic. Maybe we could even start a community band?"

***

It was almost midday when Jack finally got back from Kathy's.

"I thought you'd got lost."

"They invited me in for tea and biscuits."

"That was very nice for you. I've been slaving away, tidying up."

"Kathy asked what we were going to do with the spare bedroom."

"I haven't given it much thought. I suppose we could turn it into a home cinema."

"Kathy thought we might be thinking of turning it into a nursery."

"Ah, so that's what this is all about."

"It's not such a terrible idea, is it?"

"No, of course it isn't, but — err, we haven't really talked about that yet, have we?"

"Maybe we should. You do want kids, don't you?"

"Yeah, of course, but I always thought it was something I'd do when I was grown up."

"You're thirty, Jill."

"Twenty-nine."

"When you see the twins with their babies, doesn't it make you wish we had one of our own?"

"No, it just makes me happy that I don't have to spend all day feeding them and changing their nappies. I had quite enough of that when I was looking after them when the twins were poorly."

"It's different when it's your own baby."

"That's what everyone says. I'm not sure I believe it, though."

"I really do want children." He pulled me in for a hug.

"Me too. I'm just not sure if I'm ready yet."

"Okay." He gave me a kiss. "But let's not leave it too long. You'll make a smashing mum."

"I'm not so sure about that. I'll most likely be a nightmare."

"What do you fancy doing for the rest of today?"

"I kind of promised I'd go and support Mrs V at her hula hoop marathon. You don't have to come if you don't want to."

"Are you kidding? I wouldn't miss it for the world."

***

The hula hoop marathon was being held in Washbridge Central Rooms, which was a ten-minute walk from the high street. As we'd be having a big dinner in the evening, we popped into Coffee Games to pick up a snack for lunch.

"What time does the marathon start?" Jack said. "I don't want to miss anything."

"We've got plenty of time. It doesn't start until two o'clock."

"If it runs over, we might have to have dinner a little later than usual."

"Are you kidding?" I scoffed at the idea. "How long do you think the old yarnies are going to keep those hula hoops going? I reckon we'll be out after thirty minutes."

"You might be under-estimating them. A lot of old people keep themselves in shape these days."

"Come on, Jack. Let's face it, if they're anything like Mrs V, they'll be lucky to keep them spinning for more than a few minutes. They should have stuck with something they could manage, like the knitathon."

As soon as we stepped into Coffee Games, Jack stopped dead in his tracks. "What's going on in here?"

"It looks like blind man's buff to me." I stepped to one side to avoid a young man, wearing a blindfold, who was stumbling around, trying to tag someone.

"What's that all about?" Jack said.

"Didn't you know? They don't only do board games in here now. They do all kinds of parlour games too. Just think yourself lucky it's not pin the tail on the donkey day."

Once we had our food and drink, we managed to find refuge in a booth at the back of the shop.

"I preferred this place when it used to be Coffee Triangle." Jack took a bite of his sandwich.

"Me too. Except for triangle day."

"Oh yeah." He laughed. "I'd forgotten about your irrational fear of triangles."

"They're evil. By the way, how are you on the glockenspiel?"

"I've never played one. Why would you ask that?"

"No reason. Just curious."

***

The hula hoop marathon was way better attended than I'd expected it to be. When Mrs V spotted us, she and Armi came over.

"Jill, Jack, I'm so pleased you were able to make it."

"We wouldn't have missed this for the world, would we, Jack? And besides, it should only take a few minutes, shouldn't it?"

"I think you'll find it'll last a lot longer than that," Mrs V sounded confident. Over confident, if you asked me.

"Yeah, sorry. I'm sure you're right." Twenty minutes max.

"Yarnies!" The woman on the stage was speaking into a

megaphone. "Can I have your attention, please. The marathon will begin in ten minutes. Will all competitors please take their place on stage as quickly as possible."

"Why doesn't she use a microphone?" I whispered to Mrs V.

"That's Flo Wren. She insists she's allergic to them."

"Right."

"I'd better get going." Mrs V started towards the stage.

"Okay. Best of luck. We'll be cheering you on."

"There must be at least thirty of them up there," Jack said.

"And not one of them under seventy. This is going to be a disaster. They'll be lucky if they manage to raise twenty quid between them."

Flo Wren's voice crackled through the megaphone again. "Just a quick reminder about the rules. Once you've started the hoop spinning, you must not touch it with your hands again. If you do, you will be eliminated. If the hoop drops to the floor, you will be eliminated. Competitors are allowed a five-minute break every thirty minutes."

"That's not fair," I whispered to Jack. "Mrs V never mentioned that they'd get breaks."

"What are you worried about? You just said they'd only last a few minutes."

"True."

Flo continued, "And, finally, a reminder that the yarnie who keeps their hula hoop spinning for the longest time will have their sponsorship minutes doubled. Okay, on my count. Three, two, one, go!"

"Stop laughing!" Jack nudged me.

"Sorry." I couldn't help it. Just as I'd predicted, over half of the yarnies lasted less than a minute. The room was full of the sound of hoops hitting the stage. "I told you this would happen."

"They haven't all been eliminated yet."

He was right. A few of the yarnies had managed to keep going a little longer, but by the fifteen-minute mark, there were only seven competitors left on the stage: Mrs V and six others.

"Look at her go, Jill. She doesn't even look tired." Jack was becoming quite animated. "Go on, Mrs V!"

"Why are you cheering her on? This is going to cost us a fortune."

By the first break, there were only two competitors left. Mrs V was one of them, and she was still going strong.

When she came off the stage to get a drink, Armi, Jack and I went over to join her.

"You're doing great, petal." Armi gave her a quick peck on the cheek.

"Yeah, you're going great guns, Mrs V," Jack said. "You look like you could keep going all day."

"Don't you think you might be overdoing it?" I said. "Maybe you should call it a day now."

What? Of course I wasn't thinking about how much it was going to cost me. My only concern was for her welfare. Sheesh!

"I'm fine." She took a sip of water. "I feel like I could keep going all afternoon."

"How did you learn to hula hoop like that?" Jack said.

"I was on the hula hoop team for my school. In fact, I actually represented the country once. I guess it's something you never forget."

Flo was back on her megaphone. "The break is over, yarnies. Please return to the stage."

I grabbed Jack's arm. "We've been hustled."

"What are you talking about?"

"She never told me she was an international."

"Look. The other yarnie has dropped out. Mrs V has won!" Jack raised his hands. "Go, Mrs V."

"Well done, petal!" Armi shouted.

"Shouldn't she stop now that she's won, Armi?" I said.

"If I know Annabel, she'll keep going until she drops."

That was precisely what worried me.

And so it was that Mrs V continued to hula hoop. On and on and on it went, and all the time, all I could think about was how much money this was costing me.

Eventually, during the third break, Mrs V announced that she was going to call it a day.

Flo Wren took to the megaphone again, "Yarnies, please give it up for Annabel Versailles. According to the official timekeeper, she has clocked up an incredible seventy-five minutes."

Oh bum! At fifty pence a minute, that was going to cost me thirty-seven pounds and fifty pence.

"And, of course," Flo continued. "As the winner, her sponsored minutes are doubled to one-hundred and fifty."

Double bum! That meant I'd have to fork out seventy-five pounds.

Chapter 16

It was Monday morning and for once I was up before Jack. I'd woken early and been unable to get back to sleep, so I'd decided to fetch the journals from my car and start to work my way through them.

Progress was slow and painful. Rufus Alldig's father, Cosmo, had recorded pretty much everything he did in those books. And by *everything*, I really do mean *everything*. It was like reading someone's Twitter feed. He'd noted what he'd had to eat that day, what clothes he was wearing and what the weather was like. Every now and then, though, I did find an interesting snippet related to the graveyard. I was halfway through the first journal, and so far, I'd only found one entry related to The Shadows. Cosmo had recorded the burial of a certain Maximillian Molar who had been convicted of stealing teeth. Not dentures, but real teeth from the mouths of innocent victims. Molar's MO was apparently to tie up a dentist, and take his place. Anyone with a dental appointment that day, even for just a check-up, left the surgery minus their teeth. The journal didn't make it clear what Molar actually did with the teeth, and on balance, I decided I'd rather not know.

"Morning." Jack yawned. "How long have you been up?"

"A couple of hours."

He came to join me on the sofa, and picked up one of the journals. "What are these?"

"A gravedigger's journals."

"You always did have a weird taste in books." He half grinned, half yawned. "Are these for a case you're working on?"

"Not exactly. I followed the woman who's working in the twins' creche. She went to an unmarked grave, and I'm trying to find out who it belongs to."

"Did the twins ask you to check up on her?"

"No, they think the sun shines out of her backside."

"Why are you getting involved, then?"

"There's something about her that just doesn't feel right."

"Have you found anything so far?"

"Nothing about the unmarked grave, but I now know the man had an unhealthy obsession with mulled wine. Oh, and I'm never going to the dentist again."

"It's too early in the morning for me to try to make any sense of that. Have you eaten breakfast yet?"

"No. I thought you'd want to make it, seeing as how I'm working."

"This isn't working. This is sticking your nose in where it isn't wanted. If the twins are happy with the woman, why can't you leave well alone?"

"I'm right about Belladonna, you'll see."

"Is that really her name?"

"So she says." I put a slip of paper into the journal to act as a bookmark. "That'll do for now. I'll do some more tonight."

"You've forgotten, haven't you?"

"Forgotten what?"

"That we're babysitting for Lizzie and Mikey tonight."

"Oh bum, yeah, I had. Never mind, I can take these with me."

"No, you can't. You'll freak the kids out if they see you reading the dusty old journals of some creepy gravedigger."

Over breakfast, which I'd slaved long and hard over, Jack mused about TenPinCon.

"I promised Tony and Clare that I'd let them know what's happening with the marketing tomorrow. Can you chase up your grandmother?"

"Grandma does things in her own sweet time. My chasing her won't do any good."

"I suppose not. If she hasn't got back to you by tomorrow, I'll just have to stall them." He looked down at his egg on toast. "How come I only got one slice?"

"That's all the bread that was left. Our visitors ate us out of house and home yesterday."

"I'd better let you have my sponsorship money for Mrs V. How much was it again?"

"One hundred and fifty pounds."

"Are you sure? That sounds an awful lot."

"She did seventy-five minutes, double that because she came first. That makes one hundred and fifty."

He took out his wallet. "I don't think I have that much on me." I could almost see the cogs turning in his head. "Hold on. One hundred and fifty minutes at fifty pence per minute is seventy-five pounds by my calculations."

"Each."

"Yeah, so why did you just ask me for one hundred and fifty?"

"I didn't. I was just saying that's how much we owe."

Drat! I'd almost got away with it.

He handed me the sponsorship cash. "How's that casino case of yours going?"

"I'm making some progress, but it's a bit awkward

because I can't report back to the client."

"How come?"

"If my theory is correct, it has something to do with sups. Most are turned away, but those who are allowed inside are using magic to win. It would make more sense if the casino barred all sups from entering. Why turn a blind eye to a select few? And how am I supposed to explain any of this to my human client?"

"I can see how that might be a problem. What's your next step?"

"I'm going to pay the casino another visit. There isn't much action during the daytime, so it'll have to be tomorrow night."

***

Jack and I left the house together.

"Morning, you two," Kit called from next door.

"Pretend you haven't heard him," I whispered.

"Morning, Kit," Jack called back.

"Did Jill tell you that we ran the West Chipping half-marathon yesterday?"

"No, she didn't mention it. How did you get on?"

"A personal best time for both of us."

"Congrats." Jack gushed. "That's brilliant."

"Brilliant." I echoed, somewhat less enthusiastically.

"Did Jill tell you about our idea for a community band?"

"No, she didn't mention that either."

"Yes, I did. You must have forgotten." I began to edge towards my car. "Sorry, I really do have to get to work."

Kit continued, "The Normals first gave us the idea with

their alphorns. Then, when Jill mentioned that you played the glockenspiel, we thought why not put together a community band?"

Jack turned around just in time to see me driving away.

***

I arrived at the office building at the same time as Macabre's handyman.

"Back again?" I held the door open for him.

"Yeah. No rest for the wicked."

"What exactly has Macabre got you doing?"

"Lots of bits and bobs. Checking sticking windows, faulty radiators, that sort of thing. I've got a long list of snags to work through."

Jimmy and Kimmy were in the outer office.

"Annabel said she thought you might be able to spare us a few minutes," Jimmy said.

"Of course. Why don't we go through to my office?"

"Would you like drinks?" Mrs V asked.

The two plain-clothes clowns declined the offer.

"Have a seat. How can I help?"

"We have a shoe problem," Kimmy said.

"Are you referring to the missing clown shoes?"

"You've heard about it, then?"

"Yes. I bumped into Bingo on the stairs. He said he'd had one of his shoes stolen, and mentioned two other clowns who had suffered a similar fate. And of course one of Armi's shoes is missing too."

"There are many more than that, Jill," Jimmy said. "At first, we put it down to carelessness. We assumed people had misplaced them, but it's obvious now that they're being stolen."

"And is it always the same shoe?"

"No, everyone has their own pair of shoes."

"I meant is it the same foot each time: right or left?"

"Sorry, silly me. Yes, it's always the right foot. That's the really weird part. If whoever was doing this was stealing pairs of shoes, I'd assume they were being sold. But what good is an odd shoe to anyone?"

"Can you help us? It may seem like a trivial matter, but something like this could ruin the school's reputation."

"It's a very unusual case, but I'll be glad to help."

"Thanks, Jill. You're the best."

The two of them were on their way out of the door when Jimmy hesitated. "Will you be joining the Smallwash community band?"

"I — err — "

"Britt and Kit mentioned it to us this morning. We think it's a great idea. I used to play the accordion, but it's been a long time."

"And I've decided to dig out my old school recorder," Kimmy said. "We understand Jack plays the glockenspiel. What about you, Jill? What do you play?"

"Nothing really. Jack's the musical one in the family."

"You must join in. It'll be fun."

"I'll definitely give it some serious thought."

"Bye then, Jill. And thanks."

"You've been at it again, haven't you?" Winky jumped onto the sofa.

"What are you talking about?"

"Glockenspiel?" He laughed. "I can smell one of your

lies at a hundred yards."

"It was only supposed to be a joke."

"What are you going to play in this community band of yours?"

"I'm not. I'm steering well clear of it."

"You should play the theremin."

"There's no such thing."

"Yes, *theremin* is." He laughed at his own so-called joke. "It would suit you down to the ground because all you have to do is wave your hands around, and you do that all the time anyway."

"I do not."

"Are you kidding? Having a conversation with you is like talking to a windmill."

"Rubbish. Incidentally, did you note that I'm now going to be paid for working on the missing clown shoe case?"

"Some people have more money than sense."

Just then, Mrs V came through to my office.

"Thank you for agreeing to help Sneezy and Breezy."

"It's Jimmy and Kimmy when they aren't in costume."

"Sorry, you're right of course. But thanks, anyway."

"I'm not too confident of getting a result. I mean, who would want a load of right-footed clown shoes?"

"It's very strange, isn't it? By the way, I hate to ask, but do you happen to have my sponsorship money? The organisers are keen to get it to Yarn Aid as soon as possible."

"Of course." I took out my purse. "Seventy-five pounds, wasn't it?"

"One hundred and fifty altogether."

"That's what I meant." I handed over the cash.

"This is very generous of you and Jack."

"Think nothing of it."

"That must have hurt." Winky grinned.

"It's for a good cause."

"Yeah, but you hate parting with your money. What would you say if I offered you the chance to get it back?"

"I'm not doing anything illegal."

"It's nothing like that. I was thinking more of a small wager."

"What kind of wager?"

"Seeing as how you lost your money over hula hoop, I thought you might be up for a hula hoop challenge."

"Me versus you?"

"Yeah. A one-hundred-and-fifty-pound wager. Winner takes all."

This was a dream come true. I might not be the world's best hula hooper, but I was a thousand times better than Winky. When I'd seen him practising, he was lucky to keep it going for more than a few seconds.

"Okay, but we'll need to be clear on the rules."

"We can use the same ones as on the old bag lady's marathon."

"Fair enough. When?"

"How about Friday afternoon? That'll give you a few days to put in some practice."

As if I'd need it to beat him. "Okay, you're on."

Easy money.

***

It was the second of the W.O.W. gatherings; this one was to be held at the home of Camilla Soapling.

"I'm going out, Mrs V."

"Oh yes, it's your beetle drive today, isn't it?"

"Yeah, I'm not sure what to expect."

"You'll enjoy it. They're really exciting. I must suggest to the yarnies that we hold one soon."

I was just about to leave when I spotted something.

"I see you're wearing your clown shoes, Alistair."

"I hope you don't mind, Jill, but with all the thefts recently, I thought it better to be safe than sorry."

"Sure, that's fine. Bye, everyone."

Camilla Soapling had a luxurious apartment in what had once been an old glove factory. The complex was now called The Gauntlet.

"Come in, Jill." Camilla took me through to the living room, which had a spectacular view over Washbridge. "You'll probably recognise a lot of the ladies from Charlotte's gathering last week."

I did a quick scan of the room and was relieved to find that Gina Justice wasn't among the guests. One run-in with her had been enough.

After tea and cake, we got down to the serious business of the day.

I was seated at a table with three other witches. One of them was a similar age to me, the other two were closer to Aunt Lucy's age. Camilla went around the room, handing out sheets of blank paper and pencils.

"Have any of you played this before?" I asked the ladies at my table.

"We all play regularly," the younger witch said. "I'm Freda, by the way."

"You'll have to show me what to do. This is my first

time."

"Don't worry. It's really easy. You have to throw a six first so that you can draw the body."

On my first throw, I threw a five. "What do I get for a five?"

"Nothing. Not until you've got the beetle's body."

Five rounds later, and the other three had all thrown the six they needed to draw their beetle's body. Two of them had got the head too. If I'd been amongst humans, I might have given the dice a little *help*, but I'd never get away with using magic around witches. On my tenth turn, I eventually managed to throw a six.

"Well done." Freda beamed. "Now you can draw its body."

So I did. "What now?"

"I — err — " Freda looked a little puzzled.

"What's wrong?"

"Nothing. I'm sure there must be square beetles somewhere in the world."

Sheesh. I didn't know the thing had to be anatomically correct. "What number do I have to throw next?"

"Anything but a six, but you'll need to get the head before you can draw the eyes or the antennae, obviously."

"Obviously." I thought this game was supposed to be fun.

Ten minutes later, I'd managed to get the beetle's head, and I was feeling quite pleased with myself when Freda shouted, "Beetle!"

I thought for a moment that she'd lost her mind, but then I realised she'd managed to complete the drawing of her beetle.

"I'm getting really good at this," she said.

The other two witches on the table congratulated her. I was tempted to point out that it was simply a game of chance, involving no skill whatsoever, but instead, I said, "Well played. What happens now?"

"You have to add up how many body parts you've drawn. You get one point for each."

That didn't take much calculating. Needless to say, my score of two put me in last place in my group.

Camilla beckoned me over to her. "Did you enjoy that?"

"Err, yeah, it was great. What happens next?"

"The winners from each group play against each other to find the overall winner. The final is always the most exciting part."

"I bet." Yawn.

Freda was beside herself when she ran out the overall winner. For her prize, she received a manicure set, which I suspected was an unwanted Christmas present that had done the rounds and eventually ended up here.

An hour later, after a few more nibbles, it was time for everyone to say their goodbyes.

"I hope you enjoyed it, Jill," Camilla caught me on my way out.

"Yeah, it's been — err — great. A good attendance too."

"Actually, there are usually more ladies here than there are today."

"Oh?"

"I wasn't going to say anything, but I think it's only right you know. Several of my regulars refused to come because they said you'd approached them, and tried to get them to side with you against your grandmother."

"What? I did no such thing."

"That's what I thought. I tried to tell them that you would never do anything like that, but they were adamant it was you."

Chapter 17

As it was such a nice day, I decided to take a shortcut through Washbridge Park on my way back to the office.

Seated on one of the benches, close to the fountain, were two familiar figures: Daze and Blaze looked well and truly cheesed off.

"Hello, you two."

"Hi, Jill," Daze said.

Blaze could only manage a nod.

"What are you wearing?" I laughed. "And what's with the hairnets?"

"There are days when I wonder if I should have pursued a career in banking," Daze said.

"We're working undercover at Washbridge High School." Blaze removed his hairnet, so he could scratch his scalp. "I don't know how anyone can wear these things all day."

"They've got us working in a school canteen." Daze sighed.

"You're dinner ladies?" Blaze shot me a look. "Sorry. I meant dinner persons. What's going on at the school?"

"Nothing, apparently." Blaze replaced his hairnet. "We've drawn a big fat blank so far."

"And this is the third school we've been at," Daze added.

"What is it you're looking for?"

"According to our intel, there's a gang of dream vampires somewhere in the city."

"What's so dreamy about them?"

"Nothing, trust me. They're not actually vampires at all. They're sups called Radix, but everyone calls them dream vampires because, just as real vampires need blood to survive, the Radix need dreams."

"How does that work?"

"They feed on dreams. They literally suck them out of people's heads while the person is asleep."

"That sounds disgusting."

"It is, which is precisely why the practice has been outlawed. In the same way as vampires are required to drink synthetic blood, the Radix are supposed to feed at dream stations, which can be found in a number of locations scattered around Candlefield."

"I can't say I've ever noticed them."

"There's no reason why you would. The buildings don't have anything on the outside to identify them. They generate artificial dreams that are available free of charge to the Radix. For the most part, the system works very well."

"What about the Radix who live in the human world? Do they have access to artificial dreams here?"

"That's the thing. It's impossible to produce artificial dreams over here. That's why the Radix have been banned from ever venturing to the human world. Simply being here is an offence, which is why we're trying to track them down."

"But so far, no luck." Blaze sighed.

As I listened to them, I was thinking about Lizzie who had been complaining that she couldn't dream. I didn't speak up because I didn't want Daze or Blaze to do anything that might freak her out. I figured it would be better for me to handle it in my own way.

"What do they look like? The Radix?"

"They're ugly so-and-sos." Blaze screwed up his face.

Daze elaborated. "Fortunately or unfortunately, depending on how you look at it, they're normally invisible to the naked eye."

"How do you catch them, then?"

"Duck feathers."

"Sorry?"

"That's the only way to see them. If you cover a Radix in duck feathers, they become visible for a few minutes. Just long enough to clamp handcuffs on the little blighters."

"How big are they?"

"The size of fairies." She took something out of her pocket. "Look." It was a pair of the tiniest handcuffs I'd ever seen. "We can use these on either fairies or Radix."

"And it has to be duck feathers? Not goose or—?"

"Only duck feathers will work. Why?"

"No reason. Just curious."

Daze checked her watch. "I suppose we'd better get back."

"Good luck with the Radix."

***

I hadn't been able to spend much time with Jimmy and Kimmy earlier because I'd been due at the W.O.W. beetle drive. Now that I had a little more time, I decided to pay them another visit, to get as much information as possible on the missing clown shoes.

Macabre's maintenance man was just leaving Clown as I went in. Kimmy was behind the reception desk.

"Hi, Kimmy."

"It's Sneezy and Breezy when we're in costume."

"Sorry. Do you and Breezy have time to talk to me about the shoe thefts?"

"Of course. I'll get someone to watch the desk. Follow me, Jill."

When the three of us were seated in their office, I ran through my list of questions.

"First, I have to ask. Do you think this could be an inside job?"

"I really don't think so," Breezy said. "All of our staff are people we've known for several years, and I'd trust them with my life."

"Okay. Has there been any sign of a break-in?"

"Nothing." Sneezy shook her head.

"Typically, what's the value of a pair of clown's shoes?"

"It can vary dramatically, but one shoe by itself is practically worthless."

"That's what's been bothering me. Whoever is behind this can't be doing it for the money or they'd steal both shoes. What about your competition? Have you considered this could be sabotage?"

"Out of the question." Breezy was adamant. "The only other clown school in a hundred-mile radius is Red Nose, but they're at least an hour's drive from Washbridge. We're no threat to them, and besides Raymond is the nicest man you could ever wish to meet."

"Is he the owner of the other school?"

"Yes. His name is Raymond Higgins, but he's better known as PomPom. We've known him for years, haven't we, Sneezy?"

"That's right. The man is beyond reproach."

"Okay. Have you noticed any pattern to when the shoes

go missing?"

"Not really because some customers didn't realise that they'd lost a shoe until they unpacked their bags at home."

"I seem to remember that I-Sweat had CCTV. Do you still have that?"

"Unfortunately not. We had to make a lot of changes to the layout of the rooms, and that meant taking down the cameras. The CCTV needs a total rewire and to be honest, we don't have the money at the moment."

Just then, the biggest, ugliest cat I'd ever seen jumped onto the desk between us.

"You know you shouldn't be on there," Sneezy chided him gently.

"He's a big lad." I pushed my chair a couple of inches back from the desk.

"Bruiser," Breezy said.

"Yeah, he looks like one."

"No." Breezy smiled an enormous clown smile. "That's his name: Bruiser."

"You do know that you aren't allowed to keep animals in the building, don't you?"

"Yes, but we knew that you had a cat in your office, so we figured we'd be okay."

"If Macabre gets wind of it, you'll be out."

"What about your cat, Wonky?"

"His name is Winky. I have to hide him whenever the landlord is about. It's not worth the hassle, trust me."

"I'm sure it'll be okay." Breezy stroked the purring cat. "We couldn't throw Bruiser out."

"Okay, but don't say I didn't warn you. Talking of Macabre, I bumped into his maintenance guy on the way in."

"He's been sorting out a few odd jobs. Mainly the radiators, they all needed bleeding. And a couple of loose window catches."

"Right. I'd better get going."

"You'll keep us posted on the shoe situation?"

"Of course."

When I left Clown, Bruiser followed me out of the door.

"Hey, you!" He bawled. "You and me need to have words."

"What's wrong?"

"I heard you trying to get me thrown out."

"I wasn't. I was just saying—"

"Keep your nose out. It's got nothing to do with you."

"Please yourself."

"And you'd better tell that ugly one-eyed fleabag of yours that there's a new cat on the block, and if he knows what's good for him, he'll stay out of my way."

Charming.

Alistair was beavering away at his desk, with one finger up his nostril, but minus the clown shoes.

"I thought you were scared someone might steal your shoes?" I said.

"Sorry?" He looked up, puzzled.

"I meant your clown shoes."

"What's wrong with these?" He swivelled around on his chair. "I really like brogues."

"Err, no, yes, they're nice. Very nice indeed."

"But you just called them clown shoes."

"Sorry. My little joke. Just ignore me."

Mrs V coughed, and when I turned around, she was looking at something on the cupboard behind her.

"Is that your trophy?"

"Oh, that little thing? I didn't think you'd even notice it." She passed it to me. The inscription read:

Washbridge Hula Hoop Marathon 2018
Winner: Annabel Versailles.

"I didn't realise you stood to win a trophy."

"Neither did I. I told them they shouldn't have bothered, but Yarn Aid said it was the least they could do in view of how much money was raised. They're going to make it an annual event, and throw it open to all Washbridge residents from next year."

"I assume you'll be back to defend your title?"

"Of course." She bent down to pick up a hula hoop from under her desk. "I intend to practise regularly from now on. You're welcome to join me. It's a great way to keep fit."

"Thanks, but I already have a pretty rigorous keep-fit regime."

"Hmm."

"What on earth are you doing, Winky?"

He was breathing so hard that he could barely speak. "What does it look like?"

"Can you stop punching that for a minute."

He stepped back from the punch bag that was hanging from the ceiling. "What do you want?"

"Why do you have a punch bag, and where did you get those boxing gloves from?"

"CatPugilists.com, obviously."

"Obviously. Aren't there easier ways to get in shape?"

"This is not about getting into shape. This is about defending my territory."

"Right." Now it made sense. "I take it you know there's a new cat in *Clown*, then." I laughed. "See what I did there? Clown. Town. Get it?"

"You're as hilarious as ever. Yes, I have met him. He and I had a brief tête-à-tête earlier."

"He's a monster, Winky. He'd wipe the floor with you. I should steer clear of him if I were you."

"Is that a joke? Winky walks in fear of no cat. My reputation would be in tatters if I ran scared of a chancer like that. Even his name is a joke. Bruiser?" He scoffed. "He'll have plenty of those when I've done with him."

***

I finished work early because I needed to call at the bed shop on my way home. Mission accomplished, I arrived home just in time to see a bull and a bear come out of next door.

"Hi, Tony. Hi, Clare. I take it you have a con this week."

"Yes, it's on Saturday," Tony the bull said. "We thought about cancelling because we have so much work to do for TenPinCon, but it seemed a shame to waste the costumes."

"Can you guess what it is?" Clare the bear said.

"Err, ZooCon?"

"No."

"Is it Animals-Beginning-With-The-Letter-B-Con?"

"That's very funny, but no. It's StockMarketCon. Get it?"

"Not really."

"There's what they call a bull market, and a bear market."

"Right." It didn't make a lick of sense to me, but I wasn't interested enough to ask for an explanation. "Well, good luck as always."

"Thanks. And tell Jack we're really excited to hear his marketing plans for TenPinCon."

***

"Why have you bought a new duvet?" Jack said when he arrived home. "The two we already have are practically brand new."

"I need the duck feathers." I took out a large black plastic sack, cut open the duvet, and shook the feathers into it.

"And why do you need duck feathers?"

"To catch a dream vampire."

"Right." He pondered on that for a few seconds. "Okay, that makes no sense. How are duck feathers going to help you to catch a vampire?"

"It's not actually a vampire. People just call them dream vampires but they're really creatures called Radix."

"So why call them dream vampires?"

"Because they feed on people's dreams. I think one may be stealing Lizzie's."

"How exactly do they steal them?"

"They suck them out of your head."

"Yuk!" He shuddered. "How do you know?"

"Kathy mentioned Lizzie had been complaining that she couldn't dream. I didn't think anything of it at the time. I assumed she just couldn't remember them, but then today I bumped into Daze and Blaze. They're on the lookout for a gang of rogue dream vampires operating in Washbridge."

"Did you tell them about Lizzie?"

"No, I didn't want them to scare her. I thought it would be best if I dealt with it myself."

"I still don't get what the feathers are for?"

"The Radix are invisible. The only way to see them is to cover them with duck feathers."

"Right. You don't think Peter's parents might think it's strange if you show up with a bagful of feathers?"

"Good point. I'll leave the bag in the boot of the car until they've left."

Chapter 18

Kathy and Peter had set off for London mid-afternoon. The kids had been collected from school by Peter's parents who'd stayed with them until we arrived at just before seven o'clock.

When we got there, Mikey was playing a fishing game on the computer.

"Do you want to play, Uncle Jack?" he offered.

"Okay." Jack turned to me and whispered, "I'll take it easy on him."

"Auntie Jill, come and look at my dolls' house." Lizzie already had her PJs on.

I followed her up to her bedroom where the dolls' house was on the floor, at the end of the bed.

"Does the furniture fit in there okay?"

"Yes, Mummy says it could have been made for it." She crouched down next to the dolls' house. "Look inside."

"It looks fantastic."

"We found lots of things in the drawers and cupboards."

"What kind of things?"

"Most of it was rubbish, but we did find all these trophies." She pointed to a row of them on top of the sideboard.

"I've lost the little bear, though." She frowned.

"Never mind. It was a funny shape anyway."

"Did you have a dolls' house when you were little, Auntie Jill?"

"I don't think I did. I mainly played with my beanies."

"The ones you gave to me?"

Gave? They were stolen, more like. "That's right."

It was Lizzie's bedtime. After brushing her teeth, she climbed into bed.

"Will Mummy and Daddy be back in the morning?"

"They get back about lunchtime. Your Grandma and Grandpa will be here in the morning to take you to school." I tucked her in and gave her a kiss. "Goodnight."

"Night, night. I hope I dream tonight."

"I'm sure you will."

Downstairs, Jack and Mikey were still playing on the computer.

"Uncle Jack is rubbish at this!" Mikey shouted. "I've won every game."

Jack's attempt to look nonchalant failed miserably.

"Come on, Mikey. It's time for bed."

"Can I just finish this game, please, Auntie Jill?"

"Okay, but make it quick."

Twenty minutes later, I took Mikey up to bed. When I came back downstairs, Jack was watching TV, so I sat next to him on the sofa.

"The fishing game was a whitewash, then?" I grinned.

"I let him win."

"Every time?"

"It's a stupid game, anyway."

"You'll never guess what I saw in Lizzie's dolls' house?"

"She hasn't broken my furniture already, has she?"

"No, it's fine. She found a load of teeny tiny trophies."

"Oh no. My bowling trophies? I'd forgotten they were in the cupboard."

"You'll be pleased to know she has them out on

display."

"I suppose that's something. You never let me do that."

***

I wanted to give the kids enough time to fall asleep before I made my move, so while I waited, Jack and I had a glass of wine.

Once I was sure the kids were asleep, I crept outside and retrieved the black sack from the boot of the car.

"Is there anything I can do?" Jack offered.

"Not really. You may as well get some practice on that fishing game in case Mikey wants to play you again in the morning."

"I'm not that bothered."

Despite what he'd said, I knew that Jack would be on the computer as soon as I was out of the room.

I'd deliberately left Lizzie's bedroom door ajar, so that I didn't wake her when I crept in there. Being careful not to trip over the dolls' house, I made my way to the armchair next to the window. After hiding the bag behind the chair, I made myself invisible, took a seat and waited.

I was only too aware that this could all prove to be a total waste of time. I wasn't one-hundred percent certain that Lizzie's dream issue was the result of a dream vampire, and even if it was, I wasn't sure that I'd know when they struck.

All I could do was sit, wait and make sure I didn't fall asleep.

Ouch! I woke with a crick in my neck. Drat, despite my

best efforts I'd nodded off.

Lizzie was still fast asleep, but there was something different about her. Before my nap, she'd been sleeping peacefully, but now she was moving her head from side to side, and making an awful groaning sound.

It was possible she was just having a nightmare, but it was also possible that the dream vampire was sucking out her dreams. There was only one way to find out.

I grabbed the bag from behind the chair, tiptoed over to the bed, and tipped the feathers over Lizzie's head. As I did, two things happened: First, the tiny Radix became visible. Dreamy, it most certainly was not; the ugly, gargoyle-like creature had its long tongue inside Lizzie's ear.

"Leave her alone!"

Clearly shocked at being discovered, it withdrew its tongue, jumped off the bed, and headed towards the door, which I'd foolishly left ajar.

The second thing that happened was that Lizzie woke and sat up in bed.

"What happened, Auntie Jill?" The poor little mite was covered in feathers.

"Your pillow ripped open." I took it off the bed.

"I'm covered in feathers."

"You look like a little chicken."

"I do, don't I?" She smiled.

"Why don't you get out of bed, and brush all the feathers off you while I take this pillow and mend it."

"Okay."

I rushed downstairs.

"Have you seen it?"

"Seen what?" Jack was still playing the computer game.

"The Ridax. It came down here."

"What does it look like?"

"Just how many tiny creatures do you think there are likely to be running around down here? It's ugly and it's covered in feathers."

"Will I even be able to see it?"

"Probably not, but you'll certainly be able to see the feathers. Quick, get looking. We can't let it escape. You take the dining room and I'll take the kitchen."

Although Jack looked nervous, he didn't argue.

The kitchen was in darkness, so I switched on the light. There were no sounds, and no sign of feathers.

"Jill!" Jack called from the dining room. "Quick!"

"Have you seen it?" I met him at the door.

"No, but look over there." He pointed to a trail of feathers that led behind the drinks cabinet.

"Go and get me something to put it in," I whispered.

"What?"

"I don't know. Anything."

"Okay."

We had it cornered because the only way out of the dining room was back through the door where I was standing guard.

"Is this okay?" Jack held up a biscuit barrel. "Is it big enough?"

"Yeah. Give it here." I was just about to make my move when something rattled inside the barrel. "Why didn't you take the biscuits out?"

"I never thought to."

"Great. Hold out your hands." I took off the lid, and tipped the biscuits into his hands. "Wait here."

I crept slowly over towards the drinks cabinet. As I got closer, I could hear the tiny creature breathing, heavily. I would have to time this just right.

As soon as I showed myself, the Radix tried to make a run for it, but I was too quick. I dropped the barrel over the creature, then tipped it up, and slammed on the lid.

"Got it!"

"Well done!" Jack came over to join me.

"Jill?" Kathy was standing in the doorway. "What's going on?"

"I—err, dropped the biscuit barrel. What are you doing back?"

"Pete started to feel queasy, so we turned around and came home. He's in the loo."

"Mummy, you're back!" Lizzie must have heard her mother's voice and come downstairs.

"Why are you covered in feathers?"

"My pillow broke."

"Broke? How does a pillow break?"

"I don't know." Lizzie shrugged. "I was asleep when it happened."

"Right. Well, we'd better get you back to bed, then Auntie Jill and I can have a little chat."

"What are we going to do?" Jack said.

"We need to get rid of the Radix."

"How?"

"I'll put it in the boot of the car. While I'm out there, get the scissors, cut open this pillow, and get rid of the feathers."

"Why?"

"Because it's supposed to have ripped open."

"Right. What shall I do with the feathers?"

"I don't know. Use your imagination."

I rushed out to the car, tipped the Radix into the car boot, and slammed the lid closed. Back in the house, Jack was in the lounge, holding the empty pillowcase.

"Where are the biscuits?" I said.

"I put them in the waste bin."

"What? Why would you do that?"

"I needed both hands to sort out the pillow."

I hurried through to the kitchen, put the empty biscuit barrel on the worktop, and then rushed back into the lounge to re-join Jack.

"Let me do all the talking when Kathy comes back downstairs," I said.

"Don't worry. I intend to."

"This had better be good." Kathy had changed out of her glad rags, and she did not look happy.

"How's Peter?" I said.

"He's in bed."

"It's a pity you had to cancel your night out."

"Could we get back to the subject in hand?"

"The feathers?"

"Yes, Jill. The feathers. How did the pillow burst?"

"It was all my fault."

"I didn't doubt that for a single moment. What happened?"

"I challenged Lizzie to a pillow fight, and I got a little carried away."

"That's not what Lizzie said. She said she was fast asleep and when she woke up, she was covered in feathers."

"She's such a little love. She's obviously trying to cover for me so that I don't get in trouble."

"Oh?"

"It's okay to tear me off a strip. I deserve it. But don't tell Lizzie because she'll feel bad if she thinks I've got in trouble."

"Where's the pillow?"

"It's here." Jack passed it to her.

She studied it, and for a moment, I thought she was going to comment on the clean cut that Jack had made, but to my relief, she put it down and said, "I'm going to have a cup of tea. Do you two want one, or would you rather get off home?"

"We can't drive because we've been drinking wine. Can we sleep here tonight?"

"Of course you can, but you'll have to sleep down here on the sofas because I don't want to disturb Pete."

"That'll be fine."

"I don't know how you do it," Jack whispered when Kathy went to make the drinks.

"Do what?"

"Lie like that. You even had me believing you."

"What did you do with the feathers?"

Before he could answer, Kathy shouted, "Why are all these feathers in the cupboard?"

"You put them in a cupboard?" I looked at him in disbelief.

"I panicked."

"What was wrong with the waste bin?"

"It was full of biscuits. I thought about putting them in the washing machine, but decided that wouldn't be a good idea."

"You think?"

Kathy appeared with a tray of drinks.

"Sorry about the feathers in the cupboard." I picked up one of the cups. "Jack, tell Kathy why you put them in there."

"I—err—" He spluttered.

"Never mind." Kathy passed him a cup. "I'll sort it out in the morning."

After we'd finished our drinks, and Kathy had gone to bed, Jack and I settled down on the two sofas.

"What did you do with that vampire thing?" Jack said.

"It's in the car boot. When we get back home in the morning, I'll give Daze a call. She'll come and collect it."

"Poor little Lizzie. Fancy having that horrible thing stealing your dreams."

"I know. I'm just glad she didn't see it. She really would have had nightmares." I laughed. "You should have seen your face when Kathy asked about the feathers in the cupboard."

"I had no idea what to say."

"I thought we were in trouble when she saw the pillow. Couldn't you have made the tear more convincing?"

"It's okay for you. I'm not used to all of this subterfuge."

"It's okay. I love you anyway." I blew him a kiss. "Sleep tight."

***

Neither of us slept particularly well on the undersized sofas, but ironically, we were both fast asleep when Kathy and Lizzie came charging into the lounge at seven o'clock the next morning.

"Auntie Jill!" Lizzie was bouncing around the room. "I had a dream last night!"

"Really?" I wiped the sleep from my eyes. "That's great."

"It was a really long one too."

"She came running into our bedroom to tell us." Kathy looked thrilled.

"How's Peter?" Jack sat up and stretched.

"He's feeling much better. In fact, he's in the kitchen, making breakfast. He asked what you two would like."

"Nothing much for me," Jack said. "Cereal will be fine."

"What about you, Jill?"

"Nothing much for me either. A bit of bacon, some sausages, and eggs. Maybe some fried bread. And toast, of course."

"No mushrooms or hash browns?"

"Actually, I—"

"I'll just tell him a full English, shall I?"

"Go on, then. If you insist."

Mikey appeared in the doorway. "Why are there feathers on the stairs, Mum?"

"Morning, sweetheart." Kathy gave him a kiss. "A pillow burst."

"Do you want to play another game of fishing, Uncle Jack?"

"Of course he does," I said. "He was practising after you went to bed last night."

***

After we'd finished breakfast, I drove us both home, so we could get changed before we went to work.

"How many more fishing games did you play?" I asked.

"Another three."

"And how many did you win?"

"I don't remember."

"Was it less than one?"

"I suppose you could have done better?"

"I certainly couldn't have done any worse."

"At least I didn't resort to cheating."

"I never cheat."

"Yes, you do. At every opportunity."

Just then, a banging noise came from the rear of the car.

"It sounds like our little friend has woken up," I said.

"Have you called Daze yet?"

"No, I couldn't do it at Kathy's, could I? I'll call her as soon as we're in the house."

Once we were home, Jack showered first because he was already running late. While he was doing that, I called Daze and told her I'd captured one of the Ridax. She was just about to have a bath, but she said she'd be over within the hour.

By the time I'd showered and dressed Jack had already left for work. I was on my way downstairs when there was a knock at the door. Daze must have finished her bath and got over here quicker than she'd expected.

I was wrong; it wasn't her.

Chapter 19

"Britt?"

"Jill, I think there's something trapped in the boot of your car."

"Sorry?"

"I was just about to go for my morning run when I heard a tapping sound. I wasn't sure where it was coming from at first, but then I realised it was from your car."

"I think the exhaust is on its way out. I need to get it replaced."

"That can't be it. The engine isn't running. Maybe a cat crept in there when you weren't looking."

"That must be it. A cat. Well, I'd better get back inside, I'm running late."

"But what about the cat? It might suffocate."

"I wouldn't think so. It's a pretty big boot. There'll be lots of air inside there."

"Please, Jill. Lovely went out last night and she hasn't come back yet. It might be her."

Oh bum!

"Okay, but if it's a cat, it might be aggressive after being stuck in there. I wouldn't want you to get scratched. Why don't you go back into the house while I see to it?"

"I'm okay. I'd rather wait here until I know if it is Lovely."

Great! "Alright, just wait there a minute." I dashed inside to the kitchen, emptied the biscuit barrel and then re-joined Britt.

"What's that for?"

"Protection. In case it's aggressive."

"A biscuit barrel?"

"Trust me, they're the best protection against aggressive cats. It's been scientifically proven."

"Oh?"

"Get in the car and stay there until I've got it under control."

"But I—"

"Please, Britt, it's for your own safety."

"Okay."

Once she was inside the car, I opened the boot lid slowly. Fortunately, lots of feathers had been tipped in there with the Ridax, so the creature was still visible. It tried to escape, but I was too quick for it. I managed to get it inside the biscuit barrel and put on the lid. Then, before giving Britt the all-clear, I took the biscuit barrel back into the house.

"Okay, you can come out now. You were right, it was a cat. It wasn't Lovely, though."

"Where is it?"

"The little blighter was too quick for me. As soon as I lifted the boot lid, it shot out and ran away."

"Thank goodness it was okay."

"That's all thanks to you. Well done, Britt."

Daze arrived twenty minutes later.

"Where is the ugly little monster?"

"In there."

"You put it in a biscuit barrel?"

"It was the closest thing to hand."

"Why didn't you tell us that your niece had been having issues with her dreams? You knew we were on the lookout for dream vampires."

"I couldn't be sure it was the Ridax, and I didn't want to

freak Lizzie out unnecessarily. She told me that a lot of other kids in her school have been upset because they can't dream either."

"Don't worry. Blaze and I are going to move operations to Lizzie's school later today. Once we know which kids have been affected, we'll soon be able to track down the Ridax."

"How are you enjoying your stint as a dinner lady?"

"I'm not." She sighed. "The sooner this particular operation is over, the better. I don't think I'll ever be able to eat mashed potatoes again."

***

A tomato took my money at the toll bridge. No, I hadn't lost my mind. All will soon become clear.

"Morning, Jill," Mr Ivers stood up. "Do you like Tommy?"

"Tommy the tomato?"

"Yeah. I'm determined not to allow myself to become bored by the job this time around, so I got to thinking: what could I do to make it more interesting?"

"And you came up with hand puppets?"

"Exactly. And as luck would have it, the Hand Puppet Emporium was having a sale on vegetable hand puppets."

"That was lucky."

"What did you think of the newsletter?"

"Excellent, as always. Much better now that it's on cassette."

"Oh?"

"Yes, much better."

"I'm a little confused." I had to take his word for it—

with Mr Ivers, that was pretty much his permanent expression.

"Why's that?"

"I've discovered there's a fault on the cassettes. They were all inadvertently sent out blank." He held up another cassette. "I was going to give you this replacement."

"Right? What I meant was that although I'd enjoyed reading the newsletter, it would probably be even better on audio."

"I see. Do you have the old cassette, so I can reuse it?"

"Err, I think it's back at the house."

"No worries. Maybe you could let me have it another day."

"Of course. No problem."

***

When I arrived at my office building, there was someone blocking my way up the stairs, and for once, it wasn't a clown.

"Excuse me, Bruiser."

"Why? What have you done?" He laughed.

"Can I get past, please?"

"Did you give Stinky my message?"

"His name is Winky, and no, I didn't. He's been here much longer than you have. You should show him some respect."

He scoffed. "The only thing I'll be showing him is my fists."

"You horrible little—"

"Jill?" I spun around to find Jimmy and Kimmy staring at me in horror. "You mustn't talk to little Bruiser like that." Kimmy scooped the cat up into her arms. "You'll upset him."

"Sorry, I—err."

"I thought you were a cat lover?" she said.

"I am. I'm really sorry. I don't know what came over me. I didn't sleep well last night. That must be it."

"Fair enough, but please don't speak to Bruiser like that again. He's still feeling a little fragile in his new home."

Fragile? The cat was a psycho and a bully.

"Good morning, Jill." Mrs V took off her earmuffs. "You didn't tell me that you'd taken up boxing?"

"Sorry?"

"When I went through to your office to put the post on your desk, I saw the punch bag."

"Oh that. I thought it would be a good way to work off the stress."

Winky was knocking seven bells out of the punch bag.

"I really don't think this fight is a good idea, Winky. Every time I see Bruiser, he seems to get bigger."

"Size isn't everything. It's all about the moves, and I've got them all. Jab, jab and then the big uppercut. He won't know what hit him."

"Couldn't the two of you just talk things through? Over a bowl of milk, maybe. Perhaps you could come to some kind of agreement over—"

"Have you lost your tiny mind? This is not the time for a cosy little chat. This is war!" He gave the bag a punch for emphasis.

Oh dear. Much as I admired Winky's courage, I couldn't convince myself that he stood a chance against the monster who'd moved in next door. There was no way I could stand by and wait for the inevitable. I had to do something.

But what?

***

Was it my imagination or was Alistair's whistling even louder? I could hear the tuneless row while I was sitting at my desk. At this rate, I'd have to invest in a pair of earmuffs too.

I'd always fancied hitting a punch bag. Winky was fast asleep under the sofa, so he'd never know if I had a quick go. I could pretend it was Martin Macabre.

I swung a fist.

Ouch! That hurt!

"You're supposed to wear boxing gloves." Winky opened one eye. "It's ten pounds for ten minutes, by the way."

"What is?"

"To use my punch bag."

One punch had been more than enough for me; my knuckles were still smarting. So much so, I struggled to answer the phone when it rang.

"Get down to Ever now!"

"Good morning, Grandma. What's up?"

"I've finalised the marketing plans for your human."

"His name is Jack."

"Whatever. You'd better hurry up because I have to be at chimney sweep later."

"Right? Why do you have to see a chimney sweep?"

"Are you coming or not?"

"Sorry. I'm on my way now."

I was absolutely sure that Grandma's house didn't have a chimney, so why did she need a chimney sweep?

Julie and the other Everettes were looking as canary-like as ever.

"What do you think, Jill?" Julie touched the lapel of her jacket.

"Err, very nice. I've always liked the red."

"*Red*?" Judging by her expression, I'd clearly missed something. "Your grandmother bought these new outfits last weekend."

"Right. And that colour is one you approve of?"

"Yes, we've been pushing for the blue for some time now."

"*Blue*? Right. They look great. Anyway, I've been summoned. I'd better not keep her waiting."

When I opened the door to Grandma's office, I was almost hit on the nose by a dart.

"You should have knocked before you came charging in. That dart was headed for the bullseye."

"Sorry." She'd attached a dart board to the inside of the door. "I didn't know you played darts, Grandma."

"There are a lot of things you don't know about me, young lady. I'm the team captain of the Candlefield Arrows. We have a match against the Chimney Sweep Arms later."

"Ahh, the Chimney Sweep is a pub."

"Yes, they have one of the best darts teams in Candlefield. Not as good as the Arrows, of course." She seemed to be staring at me. "I've only just noticed. You're the spitting image of Suzi Barnstorm."

"Who?"

"She won the Candlefield Open Darts tournament. You must have seen her on the news?"

"I can't say that I have."

"She's about your height, and has a crooked nose."

"I don't have a crooked nose."

"Hmm. Anyway, we'd best crack on. I don't want to be late for the darts." She laid out her plans for TenPinCon on the desk. "What do you think of them?"

"It's a giant bowling ball and pins."

"Brilliant, eh?"

"But that's the same thing as you came up with the first time. I thought we'd agreed it was too dangerous."

"You're missing one important change that I've made." She pointed to a note at the bottom of the plans.

"Soft?"

"Exactly. The bowling ball and skittles will be soft and spongy, so there'll be no damage, and no humans will get killed. That seemed to concern you for some reason."

"I guess that could work."

"Is that all the thanks I get? This is pure genius."

"Sorry. It's great. I assume it will still require magic, though?"

"Of course. How else do you think I'm going to get a giant bowling ball and skittles? Now, do I have the green light to proceed or not?"

"I really should run it by Jack first."

"You can't tell him about the magic."

"Of course not, but I think he should at least be given the opportunity to see what you have in mind."

"Very well, but this is it as far as I'm concerned. If he

doesn't like it, he'll have to come up with his own ideas."
She stood up. "Now, if you don't mind, I have a darts
match to go to."

"Before you disappear, there's something else I need to
talk to you about."

"You'd better look sharp."

"There's something I think you need to know about
W.O.W."

"What about it?"

"It's rather delicate."

"Just spit it out, woman."

"Okay. The other day, when I was supposed to be
giving a speech at W.O.W. HQ, something weird
happened."

"Yes?"

"If you remember, you were called out of the room."

"Of course I remember."

"While you were gone, something really weird
happened."

"Belinda Cartwheel asked you to take my place as
chairman."

"You know?"

"Of course I know. I know everything."

"I turned her down, obviously."

"More's the pity. I was relying on you to take the bait."

"Hold on, I don't understand. Why would you want me
to help her to oust you?"

"Because I was hoping that would give you an *in* with
her. There's more to that woman than meets the eye, and I
thought you'd be able to find out what it was."

"But you must have known I wouldn't betray you?"

"I was certain that you would. I would have done it if

the situations had been reversed."

"You don't have a very high opinion of me, do you?"

"My opinion of you is as high as it has ever been. Now, have we done here?"

"Not yet. There's something else I need to discuss with you. I've been to a couple of W.O.W. gatherings over the last few days."

"Have you now?"

"I'm sorry if you didn't get invited."

"Of course I was invited, but I have better things to do with my time than eating cake and drawing beetles."

"Right. Anyway, according to some of the ladies there, someone is going around, impersonating me. Whoever is doing it is trying to turn people against you."

"I know."

"You do? How?"

"Because it was me."

"You were impersonating me?"

"Yes, and I have to tell you, it wasn't a pleasant experience, but needs must. I had to find out who is for me and who is against."

"You don't think it might have been a good idea to tell me what you were doing?"

"Not really. Now, if you don't mind, I have a darts match to play."

"But what about Belinda Cartwheel?"

"You'd better find out exactly what she's up to, and more importantly, who she's working with."

"Me? Why me?"

"Because you were the one who wrecked my original plan."

"By remaining loyal to you?"

"Precisely."

And with that, she disappeared.

As I made my way back up the high street, my head was still spinning. Not only had Grandma known that Belinda Cartwheel planned to ask me to take part in a coup, but she'd expected me to agree to it.

That was the bit that I couldn't get my head around: The idea that Grandma had expected me to betray her so easily.

And now, I was supposed to find out what Belinda was up to.

Fantastic!

Chapter 20

Reggie had given me the addresses of the three school governors who had been responsible for appointing Cornelius Maligarth. All three of them, two wizards and a witch, had long since retired from their primary professions. I'd elected not to phone in advance because that would have given them the chance to make an excuse not to see me. I figured it would be much more difficult for them to turn me away if I just showed up on their doorstep.

According to the very brief notes that Reggie had given me, Randolph Straightstaff was a retired lawyer who had never married.

"Can I help you, young lady?" He answered the door to his cottage wearing a smoking jacket.

"Mr Straightstaff? Do you know your jacket is smoking?"

"I thought I'd put that ciggy out." He patted his pocket. "Are you from the pharmacy?"

"Err, no."

"Pity. I'm expecting my pills. Are you sure you don't have them?"

"I'm positive. Sorry."

"I'm down to my last two. I thought I had more."

"Right. I wonder if you might spare me a few minutes of your time?"

"I have to go to the library soon. I only stayed in because I was expecting a delivery from the pharmacy."

"This will only take a few minutes."

"Okay. Come through to the study." The room was

bursting at the seams with books. The bookcases were all full, and the piles on the floor made it difficult to navigate the room. He had to clear another pile of books from one of the armchairs before I was able to take a seat. "Now, what exactly is it you wanted to see me about?"

"I understand that you're one of the governors at CASS."

"That's right."

"My name is Maggie Mantle. I'm the feature writer at The Candle. I'm doing an article on the new headmaster of CASS, Mr Cornelius Maligarth. My editor thought it would make a good sup interest story. CASS is, after all, the foremost school in Candlefield."

"Quite so. I'm not sure how I can help, though."

"I'm trying to gather a little background on Mr Maligarth. His career before he joined CASS, that kind of thing."

"Have you spoken to Cornelius?"

"He's a busy man, as I'm sure you're aware. I'm hoping to get an interview with him next week, but in the meantime, I'd like to fill in some of the gaps with your help."

"I'm still not sure how I can—"

"You see, Mr Straightstaff, I find it rather unusual that the normal searches throw up no details of the man whatsoever. Don't you find that a little peculiar?"

"Not at all. Cornelius Maligarth isn't the kind of man to court publicity, so you're unlikely to find articles about him in the popular press, but I can assure you his credentials are exemplary."

"You've personally seen evidence of his career prior to joining CASS?"

"Of course. Do you think we'd appoint someone to such an important position without vetting him thoroughly?"

"I would hope not."

"I can tell you this: the three governors were unanimous in their decision to appoint Mr Maligarth."

"Are you aware of the disruption there's been at the school since his arrival? Several teachers have already felt the need to resign."

"That can happen with a new broom, but it isn't necessarily a bad thing. Teachers, just like anyone else, can become complacent. One of the reasons we appointed Mr Maligarth was that we felt he'd be able to shake up the school."

"But some of the teachers who have left are the most—"

Just then, I was interrupted by a knock at the door.

Straightstaff jumped out of his chair. "That must be my pills. I'm sorry, Ms Mantle, but I really must go to the library now."

Randolph Straightstaff had been unequivocal in his support for the new head, and adamant that the recruitment process had been thorough. It would be interesting to see if the other two governors shared a similar view.

***

Before I visited the second school governor, I decided to drop in at Cuppy C.

"Morning, Jill." Amber was by herself behind the counter. "Your usual?"

"Just a coffee, please. I'm trying to cut down on the

muffins."

"Of course you are." She grinned.

"Where's Mindy?"

"She's had to nip out to the shops. Our milkman didn't turn up this morning, and we're almost out of semi-skimmed."

"Is Belladonna upstairs?"

"Yeah. She's got a roomful, but you'd never know it. I wish I knew her secret."

"I still have my doubts about that woman."

"Why? She's absolutely brilliant at her job, and a really nice person too."

"Don't you think it's weird how the kids react around her? It creeps me out."

"Why have you got it in for her, Jill? She's the best thing that's happened to Cuppy C in years. You should see the increase in takings since we opened the creche."

"What about the mums? Have there been any complaints?"

"Not a single one. In fact, they can't say enough good things about her."

"I followed her the other day."

"You did what? Why would you do that?"

"I have this bad feeling about her. Something doesn't ring true."

"Did she see you?"

"Of course she didn't. Have you forgotten I'm a P.I? I do this sort of thing for a living."

"You mustn't do it again. We don't want to lose her."

"Don't you want to know where she went?"

"No."

"To the graveyard. Are you going to tell me that isn't

creepy?"

"Of course it isn't. She was probably visiting the grave of a relative or friend. Did she take flowers with her?"

"Yes."

"There you are, then."

"The grave where she laid the flowers is unmarked."

"Maybe the inscription has worn away. That can happen."

"That's not it. That headstone had never been inscribed."

"It doesn't matter. You had no right to follow her or to intrude on her privacy."

"Whose privacy?" Mindy came through the door, carrying four large cartons of milk.

"Jill doesn't trust Belladonna," Amber blurted out before I could say anything.

"Why not?" Mindy put the milk into the fridge. "She's lovely."

"That's what I've been trying to tell her, but Jill has a bee in her bonnet."

"Haven't you seen how she is with the kids?" Mindy said.

"I have, yes. Don't you find it all a bit too good to be true?"

"She's just very good at her job."

Just then, a woman with a small toddler came through the door. "Is there any room upstairs?"

"Yeah, go on up," Amber said. "What can I bring you?"

"I'll have a small cappuccino and a millionaire's shortbread, please."

"What do you think of the new creche?" Amber asked her.

"It's fantastic. Just what Candlefield needed."

"What about Belladonna?"

"She's amazing. I wish I could take her home with me."

Amber shot me a 'told you so' look.

***

The second school governor on Reggie's list was Francesca Greylock, a witch and retired civil servant.

"Are you that reporter woman?" she said, before I even had a chance to speak.

"Yes. Maggie Mantle from The Candle."

"Randolph Straightstaff called me. He said you're writing some kind of article on Cornelius Maligarth."

"That's right."

"I've just spoken to Cornelius. He knows nothing about any article."

"I've been trying to get a hold of him, but he's a very busy man. Obviously, I'll speak to him before we publish anything."

"I would certainly hope so."

"In the meantime, could you spare me a few minutes?"

"You really should have called first. I can give you fifteen minutes, but then I have to go into town."

"Excellent."

"Come through to the kitchen. I'd just made myself a coffee. Would you like one?"

"No, thanks."

The kitchen looked out over the back garden, which was full of cats; there must have been at least six of them.

"You're a cat lover, I see?"

"Err, yes. Now, what do you want to know?"

I put the same concerns to her as I had to Randolph Straightstaff: the absence of any information about Maligarth in the public domain, and the detrimental effect he seemed to be having on the existing teaching staff.

Her response pretty much mirrored that of Straightstaff. She was adamant that Maligarth was well qualified for the post, and she seemed unconcerned by the resignations of some of the teaching staff.

By the time I left Francesca Greylock, I was beginning to doubt my own instincts: First Belladonna and now Maligarth. Maybe I was starting to see evil where it didn't exist.

"Young lady! Excuse me, young lady!" An elderly man was hurrying up the road behind me. "Could I have a word?"

"Sure."

He glanced behind him. "Can we go in the park? I don't want Fran to see me talking to you."

"Okay."

He led the way down the road and around the corner to a small park. Once inside, we took the bench closest to the gates.

"I'm Oswald Greylock. Francesca's husband."

"Maggie Mantle."

"I overheard you talking to Fran. To tell you the truth, I was deliberately eavesdropping. I hope you don't mind?"

"Not at all."

"This is all rather awkward. You'll probably think me a silly old goat."

"You obviously have something on your mind. You might as well tell me."

"It's just that—" He hesitated. "It's just that Fran isn't herself. She hasn't been for some weeks now."

"Not herself in what way?"

"In every way." He laughed nervously. "Like I said, I'm probably just being silly."

"Can you give me any examples?"

"There are so many. Fran has always been a tea drinker; she would never touch coffee. Now, suddenly that's all she'll drink. And the way she talks to me. She's always been a softly spoken woman, but now she's quite brash. And then there are the cats."

"What about them?"

"She's always been a cat lover."

"I noticed you have a few of them."

"That's just it. Fran always insisted on keeping them in the house with us. They were house cats, she said. Too delicate to be left outside. Now, she won't let them in the house. I'm not really a cat lover myself, but I feel sorry for them. They don't know what's hit them."

"That is rather strange."

"I don't know why I'm telling you this. I just felt like I had to speak to someone or I'd go crazy." He stood up. "You won't tell Fran what I said, will you?"

"Of course not."

"It's probably just her age." His nervous laugh was back. "I'd better get back before she realises I've gone."

What was I supposed to make of that?

The final school governor on Reggie's list was a wizard named Adrian Bowler, who had worked in advertising before he retired.

It was third time unlucky. There was no answer when I

knocked on his door, and no sign of life inside as far as I could make out. I was just about to leave when someone called to me from the adjoining house.

"Are you looking for Adrian?" The elderly wizard had a bald head and a long grey beard.

"Yes. Do you know when he'll be back?"

"I'm afraid not. He went out first thing."

"Not to worry. I'll come back later."

"Are you a friend of Adrian's?"

"I—err—"

"It's just that I'm a little worried about him. I thought maybe you'd know if there's something wrong. He won't talk to me about it."

"What makes you think there might be something wrong?"

"We've been neighbours for almost twenty years. He and I lost our wives at about the same time. Since then, we've been very close. We used to spend time together most days. Either he'd come around to my house, or I'd go over to his, for a cup of tea and a chat. But then, a few weeks ago, he stopped coming around, and whenever I call on him, he makes some excuse why he can't chat. It feels like I've done something to upset him, but I have no idea what. I thought maybe you'd have some idea what's caused the change in him. Has he been ill, do you know?"

"I'm afraid that I don't know him very well. Sorry."

"It's me who should apologise. What must you think of me, accosting a complete stranger?"

"Don't be silly. I can see you're worried about your friend."

"When he comes back, shall I mention that you called?"

"There's no need. I'd rather it be a surprise."

***

My *something isn't right* meter was buzzing.

Francesca Greylock's husband had been so concerned that his wife was acting peculiarly that he'd followed me up the street to talk to me about it. And now Adrian Bowler's neighbour had expressed similar concerns.

What about Randolph Straightstaff? He lived alone, so I couldn't check with his partner, but maybe one of his neighbours had noticed a change in him. It was worth checking, so I headed back there.

I was in luck. There was a woman in the garden of the adjoining cottage. She was standing on a stepladder, cutting the hedge that ran between the two properties.

"Excuse me." I had to shout to be heard over the electric hedge trimmer.

"Sorry?" She turned it off.

"Could I have a quick word?"

"Come in." She pointed to the gate.

"It looks like you have your work cut out."

"It's my first time doing this. I'm scared that I might take my arm off." She got down from the stepladder, and put the trimmer on the floor. "Can I help you?"

I lowered my voice. "I wanted a word about your neighbour."

"Randolph? You don't have to whisper. He's gone out."

"Is he still at the library, do you know?"

"At the bookies, more like. He spends most days in there."

"He likes a bet, then?"

"Sorry, who are you?"

"I—err, I'm a teacher at CASS. Mr Straightstaff is a governor there."

"I know. And a very good one he used to be."

"Why do you say: *Used to be*?"

"There was a time, until quite recently actually, when I would have said he was ideally suited to the role of a school governor. A learned gentleman who couldn't do enough for you."

"What's changed?"

"I wish I knew. He used to spend most of his time in the library, but now he's never out of the bookies. And then there's this." She pointed to the hedge. "He used to cut it regularly, and he always said that he was happy to do it. It had been a while since it was cut, and it was getting out of control, so I asked him when he planned to trim it again. He practically bit my head off. That's why I'm doing it myself. I blame those tablets he's taking."

"Oh?"

"I never knew him to take any medicine, but now he has tablets delivered every week. Whatever they are, they clearly don't suit him."

Chapter 21

There was now no doubt in my mind that something had happened to all three of the school governors. Had someone nobbled them? If so, that might explain the unexpected appointment of the new headmaster. I had to find out what had happened, but more importantly, who was behind it. Unfortunately, that would be much easier said than done.

I was still mulling it over when I got a call from Daze.

"If it isn't the school dinner lady."

"No longer, thank goodness. I've hung up my hairnet. I called to let you know that we've managed to round up all of the Ridax. They're now behind bars back in Candlefield."

"That's great news. The kids will be able to enjoy their dreams again. Thanks, Daze."

"It's me who should be thanking you. I'd probably still be dishing out mashed potatoes if you hadn't pointed us in the right direction. That's yet another one I owe you."

"Actually, I could do with a favour."

"Just name it."

I told her about the recent changes at CASS, and my suspicions that the school governors may have been nobbled.

"If you're right, Jill, that's terrible. CASS is a fabulous institution. I couldn't bear the thought of someone undermining it for their own ends. What can I do to help?"

"I need to find out what's happened to the school governors, and the only way to do that would be to keep them under surveillance. I can't do that by myself, so I was just wondering if you—"

"Say no more. I can't justify tying up three rogue retrievers, but we often use surveillance imps for that kind of work."

"Aren't imps bad news? I thought I'd heard they were trouble."

"Not really. They just get a bad press. There are a few bad apples, but nothing to warrant the reputation they seem to have. I've always found them very reliable."

"How much do they charge?"

"It won't cost you a penny. Our surveillance budget is in surplus this year, so there's plenty of money to cover this. And besides, if what you suspect is true, this isn't an expense that should have to come out of your pocket."

"That's great. When could they start?"

"If you give me the school governors' details, I can have the surveillance in place within a couple of hours."

"Fantastic. Thanks, Daze."

***

I wanted to grab a few hours' sleep ahead of my nightshift at the casino, but before heading home, I decided to call in at the office to check if there was anything that needed my attention.

Once again, Bruiser was on the stairs, blocking my way.

"Move!" I was done with the pleasantries.

"I hear that loser cat of yours is preparing to fight me."

"I don't know what you're talking about."

"A little bird told me he's got himself a punch bag." He scoffed. "The problem with those is that they don't hit back."

"Are you going to move, or do I have to move you?"

"I hope you have good medical cover for Stinky. He's going to need it." Bruiser moved to one side, and began shadow boxing. "I predict a first round knockout."

"Any calls, Mrs V?"

"Just the one, from Mr Macabre. He said I was to remind you that you have until the end of the week to sort out the sign. Have you been in contact with Mr Song?"

"Don't worry. It's all in hand."

Alistair took his finger out of his nostril just long enough to say, "I should have my final report ready for you tomorrow, Jill."

"Excellent. I'm looking forward to reading it."

I had to try to talk some sense into Winky.

"Stop punching that thing for a minute, would you?"

"I can't interrupt my training regime."

"This won't take long."

He moved away from the punch bag and jumped onto the sofa. "What is it?"

"You've got to give up this crazy idea. You're going to get seriously injured. Bruiser isn't messing around. Why don't you just let him have the run of the rest of the building? You'll still have this office."

"Okay."

"Really?"

"No, not really. Do you honestly expect me to back down from a fight with that tub of lard? I'd never be able to hold my head up in this town again."

"So you're prepared to get badly hurt just to protect your pride?"

"I won't get hurt. Bruiser is the one who should be worried."

"Yes, but he's a very big tub."

"Do you know what the first rule is when you're fighting a tub?"

"No. What?"

"I can't talk about it." And with that, he went back to the punch bag.

I couldn't fault Winky's courage, but if I didn't somehow prevent this fight, there was no doubt that he was going to be badly hurt.

Luckily, I had a cunning plan.

***

As I walked down the corridor to Clown, I cast the 'doppelganger' spell to take on the appearance of Martin Macabre.

"Mr Macabre?" Kimmy looked surprised to see her landlord.

"I apologise for dropping in unannounced, but this is a matter of the utmost importance."

"Would you like to come through to the office?"

"Mr Macabre?" Jimmy was seated at his desk.

"There's something very important I need to discuss with you both."

It was a toss-up which of the two, Jimmy or Kimmy, looked the more nervous. "Would you like a drink, err — can I call you Martin?" Jimmy said.

"Mr Macabre will be fine. No drink for me. I'd rather get straight down to business."

"Of course."

"When you agreed to take on these premises, I assume you were fully aware that you'd be subject to all of the conditions of the lease?"

"Yes, of course." Jimmy nodded.

"And you realise that to break any of those conditions could result in your lease being cancelled?"

"Yes, but you don't have anything to worry about because we intend to be exemplary tenants, don't we, Kimmy?"

"Absolutely. We love these premises and we don't intend to do anything to risk losing them."

"That's good to hear." I was doing my best to replicate Macabre's creepy smile. "There's just one slight problem."

Jimmy and Kimmy exchanged a worried look.

"What's that?" Kimmy said.

"The lease is very clear about keeping animals on the premises. Very clear indeed." The two of them were now fidgeting nervously on their chairs. "Wouldn't you agree?" Neither of them spoke, so he continued. "Is there anything you'd like to tell me?"

"Well, err—" Jimmy spluttered. "Actually, now that you come to mention it—"

"Yes?"

"We've been looking after a cat for a relative. Haven't we, Kimmy?"

"Err, yes. A relative."

"A cat?" I barked. "On these premises?"

"Yes, we're awfully sorry."

"I'm afraid *sorry* isn't good enough."

"It's just that we know that one of the other tenants has a—"

"I'm not here to discuss the other tenants." I cut Jimmy

off mid-sentence. "I'm here to discuss whether or not I should allow you to continue to occupy these premises."

"We're really, really sorry. I promise it won't happen again."

"And what about the cat?"

"We'll take him back to his owner."

"When?"

"Today."

"*When* today?"

"As soon as we've finished this meeting."

"Good, but let this be a warning. If this happens again, I'll have no option but to terminate your lease."

"It won't, Mr Macabre. You have our word."

"Excellent." I stood up. "Rest assured, I'll be making regular checks."

Once I was out of Clown, I reversed the 'doppelganger' spell. As I approached my office, Bruiser came running up the stairs.

"Did you tell Stinky he was a dead man?"

"No, I did not. Oh, but I did hear Jimmy calling you. You should go and see what he wants."

Snigger.

***

It was a carrot that took my money on the toll bridge on my way home. Just saying.

When I pulled onto the driveway, I saw a sight that sent a shiver down my spine. Across the road, on their front lawn, were Norm and Naomi Normal.

With their alphorns.

I had to get some sleep, or I'd be out on my feet at the casino, so I decided to have a word with the Normals in the hope that they would take pity on me.

"Hi, Jill." Norm was red in the face, no doubt from the exertions of blowing his horn.

"Hi, there. I've come home early because I'm going to be working all night."

"Poor you," Naomi said. "Remind me again what you do for a living."

"I'm a private investigator."

"Is that dangerous?"

"It can be. It's essential that I always have my wits about me, which is why I need to get some sleep this afternoon. I was hoping I might be able to persuade you to postpone your horn playing for a while."

"You're in luck. We've just finished," Norm said. "A good session it was too, wasn't it Naomi?"

"Excellent. I think we're beginning to get the hang of these now."

"Right. That's great."

"While you're here, Jill, Kit and Britt came over to see us earlier. Apparently, they've been inspired by our alphorns, and they're talking about starting a community band."

"Yeah, I seem to remember they mentioned that."

"We think it's a great idea. I believe Jack plays the glockenspiel?"

"Yes, he's something of a maestro, but he doesn't like to talk about it. He's very modest like that."

"What about you, Jill? What instrument do you play?"

"Me? None, I'm afraid. I'm not the least bit musical."

"Even so, you must get involved too. It'll be fun."

"Yeah. Maybe. I'll see." Not a chance.

"Look out, Jill!" Kimmy grabbed my arm and pulled me onto the lawn.

Toot! Toot!

Bessie, driven by Mr Hosey, came trundling down the pavement, and pulled up next to us.

"Greetings, all." He gave another toot for good measure.

"We were just telling Jill about the community band," Naomi said.

"An excellent idea." Mr Hosey nodded his approval. "I'll be digging out Henry."

"Who's Henry?" I'd asked the question before engaging my brain. Why did I even care?

"Henry is my hurdy-gurdy."

"Man, I didn't realise those things actually existed."

"It's been some time since I played it." Hosey stepped down from the train.

"Jill hasn't decided on an instrument yet," Norm said. "Maybe you could give her lessons on Henry?"

"I'd be delighted to." Hosey beamed. "What do you say, Jill?"

"I'll think about it, but I really must get going now. I need to get as much sleep as I can before tonight."

***

In the absence of the alphorns, I was able to enjoy a few hours of undisturbed sleep.

While I'd been in bed, Jack had sent me a text to say he'd be home a little late, so I made do with yet another microwave meal for dinner.

At eight o'clock, I was just about to set off for the casino when he arrived home.

"I thought you'd have gone already," he said.

"I'm just about to leave."

"Before you go, would you care to explain why it is that Kit and Britt think I play the glockenspiel?"

"I've no idea. It must be all the exercise those two get. It's drained the oxygen from their brains." I gave him a kiss and made a bolt for the door.

"We're going to talk about this!" he shouted after me.

When I arrived at the casino, just as I was about to get out of the car, my phone rang. It was Kathy, and she sounded as though she was hyperventilating.

"Are you okay?"

"I'm just so stressed about tomorrow."

"The new shop? Why are you worried? The first shop opening went okay, didn't it?"

"That's what Pete said, but I'm still worried. What if the first shop was a fluke, and this one fails miserably?"

"Now you're just being silly."

"Will you come over to West Chipping in the morning to give me some moral support?"

"I'm working undercover tonight."

"Please, Jill. Just for a couple of hours. It would mean a lot to me."

"Okay, but only for a couple of hours. What time?"

"The shop opens at nine, so if you could get there at eight, that would be great."

"I'll be there."

"Thanks, Jill. You're my favourite sister."

"Creep."

As on my previous visit to the casino, I used the 'block' spell, so the doormen wouldn't realise I was a witch. I'd come up with a plan that I hoped would allow me to get to the bottom of what was happening at Lucky Thirteen. This time, instead of moving from table to table, I planned to stay at the same one, and hopefully identify one of the big winners that night.

I opted for roulette because that was the game that I understood best. For the first couple of hours, I watched a number of humans and sups come and go. As always, the humans were mostly losers and the sups mostly winners.

Every now and then, I would wager one of the lowest value chips issued by the house, just to avoid attracting any unwanted attention.

Just before one o'clock in the morning, a witch wearing a purple evening gown joined the table. Within an hour, she'd built a large stack of chips by using magic. For someone who'd just netted a couple of thousand pounds, she looked unmoved, and if anything, a little miserable.

When she left the table, I followed her to the cashier's desk where she cashed in her chips. Outside, she headed across the car park to an old banger, which looked like it was on its last legs. That didn't make any sense. If she could use magic to make money so easily, why not invest in a decent car?

I jumped into my car and followed her. The roads were quiet, so I was able to keep my distance without fear of losing her. Twenty minutes later, she pulled onto the Washland Estate, a housing estate known for its high crime rates. The car came to rest outside a small block of flats. This too made no sense. With the ability to make large sums of money at will, why would the woman choose to live here?

I followed her into the building, and up the stairs to the third floor. As she made her way along the corridor, I picked up my pace so that by the time she reached her flat, I was standing right behind her.

"Why are you following me?" She challenged me.

"I'd like a quick word."

"What do you want?"

"Can we talk inside?"

"No. I don't know you. What do you want?"

"I'd like to ask you a few questions about the money you won tonight."

"What's that got to do with you?" She took out her phone. "You'd better go, or I'll call the police."

"Be my guest. You can explain to them how you used magic to win."

At first, I didn't understand why she looked so shocked, but then I realised that the 'block' spell was still active, so she had no idea that I was a witch.

I quickly reversed the spell.

"You're a witch!" She gasped. "How did you do that?"

"Never mind that. Can we go inside?"

"Okay." She led the way into a dingy little living room. "I haven't done anything wrong."

"I know a rogue retriever who might take a different view on that."

"No! You can't give me up to them. I don't want to go back to Candlefield. Please!"

"You'd better start talking, then. You can start by explaining why you live here. No offence, but it isn't exactly the lap of luxury, is it?"

"It's all I can afford."

"Don't give me that. I've just seen you win at least two grand, and presumably, you can do that whenever you like."

"Yeah, but it's not like I get to keep it."

"What do you mean?"

"I'm not saying anything else. I've said too much already. He'll kill me."

"Who will?"

"I'd like you to leave now, please."

"If you talk to me, I'll make sure no harm comes to you, but if you don't, the rogue retrievers will be here within the hour."

She burst into tears, and slumped into the grotty old armchair.

And then she told me everything.

Chapter 22

I managed to grab a few hours' sleep before the alarm woke me at six-thirty.

"Did *you* set the alarm?" Jack rolled over and managed to open one eye.

"Yeah."

"I thought you'd want a lie-in this morning after being at the casino last night."

"I did, but Kathy's asked me to go over to the new shop to give her moral support."

"You're a good sister."

"You're right. I am. And if you'd like to earn some Brownie points, you can make breakfast while I get showered."

"What if I'm not interested in Brownie points?"

"You can do it anyway."

Bless his little cotton socks, Jack had breakfast waiting for me when I got downstairs.

"How did things go at the casino last night?" He took a sip of coffee.

"Okay, I suppose."

"You don't sound very sure."

"I'm pretty sure I know why Kirk Sparks was murdered. The owner of the casino is a wizard named Orville Ringstone. It seems that he isn't satisfied with the house's normal cut, so he's using witches and wizards to increase his take."

"How's he doing that?"

"The sups he recruits use magic to win at the tables, but they don't get to keep their winnings. They have to turn the money over to Ringstone in return for a measly pay-out that isn't even minimum wage. I followed one of the winners home last night. She's running a clapped-out old car and living in near slum conditions. That's despite winning thousands in the casino whenever she visits."

"It's a clever scam."

"I'm positive that Kirk Sparks must have worked out what was happening."

"Even if you're right, what could he have done about it? It's not like he could have run an article about sups, is it?"

"I suspect he'd decided to take what he knew to the rogue retrievers. Ringstone must have got a whiff of what was happening, and decided to eliminate him."

"What will you do now?"

"I'll do what Kirk had planned to do. I'll pass on what I know to Daze."

"That's a result, surely?"

"I suppose so. The only problem is that I can't tell Bernie Sparks any of this."

"What will you tell her?"

"That I can find no evidence that points to her husband being murdered. It stinks, but what else can I do?"

"You did your best." He kissed the top of my head. "At least you have something to look forward to tonight."

"What's happening tonight?"

"Have you forgotten? You're going to the circus with the twins and Aunt Lucy."

"Oh bum! I'd forgotten about that stupid thing."

"It'll be great. I wish I could come with you."

"I wish you could go instead of me."

"You'll enjoy it when you get there."

"At least there are no clowns."

"How come?"

"Apparently, the clown troupe have handed in their notice."

"What good is a circus without clowns?"

"If I had my way, there would be no more clowns anywhere."

"You should see a therapist about that phobia of yours."

"I don't have a phobia. I just don't find them funny."

"If you say so. I don't suppose your grandmother has been in touch about the marketing for TenPinCon, has she? The big promo is supposed to be this weekend."

"She has actually. She called me down to Ever yesterday."

"So? Don't keep me on tenterhooks. What has she come up with?"

"It's pretty much the same idea as she had originally."

"With the giant bowling ball and pins? I thought we'd agreed that would be too dangerous?"

"We did, and it would be, but now she's going to make the ball and skittles spongy so that there'll be no damage, and no one will get hurt."

"Do you trust her?"

"I—err—"

"Jill?"

"Yes. Absolutely." Fingers crossed. "She knows what she's doing."

"Fair enough. Am I okay to let Tony and Clare know about the plans now?"

"Yeah. I don't see why not."

"Great." He hesitated. "I've just remembered something; I have a bone to pick with you."

"What have I done now?"

"One word: glockenspiel."

"Is that the time? I'd better rush or Kathy will give me grief." I grabbed my bag and coat, and hightailed it towards the door.

"Sooner or later, we *will* talk about this, Jill."

***

"I didn't think you were coming." Kathy unlocked the door, and let me into the shop.

"It's only five-past." I glanced around the place. "This all looks great."

"Thanks. Pippa has done most of the work."

"Where is she?"

"In the back, putting the nibbles on plates."

"Morning, Jill." Pippa must have heard us talking. "Will you tell your sister to stop panicking. I've tried, but she won't listen to me."

"What if no one turns up?" Kathy said. "Maybe it was a mistake opening a shop in West Chipping."

I rolled my eyes at Pippa. "I was just saying to Kathy that everything looks great. It's bigger than your other shop, isn't it?"

"Yes." Kathy adjusted one of the wedding gowns on display. "It's almost twice as big. Are you sure this display looks alright?"

"It all looks fantastic. Why don't we have a small glass of bubbly? It might calm your nerves."

"Okay, then." Kathy nodded.

"Shall I get it?" Pippa offered.

"It's okay. I'll see to it." I walked through to the stockroom at the back of the shop. There were half a dozen bottles of champagne in ice buckets on a small table, so I grabbed the nearest one, with almost disastrous results. It slipped from my hand, but luckily, with my razor-sharp reflexes, I managed to catch it before it smashed on the floor.

Phew! Disaster averted.

I picked up three champagne flutes, and walked through to the shop. After putting the glasses on the counter, I removed the wire cage from the bottle, and grasped the cork.

Just then, Kathy who had been making further adjustments to one of the gowns, turned around and screamed in horror, "Don't open that in here."

The champagne exploded out of the bottle. In a panic, I turned back towards the stockroom, but in doing so, I managed to spray champagne over every dress in the shop.

For the longest moment, there was an eerie silence, but then Kathy became hysterical.

"Look what you've done! Everything is ruined!"

She was right. The gorgeous dresses were all now soaked in champagne. There was only one thing to do. I cast the 'take-it-back' spell, followed quickly by the 'forget' spell.

While Kathy was still feeling a little fuzzy, I turned to Pippa. "Act as though nothing happened."

"Okay."

I hurried back into the stockroom, opened the champagne, but this time with a towel over the top of the bottle. Then I poured out the bubbly and took the three glasses through to the shop.

"I'm not sure I should have a drink." Kathy took the

glass anyway. "I already feel a little light-headed."

But she did take one, and moments later, the three of us drank a toast to her new venture.

***

It was almost ten o'clock when I left the shop. Kathy needn't have worried because within minutes of opening, she had twelve customers through the door. All of them seemed to approve of the shop, and at least two of them tried on dresses.

Kathy's business was going from strength to strength, and it was way past time that I did something to boost my own. The first step in that process would be to listen to the ideas that Alistair had been formulating since he arrived. The previous day, he'd indicated he was ready to have a discussion with me, and I was eager to hear what he'd come up with.

"Morning, Mrs V. Morning, Alistair. Shall we make a start?"

"Sorry?" He looked puzzled. "On what?"

"You said you were ready to discuss your findings?"

"Err, no. I'm not quite ready yet. I should have everything finalised by Friday, though."

"I thought you said—err, never mind. Friday it is, then."

"You can call me champ." Winky thumped the punch bag.

"You mean *chump*, don't you?"

"Nothing you can say will upset me today. Are you

ready to admit you were wrong?"

"About what?" I took a seat at my desk. "I have no idea what you're talking about."

"Bruiser has done a runner. He knew he was in for a beating, so he took the coward's way out, and did a moonlight flit."

"I think Kimmy and Jimmy may have had to get rid of him. You know how the landlord feels about tenants keeping pets."

"That's what Bruiser would like us to believe, but he's just trying to save face. There's only one reason he's left, and that's because he was scared of yours truly." Winky gave the punch bag a couple more thumps. "I'm the greatest."

"I hear you float like a bee and sting like a butterfly."

"Not funny."

***

At my request, Daze and Blaze had come over to the office.

"Before you start, Jill," Daze said. "I thought you'd like to know that the surveillance imps are tailing the three school governors. I'll let you know as soon as they have anything to report."

"That's great. And you're absolutely sure that the imps are reliable? I've heard some dodgy things about them."

"You have nothing to worry about. We've worked with the surveillance imps on numerous occasions, and we've never had a spot of bother, have we, Blaze?"

"No." He hesitated. "Apart from the flatulence."

"Don't be ridiculous." She shot him a look.

"You weren't the one who was trapped in the lift with three of them on the Buckland case." He screwed up his nose. "I was stuck in there with them for two hours. It was not a pleasant experience."

"Take no notice of him, Jill. He's exaggerating as usual."

"All I'm saying, Jill." Blaze had no intention of being silenced. "Is that you should avoid any confined spaces when you're with them."

"I'll bear that in mind." Those two made a great double act. "Now to the reason I asked you to come over today. I have a rogue for you."

"Oh?" Daze took out a notepad. "Who's that, and what have they done?"

"There's a casino halfway between here and West Chipping; it's called Lucky Thirteen. The owner is a wizard who's running a scam to fleece all the humans who venture inside."

I explained how vulnerable sups were being used to win money, which they were then forced to hand over to the casino owner.

"That seems pretty clear cut," Daze said. "And another feather in your cap, Jill."

"It doesn't feel much like it."

"Why's that?"

"I originally became involved in this case because a reporter was killed outside the casino. He was crushed to death by two giant dice, which had supposedly been dislodged by a random lightning strike. His wife asked for my help; she wanted me to find proof that it wasn't an accident. She believes he was killed because he was working on a story about the casino."

"Was she right?"

"I believe so. What she didn't know was that her husband was a sup. He'd figured out how the scam worked, and I'm pretty sure he was about to contact you guys. That's when the 'accident' happened."

"You think the lightning strike was caused by magic?"

"I'd bet my life on it, but there's no way I can prove it, and even if I could, I can't take any of this to the human authorities."

"Maybe not, but whoever's responsible is going to spend an awfully long time behind bars back in Candlefield."

"Which is all well and good, but I still can't tell the deceased's widow anything. It stinks."

"I agree, but I don't see what more you can do. Who is the casino owner anyway?"

"His name is Orville Ringstone."

Daze and Blaze exchanged a look.

"Have you two heard of him?" I said.

"Maybe, maybe not. We've been on the lookout for a wizard called Stonering for some years now. Norville Stonering. He's wanted for gambling related offences back in Candlefield."

"Do you reckon it's the same guy?"

"If not, it's one heck of a coincidence. If it is him, then there may be other options open to us. Can you give us twenty-four hours on this one?"

"What other options?"

"I'd rather not say until we've had a chance to make some enquiries. The first thing I'd like to do is make sure they're one and the same guy. Is it okay if I get back to you tomorrow?"

"Sure."

As soon as Daze and Blaze had left, Winky took out the hula hoop, which he kept under the sofa. "You haven't forgotten it's our head-to-head competition on Friday, have you?" He gave the hoop a spin, and moments later, it dropped to the floor.

"I haven't. I'm very much looking forward to it."

"If you'd rather call it off, I'll understand." It was obvious that he was starting to get cold feet. "I realise your personal finances aren't the best."

"Not at all. In fact, I'd be happy to double the wager if you're up for it."

"I couldn't take your money, Jill. It wouldn't be fair."

"Don't give it a second thought. I'm more than happy to double the original stakes."

"Fair enough." He spun the hoop again, and this time managed to keep it going for all of twenty seconds.

This was going to be the easiest money I'd ever made.

Chapter 23

I left the office a little earlier than usual because I wanted to spend some time going through Cosmo Alldig's journals, and I knew I'd get more done if Jack wasn't around to distract me.

First, though, I had to call in at the corner shop because we were out of bread. Ideally, I would have used the shopping app, but I wasn't buying enough to cover the minimum order. And besides, I always enjoyed my conversations with Little Jack.

When I arrived at the shop, I was rather surprised to find a bike rack on either side of the door. Both racks were full of bikes, all of which had baskets on the front. I was in for an even bigger shock once I stepped inside the shop. Normally, there were no more than two or three customers in there at a time, but today, it took a while to get inside because the place was full of customers — most of them teenagers.

It was a bit of a struggle, but I eventually managed to grab a loaf, and make my way to the counter, behind which was Little Jack (on his stilts), Lucy Locket, Peter Piper, and a cast of thousands. To say that Little Jack looked harassed would have been an understatement.

"Could I just pay for this loaf of bread, please, Jack?"

"Sorry, Jill, I didn't see you standing there."

"You're very busy today. Are you running a promotion or something?"

"These aren't customers. They're all the staff I've had to take on to cope with the orders generated by the shopping app."

"Oh? That explains all the bikes."

"Is that all you need today, Jill? No custard creams?"

"No, thanks. Just the bread."

By the time I'd managed to fight my way back out of the shop it was a wonder the bread wasn't stale. I was beginning to think that Little Jack hadn't thought through the shopping app and delivery service.

There had always been a line of bushes in between what was now the Normals' house and their next-door neighbours, but until today, no one had tried their hand at topiary on them.

"What do you think, Jill?" Naomi called to me as I got out of the car. "Norm has always wanted to have a go at this. He's a natural, wouldn't you say?"

"Err, yeah. The chicken is very good."

"It's a lion."

"Did I say chicken? I meant lion. What's that next to it? Is it some kind of fish?"

"It's a unicorn."

"Of course it is. I can see that now. And the last one?"

"A bear."

"Right. It's quite a small bear. Is it a koala?"

"No, it's a brown bear. It started off much bigger than it is now, but Norm slipped and cut it off at the groin."

"Painful."

"Aren't you going to ask why he chose the lion, unicorn and bear?" The truth was, I didn't give even the smallest— "I'll tell you. It's to represent our family coat of arms."

"You have a coat of arms?"

"Of course. Don't you?"

"Not that I know of."

"You should try to find out. Would you like to know what our family motto is?"

"Sure."

"normalis semper. Can you guess what that means?"

"Alphorn player?"

"You're obviously not a Latin scholar." She laughed. "It means always normal."

"Great. Anyway, I'd better get going."

"Blast!" Norm dropped the hedge trimmer.

"Are you okay?" Naomi shouted. "Did you cut yourself?"

"No, I've just lopped off the unicorn's horn by mistake."

I made myself a cup of tea, and settled down at the kitchen table with the pile of journals. They were so mind-numbingly boring that I might have nodded off, had it not been for the dust, which kept making me sneeze.

Two hours later, and with five journals still to go, I could take no more. Once I'd finished the last few pages of the current book, I'd leave the rest until tomorrow.

But then, I spotted it.

The entry was headed: Griselda The Vile. The details were sparse, but it left me in no doubt that it referred to the unmarked headstone I'd seen Belladonna visit. Cosmo Alldig's entry read:

I fought long and hard to persuade them not to accept her body, but the authorities insisted that everyone was entitled to a burial. I said they should have fed her to the rats, but that didn't go down very well. In the end, I had no choice but to accept their decision. It was either that or lose my job, and I couldn't afford to do that. Obviously, the grave is situated in The Shadows, and the headstone has been left blank. I hope she rots in Hell.

Strong words indeed, but who was this woman known as Griselda The Vile, and what had she done to deserve such contempt? Inspired by my find, I ploughed through the remaining journals in case there was more information to be found on the woman in the unmarked grave, but there was nothing.

***

When Jack arrived home, he was weighed down with books.

"Have you joined the library?" I took a few from him before he dropped them.

"These are your tortoise's poems."

"They've made a really good job of them. They look great."

"They should do. They cost an arm and a leg."

"Don't worry. Rhymes will repay you."

"When?"

"I'll drop them off later on my way to the circus."

"Oh, and this came with them." He handed me a sheet of paper.

"What's this? A competition?"

"Yeah. Apparently, everyone who has a poetry book published by that company is automatically entered into the competition. There's a trophy up for grabs, apparently. Let's just hope he doesn't win. That could prove to be a little awkward."

"You've read his poems. I don't think there's any chance of that."

"By the way, Jill, did you see the Normals' hedge?"

"I did." I laughed. "I've never seen anything quite like

it."

"They may be a little strange, but the man certainly has talent."

"I assume that's a joke?"

"No. Those three dolphins are amazing."

"Those three *dolphins* are a lion, a unicorn and a bear."

"No, they're not. They're clearly dolphins."

"Naomi called me over to look at them, and I'm telling you, they're supposed to be a lion, a unicorn and a bear. They're from the Normals' coat of arms."

"They have a coat of arms?"

"They certainly do. And their motto is normalis semper."

"What does that mean?"

"I believe a rough translation is: Nutjobs are us."

"That's not very nice."

"Accurate, though."

"I'd kill for a cup of coffee."

"Me too. Thanks for offering."

We went through to the kitchen where the journals were still on the table.

"Haven't you finished with these dusty old things yet?"

"Yeah, just now. I've found what I was looking for."

"You've found out who the grave belongs to?"

As he made coffee and I put away the journals, I told Jack what I knew about Griselda The Vile.

"What do you think she did to be so reviled?"

"I've no idea, but I intend to find out."

"How do you plan to do that?"

"Now that I have a name, I can make some enquiries at Candlefield library."

"Will their records go back that far?"

"I won't know until I ask."

"Enjoy the circus." Jack passed me Rhymes' poetry books, which he'd put into a spare cardboard box. "And make sure you get that tortoise to *shell* out for these." He laughed. "*Shell out*? Get it?"

"That's awful."

"Your problem is that you don't recognise comedy genius when you hear it."

"Hmm. I suppose I'd better get going. I'll see you in a few minutes." I gave him a kiss and then magicked myself over to Candlefield.

"What do you have there, Jill?" Aunt Lucy was in her glad rags.

"They're Rhymes' poetry books."

"Oh good. He's been so looking forward to getting those."

"What time are the twins coming?"

"If they're punctual, they should be here in five minutes."

"So about a quarter of an hour, then?"

"If we're lucky."

"I'll take these books up to Rhymes."

"Jill!" Barry came charging over to greet me, and almost knocked the box of books out of my hands. "Are we going for a walk?"

"No. You've already had your walks today. I'm going to the circus with Aunt Lucy and the twins."

"What's a circus?"

"It's err — a big tent."

"That sounds boring."

"It is, but I have to go."

"That's okay. I'm busy working on my drawings, anyway."

"You're still at it, then? I thought you might have got fed up by now."

"No, I love it. Dolly is still trying to arrange an exhibition for me."

"Right. You mustn't build your hopes up too high. Exhibitions aren't easy to organise."

"But Dolly promised."

"Right." That woman had better know what she was doing. If she let him down now, he would be inconsolable. "Where's Rhymes?"

"He's asleep under the bed. He's been there for ages."

Oh no! Please don't let him be hibernating. I crouched down, and peeped under the bed. "Rhymes? Are you awake?"

Thankfully, he was only sleeping. One yawn and a stretch later, he crawled out. "Hello, Jill. I didn't realise you were — " That's when he spotted the box. "Is that? Are those?"

"Your books? Yes."

"Show me! Please!" I passed him one, and he flicked through it. "I love it! Thank you so much, Jill!"

"No problem."

"Take one for yourself."

"Err, right. Thanks."

"I'm going to give them to all of my friends. They'll be so proud of me."

"And so they should be."

"Jill is going to the circus," Barry said.

"What's a circus?" Rhymes looked up from the book.

"Jill says it's a big tent."

"Oh? That doesn't sound very interesting."

"I'd better get going." I stood up. "There's just the question of the money."

"What is money?"

I thought at first Rhymes was joking; tortoises can be such kidders, but it soon became obvious that he had no idea what I was talking about.

Oh bum!

When I got back downstairs, the twins had arrived.

"We hear you've had Rhymes' poetry published." Pearl grinned.

"Did you *shell*-f-publish it?" Amber quipped.

The twins and Aunt Lucy all dissolved into laughter.

"Very funny. Rhymes doesn't have any money to pay for them."

"What did you expect?" Pearl wiped a tear from her eye. "Why would a tortoise have any money?"

"It's just that—err, Winky is rolling in it."

"It looks like someone is out of pocket," Amber said.

"Yeah. Jack. I don't think he's going to be too impressed when I tell him."

***

The big top was in Candlefield Park, and judging by the huge queues, it was very popular.

"Oh no. Look at all those people." I did my best to sound disappointed. "We'll never get in. We'd better go back home."

As I tried to turn back, Amber grabbed my arm. "We already have our tickets."

"Oh? That's great."

Fifteen minutes later, we'd taken our seats inside the huge tent.

"These are brilliant seats," Pearl said.

We were a bit too close to the front for my liking, but at least I didn't have to worry about stupid clowns.

"Ladies and Gentlemen." The ringmaster's uniform was green rather than the more familiar red. "Welcome to Circus Fantastico. Before we begin, I have some exciting news. You may have read in the press that we recently lost our clown troupe. I'm very pleased to tell you that we have now signed a new troupe who'll be making their debut this evening." The crowd roared their approval — all except me, of course. "Ladies and gentlemen, please give a warm welcome to Clowns Cyclopper!"

Everyone got to their feet and cheered.

"What kind of name is cyclopper?" I said to Aunt Lucy.

"Haven't you heard of them?"

"No, should I have?"

"The cycloppers are one of the rarer sups. They live mainly in the countryside, and usually keep themselves to themselves. I'm surprised that some of them have chosen to form a clown troupe."

Just then, the clowns came tumbling into the arena. Now, as far as I'm concerned, all clowns are freaky, but these guys really took the biscuit. The cycloppers had only one eye, in the centre of their faces. They also had only one leg.

The head cyclopper took the mic. "Thank you for that

warm welcome! We're so very pleased to be here with you tonight. Clowns Cyclopper is a brand new troupe; this is our very first show. In fact, we very nearly didn't make it tonight because our shoes, which have to be specially ordered, didn't arrive in time. But, luckily, we were able to make alternative arrangements, so here we are. We hope you have fun!"

Ten minutes into their act, and the crowd were lapping it up.

"They're great, aren't they, Jill?" Amber gushed.

"Yeah. Fantastic."

"She's terrified of them." Pearl laughed.

"No, I'm not." If they came any closer, I was out of there.

Just then, a freaky clown jumped onto one of the bales of hay that edged the ring.

"He's coming to get you!" Pearl screamed at me.

By rights, I should have been terrified, but I was too busy staring at his foot. All of the cycloppers were wearing a single clown's shoe, and I had a feeling I knew where they'd got them from.

***

Two hours, and what felt like several lifetimes later, the show finally drew to an end.

"That was fantastic," Amber said once we were outside.

"I thoroughly enjoyed it." Aunt Lucy turned to me. "What about you, Jill?"

"It was great."

"Do you want to come back to the house for a cuppa before you go home?"

"Err, no thanks. I'm going to get back."

"Don't have nightmares about the clowns," Pearl said.

"Very funny. I'll catch you all later."

Instead of going home, I magicked myself to the rear of the big top where the artistes had their caravans and mobile homes. Fortunately, no one questioned my presence, so I was able to search for the cycloppers without interference. A few minutes later, I came across several caravans with the name Clowns Cyclopper screen-printed on the side. The caravans were parked in a circle, and in the centre, a small bonfire had been lit. The clowns, who were still wearing their ridiculous costumes, were all gathered around the fire, eating, drinking and no doubt celebrating their successful debut.

Little did they know that I was about to rain on their parade.

"Hey! You lot!" I walked over to the bonfire. "I have a bone to pick with you cycloppers!"

"Who are you?" The head cyclopper, who had spoken in the ring earlier, shouted at me.

"My name isn't important. What is important is that you have stolen property from the human world, and I intend to report you to the rogue retrievers."

"How dare you?" Another cyclopper shouted.

"Yeah, what right have you to call us thieves?"

"Don't come the innocent with me. You said yourself that your shoes didn't arrive on time, and that you'd had to make *alternative arrangements*."

"That's right. We did."

"You stole those shoes from the human world."

"What? Are you crazy?"

"The game's up. You may as well accept it."

"We paid good money for our shoes, and I'll prove it. Wait there!" He disappeared into one of the caravans, and moments later, came back with a large box full of shoes. "See! We had no choice but to buy pairs of shoes even though we'll only ever use one from each pair. I can show you the receipts if you like."

And that's when I noticed that they were all wearing left-footed shoes. The ones in the box were all right-footed.

Oh bum and treble bum!

"Right." I started to edge slowly away from the fire. "You'll be pleased to know that you've all passed the test. Congratulations."

"What are you talking about? What test?"

"I'm from the CCIA."

"The CIA?"

"No. It's CCIA. It stands for the Candlefield Circus Inspection Authority. We have to satisfy ourselves that all clowns are not only able to make people laugh, but that they're also able to take a joke. I'm very pleased to confirm that you've passed with flying colours. Thanks very much for your time. Goodnight."

And with that, I fled.

Chapter 24

"Did Rhymes say when I'd get my money?" Jack asked the next morning.

"I told you last night; he'll draw out the cash the next time he goes to the bank."

"Do tortoises have banks?"

"Apparently."

"I hope he doesn't stiff me. I'm already short because of the money you cost me on the hula hoop sponsorship."

"Rhymes wouldn't do that. He's a good little guy."

"Do your Aunt Lucy and the twins know you made a fool of yourself with the clowns last night?"

"First, I didn't make a fool of myself. It was a simple mistake that anyone could have made. And no, the twins and Aunt Lucy weren't with me when I confronted the clowns."

"Where does that leave you with the mystery of the missing clown shoes?"

"Back at shoe one. I'll probably have to tell Jimmy and Kimmy I can't help them."

"Oh well. Win some, lose some. It'll soon be weekend. I'm really looking forward to seeing the TenPinCon promo that your grandmother is organising, aren't you?"

"Yeah, it's the favour that I was forced to promise her that worries me."

"She'll probably have forgotten all about that."

"There's no chance of that. She never forgets anything."

***

Macabre's maintenance man arrived at the office

building at the same time as I did.

"Back again?" I said.

"Yeah. No rest for the wicked."

"Has Mr Macabre asked you to do any work in my office?"

"No. Just in the common areas, and in the offices of that new clown place."

"Right."

That didn't seem fair. There was work that needed doing in my offices too. Maybe I'd have a word with Macabre.

When I pushed open the door to the outer office, it hit something, and there was a loud yell.

"Ouch!"

Alistair was holding his bloody nose.

"Are you okay?" I'd had no idea he was standing right behind the door, which had hit him full in the face.

"Here!" Mrs V hurried around her desk with a box of tissues.

I grabbed his chair. "Sit down. I'm really sorry. I had no idea you were behind the door."

"It's okay." He pressed a handful of tissues against his nose to stem the blood.

"He'll be okay," Mrs V assured me. "I'll see to him."

"Okay. I really am very sorry."

Poor old Alistair. Still, it might stop him picking his nose.

What? It was a joke. Sheesh.

"I know doliphant boy is pretty useless," Winky said. "But that was brutal."

"It was an accident. And how do you even know what

happened? Do you have x-ray vision?"

"Winky is all-seeing and all-knowing."

"What have I told you about referring to yourself in the third person?"

"Sorry. Winky won't do it again." He laughed.

***

Daze popped into the office just before eleven o'clock.

"I hoped I might catch you, Jill."

"You were lucky. My feet have barely touched the ground this week." I ignored Winky who was rolling his eyes at me.

"What happened to that office manager of yours? It looks like someone has punched him in the face."

"Alistair? He walked into a door." Cue more eye-rolling from Winky.

"Poor guy. I came over because I promised to get back to you when I'd had the chance to check on that casino owner."

"Ringstone."

"He may call himself that now, but as I suspected, his real name is Norville Stonering."

"Are you saying it's the same guy who's already wanted back in Candlefield?"

"There's no doubt about it."

"I suppose that means he'll end up behind bars, even if it isn't in the human world. It's just a pity my client will never know."

"Actually, that's what I wanted to talk to you about. There may be a way for your client to see Ringstone, Stonering or whatever he calls himself, brought to justice here in the human world."

"Oh? How's that?"

She went on to outline her thought process.

"Thanks, Daze, that's a brilliant idea."

"Do you think you'll be able to pull it off, Jill?"

"I hope so for my client's sake. I'll keep you posted."

***

It stuck in my craw that Macabre was sorting out all of Jimmy and Kimmy's little snags, but hadn't asked his maintenance man to attend to any of the issues in my offices. What exactly was I paying him the service charge for?

I gave him a call.

"Mr Macabre? It's Jill Maxwell. No, I haven't forgotten about the sign. Yes, I do know it has to be sorted by end of business tomorrow, but that's not why I called. I want to know why your maintenance man isn't going to do any repairs in my office. I have a few things that need—" That was as far as I got because what he told me next stopped me dead in my tracks. "Right. Sorry to have troubled you, Mr Macabre. Yes, I'll make sure the sign is sorted. Bye."

Alistair was at his desk; he looked awful.

"Are you okay?" I asked.

"Just about." He was still holding the tissues to his nose.

"I reckon he'll have a couple of black eyes in the morning," Mrs V said. "His face is already starting to swell below his eyes."

"Perhaps you should go home," I suggested.

"Maybe I will. Is that okay?"

Of course. I'm really sorry about what happened."

"You haven't forgotten I'm not in this afternoon, have you, Jill?" Mrs V said. "I have my annual medical check-up."

"I had forgotten, but don't worry about it. I'll be here for most of the afternoon."

After seeing Alistair off, I made my way down the corridor to Clown.

Kimmy was behind the desk.

"Hi, Kimmy. Is Jimmy in? I'd like a word with you both."

"It's Breezy and –"

"Yes, yes, but if I could just speak to you both. It's about the stolen shoes."

"Of course. Come through to the office."

"Do you know who the thief is?" Breezy said.

"Before I get into that, where's the maintenance man?"

"Why?"

"Humour me, please."

"He's in the small classroom. We don't have any classes in there for an hour."

"Take me there, would you?"

"I don't understand, Jill."

"All will become clear."

The maintenance man was sitting on the floor next to one of the radiators. He seemed surprised to see us. "I thought I was okay to work in here for the next hour?"

"You are," Sneezy said. "Jill wants a word with you, I believe."

"Hello again." I walked over to him.

"Hi?"

"Would you mind showing me what's in your tool bag?"

"Sorry?"

"You heard me." I grabbed it, undid the zip, and emptied out the contents: three spanners, a screwdriver, a hammer and a clown shoe. "You're busted, buddy!"

"Who are you?" Sneezy demanded.

"It was only a joke," the man spluttered.

"Do you see anyone laughing?" Breezy looked as though he wanted to rip the man's head off. "Why have you been stealing the shoes?"

"I was paid to do it, but the guy who hired me said it was just a joke between you and him. He said you were always pulling practical jokes on one another."

"What man?" Breezy demanded.

"Raymond Higgins."

"Raymond?" Sneezy looked shocked.

"PomPom?" Breezy shook his head in disbelief.

"Isn't he the guy who runs the other clown school?" I said.

"Yes. The Red Nose school. I just can't believe Raymond would do something like this."

"You're not going to turn me in to the police, are you?" The phony maintenance man put his tools back into his bag. "I would never have done it if I'd realised it was anything other than a practical joke."

"That's up to these two." I gestured to Sneezy and Breezy.

"What good would it do?" Breezy sighed. "It's PomPom who has to answer for this."

"There's something I'd like to know," I said. "Why did you only take one shoe?"

"I didn't have room in my bag to take both."

"And why did you always take the right shoe?"

"I didn't realise I had. I just grabbed the first one I saw."

***

Orville Ringstone lived in a fabulous mansion located ten miles south of Washbridge. The property was surrounded by a huge wall. The only access was through a large gate, manned by a guard.

None of that was any match for my magic.

After levitating over the wall, I strolled across the huge rear lawn, and took a seat next to the swimming pool. I'd only been there a few minutes when I spotted a man's face at the French windows.

Not wishing to be antisocial, I gave him a little wave.

"Who are you?" He came storming out of the house. "How did you get in?"

"What kind of greeting is that for a fellow sup?"

"You have no right to be here. If you don't leave immediately, I'll have you thrown out."

"Oh yes. I'd forgotten that you don't like sups on your properties. Particularly not in your casino."

"You have one minute to leave!"

"Except that you do allow certain sups into the casino, don't you? As long as they agree to hand over their winnings to you."

That seemed to knock the wind out of him momentarily, but he quickly recovered. "Are you a reporter?"

"What would you do if I said I was? Drop giant dice on my head? Like you did to Kirk Sparks."

"Who are you?"

"My name is Jill Maxwell. I'm working for Kirk's wife. She came to me because she suspects Kirk's death wasn't an accident."

"Of course it was. The inquest said so."

"Yes, but you and I know that the humans who conducted the inquest weren't aware that a lightning strike could be caused by magic, were they?"

"You think you're clever, don't you?" He laughed. "I'd like to see you prove any of this."

"There's no need for me to prove anything because you're going to present yourself at Washbridge police station. Once there, you're going to confess to embezzling funds from the casino, and tax evasion."

"Embezzlement? I own the business."

"The casino is operating as a limited company. You and it are separate entities. You've been stealing from the business."

"*I'm* not going anywhere, but you are." He took out his phone. "I can have someone here to remove you in a couple of minutes."

"Before you make that call, I have just one word to say to you: Rondan." All the colour drained from his face and he dropped the phone. "I take it the name rings a bell?"

"What about him?"

"As I understand it, Rondan was your partner in the last scam you ran back in Candlefield. I also heard that you took all the money, and then left him to carry the can."

"He's locked up."

"He is indeed. In Candlefield High Security Prison."

"What does that have to do with me?"

"I'm glad you asked. I was talking to a friend of mine

earlier. You might have heard of her. Her name is Daze. She's one of the — "

"I know who she is."

"Good. Apparently, she has a list of charges, as long as her arm, to bring against you. She also happens to have a lot of influence with the judiciary back in Candlefield. When you're convicted, there's a one-hundred percent chance that you'll be incarcerated in Candlefield High Security Prison, alongside your old mucker, Rondan."

"He'll kill me."

"Yeah, that's pretty much what Daze said."

"I can't go back there."

"There may be a way to avoid it."

"What is it? Tell me, please!"

"Luckily for you, Daze just happens to be a very good friend of mine. She's agreed that if you hand yourself in to the authorities here in the human world, she won't drag your sorry backside back to Candlefield and Rondan."

"Hand myself in and tell them what?"

"That you fixed the tables so that certain people would win. And that those people would then hand the cash to you. Obviously, you'll have to leave out the bit about them using magic."

"And if I do this, I won't have to go back to Candlefield?"

"Correct."

"How about I give you some money instead? I'm a very rich man."

"You wouldn't be trying to bribe me, would you? Because if you were, I'd be forced to tell Daze."

"No, no. I wasn't. I promise."

"Good. In that case, you'd better hurry. You're due at

the police station."

"I'll need time to put my affairs in order. A month ought to do it."

"You have two hours. If you haven't handed yourself in to the police by then, you can expect a visit from the rogue retrievers."

"But, I—"

"Goodbye, Mr Ringstone. I can see myself out."

The information Daze had provided to me had been invaluable. As she suspected, Ringstone was terrified at the idea of going back to Candlefield because he knew his ex-partner would kill him. Even so, the sentences he'd receive for the theft and tax evasion were nothing compared to the life sentence he deserved for the murder of Kirk Sparks. I consoled myself that it would at least allow Bernie to see the man she believed responsible for her husband's death put behind bars.

There was also one minor point that I'd omitted to mention to Ringstone. Daze had assured me that once he was released from prison in the human world, he would immediately be arrested and taken back to Candlefield, where he would spend many more years behind bars. I asked if he'd be incarcerated with Rondan, but Daze thought that might be a step too far.

I'm not sure I agreed.

***

Having sent Alistair home, and with Mrs V at her medical check-up, I expected to find the office locked, but the door was open.

Inside, there was no sign of Mrs V, but to my surprise, Alistair was at his desk. Even more surprising was the fact that his eyes and nose showed no sign of the injury I'd accidentally inflicted on him that morning. When I'd sent him home, his eyes had already started to close, and his nose was crusted with blood.

"What's going on with your nose?"

"Sorry." He took his finger from his nostril. "It's a disgusting habit I know. I'm trying to stop."

"I'm not talking about you picking your nose, I'm talking about the bruising."

"*Bruising*? Right. I — err, I — "

While he stumbled to come up with an explanation, the penny dropped.

"Who are you really?"

"Sorry?"

"Are you Alistair or are you Craig?"

"I — err — "

"Don't you dare lie to me!"

"I'm Craig."

"And who was sitting at that desk this morning?"

"That was Alistair."

"I thought I was going crazy. I couldn't work out why you swapped your tie at lunchtime every day, or why you whistled in the morning, but not in the afternoon. And the clowns. And the bike."

"I can explain."

"Don't bother. I want to see both of you in my office tomorrow afternoon. You can both explain then."

"What shall I do for the rest of the afternoon?"

"Get out of my sight before I give you a pair of black eyes too."

"Right." He grabbed his coat. "Sorry."

"Priceless!" Winky was in hysterics.

"I'd be careful if I were you. I've already given one person a black eye today."

"You call yourself a P.I, and yet you didn't even realise that you had two of them working for you."

"Neither did you."

"Of course I did. I just wanted to see how long it would take for you to work it out."

"You're such a liar."

Chapter 25

By the time I'd crawled out of bed the next morning, Jack had already finished his breakfast.

"Morning, sweetheart." I gave him a kiss. "You're looking particularly handsome this morning."

He eyed me suspiciously. "What are you after?"

"I don't know what you mean."

"I normally struggle to get more than two words out of you when you first get up. You obviously want something."

"No, I don't. I just thank my lucky stars every day that I ended up with someone as kind and generous as you."

"Now I definitely know you want something. You might as well spit it out."

"It's nothing, really. You know the casino case I've been working on?"

"Yeah?"

"If things have gone according to plan, the owner of the casino, a certain Orville Ringstone, will have handed himself in to the police yesterday, and he'll have confessed to embezzlement and tax evasion."

"I thought it was a murder you were investigating?"

"It was, but there's no way I could make that stick here in the human world, so I had to settle for these lesser charges."

"What makes you think he will have confessed?"

"It was either that or be taken back to Candlefield where he'd be incarcerated with a psychopath who is baying for his blood."

"And where exactly do I come into this?"

"I want you to confirm with Washbridge police that he

did in fact hand himself in, and that he's been charged."

"No."

"What do you mean, no?"

"It's very simple. I won't do it."

"Why not?"

"Because the last time I helped you, I told you I wouldn't do it again."

"I don't remember that."

"Yes, you do. It was when you asked me to find out what the Washbridge police had on Josh Radford."

"I thought you were just joking."

"No, you didn't. You were just hoping I'd forgotten."

"But this is such a teeny little thing to ask."

"The answer is still no."

"You're a meanie."

"I thought I was handsome, kind and generous?"

"I lied about that."

He was right of course. I shouldn't have asked him to use his position to get information for me.

But he was still a meanie.

"Jill!" he called from the lounge. "I think you'll want to see this."

The TV was tuned in to the local news station.

"I thought you were watching TenPin TV?"

"I was just about to switch to it when this came on."

On screen, there was a picture of the Lucky Thirteen casino.

"Turn it up." I sat on the arm of the sofa.

"We have just learned that the Lucky Thirteen casino, located between Washbridge and West Chipping, has closed with immediate effect. No official statement has been released, but an

unofficial source is reporting that the owner, Mr Orville Ringstone, has been charged with a number of offences."

"Result!"

***

I'd parked the car in Washbridge, and was walking towards my office building when my phone rang.

"Jill, it's Bernie."

"Hi."

"I've just seen the news about the casino closing down and the owner being arrested. Did you know about it?"

"Yeah. In fact, I may have had a small hand in it."

"Are they going to charge Ringstone with murder?"

"I'm afraid not. I believe he was responsible for Kirk's death, but there's simply no way to prove it. At least this way, he'll do some time behind bars, and the casino has been closed down."

"I guess that's better than nothing. Did you find out what story Kirk was working on?"

"No. It's like you said, those notebooks of his were indecipherable, but at least my investigation uncovered Ringstone's theft and tax evasion."

"Do you think it's possible more evidence might come to light that will prove he was behind Kirk's death?"

"I think it's unlikely, but if it's any consolation, I have a feeling that this may not be the end of Ringstone's woes."

"I do hope you're right. Thanks again for your help. I assume you'll send me your bill."

"It'll be in the post today."

Mrs V was at her desk.

"I don't think we'll see Alistair today, Jill." She was knitting yet another clown sock. "The poor lad must still be in pain."

"Not as much pain as he'll be in when I catch up with him."

"What did you just say?" She looked appalled.

"Nothing. Ignore me. I didn't sleep well last night. Can you make up the bill for Mrs Sparks, and let me see it? I'd like to get it in tonight's post."

"Will do. Do you think I should give Alistair a call to see if he's okay?"

"I wouldn't bother. I have a feeling he'll be in a little later."

"I'm excited about this afternoon," Winky said. "Are you ready?"

"Am I ready for what?"

"Don't tell me you've forgotten our hula hoop contest, have you?"

"I'm going to have to postpone it."

"What? Why? Are you chickening out?"

"No, but I'm too busy today. We can do it tomorrow morning."

"Saturday?"

"Why not? I have to come into town for the stupid TenPinCon promo, so I'll pop in here first. It shouldn't take long to beat you. Besides, I still have to buy a hula hoop."

"You can borrow mine."

"Do you think I'm stupid? I know you and your little tricks. You'll weigh it down, or find some other way to sabotage it when it's my turn."

"You're not very trusting, are you?"

"When it comes to you, no."

"So how come you're so busy today? Paperclip drawer need sorting again, does it?"

"Have you forgotten? I have the Robinson twins coming in this afternoon. And before that, I have to do some research into a woman called Griselda The Vile."

"I know her brother: Godfrey The Tile. If you need your kitchen or bathroom tiling, he's your man."

"You're hilarious. Let's see if you're still laughing tomorrow when I wipe the floor with you."

"Dream on. You aren't going to sulk when I take your money, are you? I know what a bad loser you can be."

"First, I am not a bad loser, and second, there is zero chance of you winning."

***

The witch behind the desk at Candlefield Library was fresh-faced and eager to be of assistance.

"Hi, I'm Trixibelle. Can I help?"

"Hi. I don't think I've seen you in here before, have I?"

"I only started last week. I'm so lucky to be here. This has been my dream job ever since I started school."

"Right. I'm hoping to find some information about a criminal named Griselda The Vile."

"I see. Is she still alive, do you know?"

"No. She died many years ago—more than a century, probably. I don't have a precise date, I'm afraid."

"We do have a section devoted to crime, but all of the books in that section are fiction. Let me just check the index to see if I can find the name." She clicked the mouse, and began to study the computer. "Griselda—?"

"The Vile."

"You wouldn't happen to know her real surname, would you?"

"I'm afraid not."

"Hmm. The only Griselda I can see is a book called Griselda The Green Mouse, which is in the children's section."

"That's rather disappointing."

"Have you tried CMOC?"

"What's that?"

"Candlefield Museum of Crime."

"I didn't realise there was a museum of crime."

"Not many people do. It's a tiny building at the rear of the police station. It might be worth a try."

"Right. Thanks, Trixibelle, you've been a great help."

"My pleasure."

How very nice it was to have finally met someone with customer-facing skills to match my own.

When Trixibelle had said the museum was tiny, she hadn't been kidding. I'd walked past it three times before I realised that the door, which had peeling green paint, was in fact the entrance to CMOC. I'd expected to see a sign of some kind, but it was only when I was right next to the door that I noticed a miniscule plaque bearing the letters: CMOC.

Once inside, I found myself in a tiny reception area; the only furniture in there was a single chair and a coffee table. A small sign next to a frosted window gave instructions to press the button, so I did. I expected to hear a bell ring, but there was no sound. I waited a couple of minutes and tried again. Was it even working?

Exasperated, I pressed the button and this time held my finger on it. Moments later, I heard footsteps.

"Whatever happened to patience?" A tiny man slid open the window.

"Sorry. I wasn't sure if the button was working."

"I was in the basement. There are lots of steps to climb."

"Sorry again."

"Get it over with, then. You may as well say it. Everyone does."

"I don't know what you mean."

"Aren't you going to say that you didn't think anyone was *gnome*."

"I didn't even realise you were a—err. That's to say, I'm used to seeing gnomes with—err, never mind."

"You live in the human world, don't you?"

"I do, yes."

"I can always tell. I suppose you expected me to have a fishing rod or a wheelbarrow?"

"Well, I must admit, I—"

"It's a travesty the way we're represented over there. We don't all like fishing or gardening, you know."

"I'm sure."

"Personally, I enjoy rock climbing, but I bet you haven't seen any gnomes in the human world, dressed in climbing gear, have you?"

"Now you mention it, I don't think I have."

"Did you actually want something? I can't stand here all day, chitter chattering with you."

"Sorry, yes. The young lady at Candlefield Library suggested I might find information here on a criminal who died some centuries ago."

"Name?"

"I'm Jill Maxwell."

"Not your name! The name of the person you're interested in."

"I don't know her full name."

"In that case, you're probably wasting your time and mine."

"She was known as Griselda The Vile."

Upon hearing that, he visibly flinched. "Why would you be interested in that lowlife?"

"You've heard of her, then?"

"Unfortunately, yes. I repeat my question: what's your interest in her?"

"I came across her unmarked grave."

"In The Shadows?"

"That's right. I've spoken to the current gravedigger, whose father had held the same post before him. It was his father's journals that gave me Griselda's name."

"My advice to you would be to forget all about her. The crimes that woman committed are another level of evil. You're better to remain oblivious. I wish I had."

"I'm sorry, I don't know your name."

"Jerome."

Jerome the gnome? I loved it.

"I appreciate your advice, Jerome, but I really do need to find out what this woman did."

"Very well. On your head be it." He gestured to a door at the far side of the room. "I'll see you through there."

I followed him down a corridor to a tiny office with a single desk and chair.

"Wait there. I'll go and fetch the relevant texts."

He was gone for almost fifteen minutes, and I was just

wondering if I should go and look for him when he returned carrying a number of dusty books, which had obviously come from the basement.

"Thanks."

"Are you absolutely sure you want to do this?"

"Positive."

"Alright, then. I'll leave you to it."

An hour later, I thanked Jerome, and left. After being stuck in that stuffy office, the fresh air was very welcome, but it did little to ease the nausea I was now experiencing. Nausea that had no doubt been brought on by what I'd just read.

***

Back at my office, my head was still spinning. I now knew exactly who Griselda The Vile was, what she'd done to deserve the nickname, and why Belladonna took flowers to her grave. But what should I do about it?

My phone rang; it was Aunt Lucy.

"You'll never guess what, Jill."

"You can't get into your house for Barry's pictures?"

"Close, but no. I'm coming to Washbridge tomorrow."

"Wow! I wasn't expecting that."

"The twins persuaded me that I should. I'm a bit nervous, but I'm looking forward to seeing the parade."

"Are you planning to stay here overnight?"

"Goodness, no. I only agreed to do it because it will only be for a few hours. You and Jack will be there, I assume?"

"Yes. Kathy, Peter and the kids too."

"Fantastic! I can't wait to see you all. See you tomorrow."

"Okay, bye."

I'd totally forgotten the twins had said they might come over. I'd grab a quick word with them at the parade, and let them know what I'd found out about Belladonna.

"Jill." Mrs V came through to my office and closed the door behind her. "Alistair is here." She hesitated. "But there are two of him."

"Send them both in, would you?"

The Robinson brothers looked a little sheepish. It was certainly easy enough to tell them apart now. Alistair had the dolphin tie; Craig had the elephant tie.

Oh, and of course, Alistair had two black eyes.

"Take a seat, please."

Before I could say anything else, Alistair apologised. "We're really sorry for the subterfuge, Jill."

"It was unforgiveable," Craig said.

"I don't understand why you did it. What was the point?"

They looked at one another, neither of them seemed keen to do the talking. Alistair eventually folded.

"We both applied for the same job."

"I already know that."

"Yes, but we did it twice. Craig and I unknowingly applied for the same two jobs. You offered me this one, and Craig was lucky enough to land the other."

"That still doesn't explain why you did this."

"I know. Neither of us was sure which of the two jobs we'd be best suited to, so when we landed both, we thought why not try them out for a couple of weeks, and then decide which one of us would take which job."

"Or, you could have — and this might sound like a crazy idea — taken the job you were offered!"

"You're right," Craig said. "With hindsight, that's what we should have done, but we thought we could pull this off without anyone noticing."

"That didn't quite work out, did it? I have to tell you that you aren't as similar as you think you are."

"We've come to that realisation ourselves."

"This whole thing is ridiculous, but the truth is it was a toss-up which one of you I offered the position to in the first place, so you might as well decide between you who is going to do this job, so we can all move on."

For the longest moment, there was a stony silence, and then Alistair spoke, "The thing is, Jill. Another vacancy has come up with the other company, and we've both decided that we'd rather work there."

"What? Who is this other company?"

"It's the marble works on the other side of Washbridge. They're called Top Marble."

"Do they make worktops?"

"No. Just marbles. You know the little round glass — "

"I know what marbles are, thank you."

"We've both been fascinated by marbles ever since we were kids, so this is kind of our dream job."

"But what about this place? Don't you find the work I do exciting?"

They looked at one another and then both shook their heads.

"There is one thing I'm going to miss, though," Alistair said.

"What's that?"

"Having the clown school right next door was great."

After the brothers Robinson had left, Winky jumped onto my desk.

"Don't you dare say a word!" I threatened him.

"Good riddance if you ask me."

"I suppose you'll want the job now?"

"Me? No chance. I must have been out of my mind to even consider doing it. You're on your own."

"That's fine. In fact, I'm glad they decided to quit. I've always worked best by myself. The Lone Ranger, that's me."

"There's always a *silver* lining."

"You do realise that no one appreciates your funny quips, don't you?"

"*Hi, ho.*" He shrugged.

"Give me strength. And what am I supposed to do with the orange dolphin desk?"

"Fifty quid."

"Okay, it's yours."

"I don't want to buy it. I'll take fifty-quid to dispose of it for you."

I'd had just about enough, so I decided to call it a day. I needed a long hot bath, and a glass of wine.

Oh no! I'd totally forgotten about the sign. Macabre had given me until close of business today to get it sorted. Still, not to worry, a little magic would soon shrink it to an acceptable size.

Fortunately, the street outside was quiet before the rush hour stampede, so no one would notice what I was doing. The spell was easy enough — just a small reduction in size was all that was needed.

I'd just begun to cast the spell when several cars beeped their horns, and came screeching to a halt. I turned around to see what was happening, and soon saw the source of the problem. A cat had run straight across the busy road, and had been lucky to escape with its life. Perhaps Winky's idea for the Cat Zip had not been so crazy after all.

"Look out!" someone yelled.

The next thing I knew, a man had pushed me to the ground. I was just about to lay into him when the sign came crashing to the floor next to us.

"Phew!" The man helped me to my feet. "That was close."

"Thanks. You saved my life."

"Think nothing of it. You should sue whoever's sign that is. Are you okay?"

"Yeah, I'm fine, thanks."

"I'd better get going. I have a bus to catch."

"Thanks again."

I was such an idiot. At the critical moment, I'd been distracted by the cat, and instead of shrinking the sign, I'd enlarged it. The additional weight had been too much for its fixings, and it had come crashing to the ground where it had broken into several pieces.

The incident had attracted quite a crowd, so there was no chance of using the 'take it back' spell.

Great! Now I had no signage again.

Chapter 26

"Today's the big day!" Jack was as excited as a little kid at Christmas.

"It certainly is. This is going to be easy money."

"What are you talking about?"

"The money I'm going to take off Winky in the hula hoop contest. Why, what are *you* talking about?"

"The promo for TenPinCon, of course."

"Oh yeah. Obviously, I'm excited for that too," I lied.

"What makes you so sure that you'll beat Winky at hula hoop?"

"Because I've seen him. That cat doesn't have the first clue how to do it."

"He might try to cheat. What if he tampers with the hula hoop?"

"I've already thought of that, which is why I'm going to nip into town early to buy one."

"Are you going to take your own car, then?"

"Yeah. Where shall I meet you?"

"I told Kathy we'd see them outside of Ever. Where did you tell the twins to meet us?"

"I didn't, but they'll know where to find us."

"Make sure you're on time. There's likely to be a big crowd."

"Don't worry. It won't take me long to beat that cat."

***

The question now was: where would I get a hula hoop from? I rarely visited toy shops. At least, not since the horrific Total Dream Office incident—I still had nightmares about that.

I drew a blank in the first three shops I tried, and I was just starting to worry when the young woman in Washbridge Toys made a suggestion.

"Have you tried Hula Hoop Heaven?"

"Is that online? Only, I need it today."

"No, it's here in Washbridge. Do you know Harry's Hot Cakes?"

"Is that the bun shop near the railway station?"

"That's the one. Hula Hoop Heaven is just around the corner from there."

You could have knocked me down with a feather. Who knew there was even such a thing as a shop that specialised in hula hoops? And how very fortunate that it was right here in Washbridge.

"Good morning, madam." The young man behind the counter was wearing a cute beret. "Welcome to HHH."

"Like the pencil?" I laughed.

"Sorry?"

"3H—pencil lead."

"Huh?" He was obviously none the wiser.

"Never mind. I need a hula hoop."

"You're in the right place. Can I ask, is it for pleasure or competition?"

"Definitely competition."

"Which team are you with? I don't recall seeing you in any of the league matches."

"I'm not actually in a team. I just have a contest with my—err—my friend."

"Right, in that case, I would recommend the Hula3899."

"Is it light?"

"Very light with excellent balance."

"That sounds like what I'm looking for."

He took one from the rack. "Try it for size."

"Do you have it in other colours?"

"I'm afraid not. Only green."

"Okay." I stepped into it, and gave it a twirl.

"Have you considered taking lessons?" he said. "We hold them for all levels."

"Thanks, but I won't be needing them. This one is fine. How much does it cost?"

"You're lucky. It's on offer this week at only thirty-two pounds."

"Thirty-two?"

"It's normally forty. There's twenty percent off this week."

It was much more than I was hoping to pay, but I'd soon have recuperated that and more. "Okay, I'll take it."

"Would you like me to wrap it?"

"No need. This bad boy is going to be seeing action in a few minutes."

***

"Well, well, well." Winky jumped down from the sofa. "I was sure you were going to chicken out."

"No chance. This is going to be the easiest and quickest money I've ever made."

"Is that the Hula3899?"

"It is." I held it aloft. "Eat your heart out, sucker."

"How much did that cost you?"

"Only thirty-two pounds. It was on special offer."

"I paid seventy pence for mine, from the market."

"Pah. How gullible do you think I am? I don't believe that for a minute."

"Please yourself. How are we going to do this?"

"Grab your hoop, and on three, we start. The one who keeps it going longest is the winner. Okay?"

"Sounds good to me." He stepped into his hoop. "Let's do this."

"Here goes. One, two, three. Go!"

I was pleasantly surprised at the ease with which I hit my rhythm. This was going to be a doddle. Another minute, two at the most, and I would have won back all the money that Jack and I had been forced to pay out for sponsoring Mrs V.

But that's when I noticed that Winky too seemed to have hit a rhythm. When I'd watched him practising before, he'd been awkward and uncoordinated, but today, he seemed to be much more relaxed and comfortable. I wasn't worried, though. He wouldn't last long.

Fifteen minutes later, I was starting to flag. I'd lost all sense of rhythm, and it was getting harder and harder to keep the hoop spinning. Meanwhile, Winky could not have made it look any less effortless.

Breathless, I could go on no longer. My hoop hit the floor with a sickening sound.

"I win, I believe." Winky grinned.

"You conned me."

"How about I give you a chance at double or nothing? Do you want to bet I can't keep this going for another hour?"

"No, I don't." I threw the Hula3899 across the room. "You're nothing more than a con artist." I started for the door.

"What about my money?"

"You'll get it."

"By the way, Jill, what happened to the sign?"

I couldn't believe I'd allowed it to happen again. As soon as he'd issued the challenge, I should have realised what he was up to. What was I going to tell Jack? I'd promised him that I'd win our money back, and now we were even deeper in the hole.

Oh bum!

***

"I thought you weren't going to make it," Jack said when I arrived at Ever. "Did you win our money back?"

"I — err — "

"Hi, Jill!" Amber was hurrying towards us; Pearl and Aunt Lucy were a few yards behind her.

Phew! Saved by the bell. "Hi, everyone."

"Hey, you lot!" Kathy, Peter and the kids arrived from the other direction.

We were all chatting away happily, and I thought I'd got away with having to tell Jack the bad news about the hula hoop contest when he appeared at my side. There was no escape, I would have to come clean and confess.

"Jack, about the — "

"I think I should go and thank your grandmother before the parade starts."

"What? Why?"

"For all the work she's put into this. Just look at the crowd. I would never have been able to pull off something like this."

"But we'll miss the parade."

"We've got ten minutes. Come on." He led the way into Ever, which was manned by a skeleton staff of just two.

"Is my grandmother in?"

The Everette nodded and pointed to her office. I knocked once.

"Come!"

She was at her desk, sucking on a lemon.

"Hi, Grandma."

"Who's your friend?"

"You know who he is. It's Jack."

"Oh, yes. I remember him now."

"He wants to have a quick word."

She took another suck at the lemon. "Go on, then. What is it? I'm a busy woman."

Jack stepped forward nervously, and spent the next five minutes thanking Grandma for all the work she'd put into today's event.

"Is that it?" She took a bite of the lemon skin.

"Err, yes."

"Right. You may leave now." She dismissed him with a wave of her hand.

We both turned to go.

"Jill, wait here a moment."

"I'll see you outside, Jill." Jack made a bolt for the door — the coward.

"What is it, Grandma? The parade will start soon."

"This will only take a minute. Do you remember you promised to do me a favour, in return for my help with today's events?"

"Yes, but I — err —"

"Good. You'll just have time to fulfil your part of the

bargain before the parade starts."

"What do I have to do?" I glanced at her feet, and was relieved to see she had her shoes on.

"Over there." She pointed to a small pan on a mini-hob. In it was a yellowish liquid, bubbling to the boil.

"You don't expect me to drink that stuff, do you?"

"Of course not. Why would I ask you to drink wax?"

What a relief. "What do you want me to do with it, then?"

"Look underneath the table, and you'll find a candle mould."

"Got it."

"Good. Pour the wax into the mould, and don't spill any."

"Okay." I lifted the pan from the hob and began to pour.

"Be careful!"

"Sorry, I only splashed a little." I put the empty pan back on the hob. "Is that it?"

"Yes, you can go now."

Phew! That was far less painful than I'd expected it to be.

***

The parade was even more spectacular than the ones that Grandma had organised previously.

At its head was a troupe of clowns. Thankfully, these were of the two-eyed, two-legged variety. It was only when I spotted Sneezy and Breezy that I realised it was the clowns from the school.

I managed to grab a quick word with Breezy as they

passed by.

"Hi, Jill."

"How come you got involved today?"

"The organiser asked if we'd like to take part. We figured it would be good publicity for the school."

Next in line was the Everette Steel Band, led by Julie, and sounding even better than the last time I'd heard them.

"I like their yellow uniforms," Jack said.

"If I were you, I wouldn't mention the yellow to any of them."

Next came the jugglers who were all juggling bowling pins. Behind them, were the acrobats, and although there was no doubt they were talented, I couldn't help but feel it was a case of: seen one acrobat, seen them all.

"What's that awful sound?" Amber put her hands over her ears.

Everyone was looking around, trying to figure out what could possibly be making such a terrible racket.

"It's the Normals!" Jack pointed.

Sure enough, behind the acrobats, were Norm and Naomi, playing their alphorns.

"I might have known." I cringed.

"It's clever how they've adapted those wheelbarrows to support the horns," Jack commented.

Norm managed a quick wave on his way past.

Behind the Normals, at the rear of the parade, was the marching band who proved as popular as ever.

Once the parade had finished, we moved onto the main event of the day: The giant ten pin bowling. Everyone who wanted to take part was allowed a single go. The twins were useless, and both managed to knock over only one pin. Aunt Lucy managed four, and I did a little better with six. Needless to say, Jack and Peter were as competitive as ever, and they ended up tied for the lead on nine pins each.

"It looks like we're going to be joint winners," Jack patted Peter on the back as the competition was drawing to a close.

"What about Lizzy?" I said. "She hasn't had a turn yet."

"The ball is too big for her." Mikey, who had managed to score a respectable seven, scoffed at the idea.

"No, it isn't. Would you like a go, Lizzie?"

"I don't think I can do it, Auntie Jill."

"Of course you can. Come on."

She stood behind the giant soft bowling ball, and gave it a gentle push.

"That's rubbish!" Mikey laughed.

But then, as if by magic, the ball picked up pace and hit the pins in the sweet spot.

"Strike!" Kathy yelled. "Well done, pumpkin!"

Jack shot me an accusatory look, but I just shrugged. Snigger!

***

When the day's events finally came to an end, I told Jack that I'd meet him back at the house. Before I headed home, I wanted to have a word with Amber and Pearl. I had to tell them what I'd learned about Belladonna.

"I've really enjoyed myself," Aunt Lucy caught me as I was on my way to speak to the twins.

"I'm pleased you came over. It seems to have been a

great success."

"Credit where credit is due. Your grandmother certainly knows how to organise this kind of event."

"And the price I had to pay wasn't too bad."

"She didn't actually charge you for doing this, did she?"

"Not cash, but she did ask me to do her a favour in return. I was expecting something terrible, but as it turned out, it wasn't too awful. She just wanted me to pour some wax into a candle mould."

"Oh dear." The colour seemed to drain from Aunt Lucy's face.

"What's wrong?"

"Nothing." She looked as though she was about to be sick.

"Are you sure? You've turned a strange colour."

"It's just that your grandmother has always had this theory that the best kind of candles are those made from — err —" She hesitated. "But, like I said, I'm sure it's not that."

"From what, Aunt Lucy?"

"From earwax. She keeps it for decades until she has enough to make one." Aunt Lucy took me by the arm. "Jill, are you okay?"

***

When I arrived home, I was still feeling a little queasy. I wasn't sure I'd ever be able to get the image of Grandma's earwax candle out of my head. After that ghastly revelation, I hadn't been able to face speaking to the twins. I'd have to tell them about Belladonna another day.

Jack's car was on the driveway, but there was no sign of him anywhere in the house. Where could he have gone?

When I looked out of the front window, I had my answer. Moments later, I was standing next to the tree in the Normals' front garden.

"You're looking really *wood*, Jack." I laughed.

"Shush! I'm supposed to be undercover."

"Are you working for special *branch*?"

"This isn't funny."

"From where I'm standing, I'd say it was *tree*larious."

"You never told me what happened with the hula hoop contest."

"I — err — , I should go and make a start on dinner."

"Jill! What about the hula hoop money?"

"Sorry, I can't hear you. See you later."

As I walked up our driveway, someone shouted.

"Hey! I have a bone to pick with you!"

I looked around to find Bruiser standing there.

"What are you doing here?"

"Don't come the innocent. I know it was you who got me thrown out of Clown."

"I don't know what you're talking about. I assumed you'd been taken to the cat rehoming centre."

"My two-leggeds would never do that to me. They've said I can live with them in their house."

Oh bum!

ALSO BY ADELE ABBOTT

The Witch P.I. Mysteries
(A Candlefield/Washbridge Series)

Witch Is How... (Books #25 to #36)
Witch is How Things Had Changed
Witch is How Berries Tasted Good
Witch is How The Mirror Lied
Witch is How The Tables Turned
Witch is How The Drought Ended
Witch is How The Dice Fell
Witch is How The Biscuits Disappeared
Witch is How Dreams Became Reality
Witch is How Bells Were Saved
Witch is How To Fool Cats
Witch is How To Lose Big
Witch is How Life Changed Forever

Susan Hall Investigates
(A Candlefield/Washbridge Series)
Whoops! Our New Flatmate Is A Human.
Whoops! All The Money Went Missing.
Whoops! Someone Is On Our Case.
Whoops! We're In Big Trouble Now.

Web site: AdeleAbbott.com
Facebook: facebook.com/AdeleAbbottAuthor
Instagram: #adele_abbott_author

23337006R00175

Printed in Great Britain
by Amazon